"I love you," she said. "I have loved you for a long time, but I have hardly dared to admit it to myself. I had no idea that you loved me. I only knew that it thrilled me to see you, to know that you were near. Tonight I have been happier than I've ever been in my life."

The coldness which had held her captive broke; she was conscious only of the emotions which possessed her, passionate, intense, and demanding. Then she held out her arms, held them out with a gesture of complete surrender.

"Oh my darling," she cried. "I love you!"

And at last unable to prevent himself, he took her into his arms.

Also in Pyramid Books

by

BARBARA CARTLAND

OUT

OF

REACH

Barbara Cartland

▲PYRAMID BOOKS   •   NEW YORK

OUT OF REACH

A PYRAMID BOOK

Pyramid edition Published December 1973

ISBN 0–515–03242–5

Pyramid Books are published by Pyramid Communications, Inc. Its trademarks, consisting of the word "Pyramid" and the portrayal of a pyramid, are registered in the United States Patent Office.

Pyramid Communications, Inc.

919 Third Avenue   New York, New York 10022

CONDITIONS OF SALE

1

"Captain Graham, madam."

The grave young officer entering the room apprehensively stood for a moment irresolute. The blinding sunshine outside had dazzled his eyes and made it difficult for him to perceive the figure of a woman sitting by the flower-filled fireplace.

Then she spoke in a cool, well-modulated voice. "How do you do?"

He started and moved across to her, his eyes gradually growing accustomed to the shaded light which, diffused by green sunblinds, gave him an impression of swimming in water. As he reached her side, she held out her hand and he looked into her face.

"Madam Razoumovsky?"

"Yes, but I am known here as Mrs. Stanfield. That is my husband's real name, you know. Won't you sit down?"

She indicated a chair on her right, and for the first time he realised why she had not risen at his approach, and noted with a growing surprise the heavy invalid chair with its big rubber wheels and the light rug which covered her to the waist.

Lydia Stanfield smiled and the man beside her saw that she was beautiful.

"Amazingly beautiful," he told himself in astonishment.

"I'm sorry I had to ask you to come all this way on such a hot day," she said.

"The train was rather overcrowded," he replied, and found himself speaking naturally. "I don't believe that all the travellers were evacuees either. I think they were just holiday-makers determined to have a day in the country."

"We don't get many evacuees down here; this is very much a danger area—just outside the balloon barrage, you know. But it is our home and we love it. Nothing short of a direct hit would evacuate us."

The man glanced round the room and was not surprised at the pride in Lydia Stanfield's voice. The possessions with which she was surrounded were indeed lovely.

Even to his amateur eye the furniture was rare and chosen with exquisite taste. And yet he realised that the room itself with its soft colourings and elaborate furnishing was only a frame for the woman who owned it.

"She is lovely," he told himself again.

What exactly was it he had expected? It was difficult to know. Something exotic, Bohemian, vaguely Oriental, he supposed.

Not, at any rate, this gem of a manor house hidden among the Surrey woods only an hour's train journey from London, but quiet, secluded and perfectly in keeping with the country.

Certainly not a chatelaine whose bearing and voice proclaimed her both English and county.

Abruptly he bent forward and heard the embarrassment and rawness in his own voice as he started to speak.

"Madam Raz . . . I mean, Mrs. Stanfield, you asked me to come here and see you."

"I think, Captain Graham, you know what it is about," Lydia Stanfield said evenly. "Let us speak quite frankly, it makes things so much easier. I have heard—and on very good authority—that you intend to divorce your wife, citing my husband as co-respondent. Is that right?"

"Yes, that is true, but I don't know who could have told you."

"You will forgive me if I don't reveal the name of my

informant; it was a friend someone who has my well-being very much at heart and incidentally—yours."

"Mine?" Timothy Graham asked the question abruptly.

"Yes, yours as well. You will forgive my speaking plainly and not think it an impertinence, but I understand that you are very fond of your wife?"

Timothy Graham scowled and made no reply.

After a moment Lydia Stanfield continued:

"In which case is there anything to be gained by forcing an issue over something which is already finished and done with?"

"Finished and done with!" Timothy Graham ejaculated. "That isn't true! Mona loves the swine . . . I beg your pardon . . . loves your husband; she told me so herself. If you only knew what I . . ."

With an effort he controlled himself, silencing the words which in his indignation threatened to overflow.

"What's the use of talking?" he muttered.

Lydia sighed.

"Captain Graham, may I explain that I do understand what you are feeling, that I am terribly sorry for you. I asked you to come here simply and solely because I believed that good could come of our meeting. Let me tell you that my husband knows nothing of your visit nor of my intention to ask you here."

"But you've spoken to him about . . . about the divorce?"

Lydia shook her head.

"No, I've not spoken to my husband about your wife; in fact, to be quite honest, I had never heard her name or yours until I was informed by the friend who is nameless that you intended to start proceedings."

"But then . . . what do you know about it?"

"I know my husband."

Lydia spoke softly, and yet somehow her words carried conviction to the man listening to her.

"You see, Captain Graham, he is rather an exceptional person."

7

"Oh, I know he's a wonderful musician, almost worshipped by those who care for that sort of thing; but I never believed that my wife took it very seriously—music, I mean—until now."

"I expect she was swept off her feet," Lydia said. "You see, Ivan often has that effect on women."

She saw Captain Graham's lips tighten and the anger in his eyes.

"I'm sorry to put it in the plural," she said, "but, you see, this isn't the first time it has happened."

"Not the first time? And you stand for it?"

Lydia smiled, and despite his agitation Timothy Graham could not help thinking how it transfigured her face.

"I love my husband and I understand him. I am sorry to keep harping on the fact that he is different, but once you realise that, you don't expect from him the same standards as you would expect from other men."

"That's all very well," Timothy Graham said sharply, "but I do expect certain standards from my wife. Besides, she's in love with the fellow; she's told me so. She's asked me, even begged me, to divorce her."

"But what good would that do her?" Lydia asked. "You see Ivan will not marry her."

"Not marry her? He'll damn well have to."

Timothy Graham half started from his seat and Lydia put out her hand as if she would restrain him. She did not touch him, but instinctively he sank back.

"Listen, Captain Graham. I shall not divorce my husband, and once again I want to be very frank. He isn't in love with your wife."

"Not in love with her? But . . . they've been away together. He said . . ."

Lydia put up her hand once again as if to check the words which came from his lips.

"Yes, yes, I know. Ivan does those things. But it's over for him; it's a passing phase, a charming episode, if you like, but nothing more. Already he has reverted to

8

his old life, to the interests he had before he met your wife. I wouldn't be so brutal as to say he'd forgotten her, but it wouldn't surprise me if he had."

"But, I say! How do you know all this?"

"I've been married twenty-two years, Captain Graham. I ran away with my husband when I was eighteen. He wasn't famous then, but I watched him gradually grow to fame.

"No man with Ivan's temperament could be expected to accept all the adulation and flattery which he receives and remain a normal, conventional English husband. Besides, he is half Russian.

"The world thinks he is wholly Russian, but Razoumovsky was his mother's name. By birth my husband is English—Ivan Stanfield."

Timothy Graham rose from the chair in which he had been sitting and walked to the window.

"I don't know what to say or think," he said. "This is all a revelation to me. I intended, as apparently you know, to divorce my wife because I believed your husband would marry her and that she would find with him the happiness which she assured me was hers for the taking."

"When did you last see your wife?" Lydia asked.

"About ten days ago. She went to her mother after we'd had a flaming row over this very matter."

Lydia bent forward.

"Captain Graham, go and see her. Forgive her and ask her to come back to you. I think you'll find that she will."

"But she was so certain—so sure, when she told me that Razoumovsky . . . your husband . . . was her lover. She told me the only thing they lived for, both of them, was to be together—to be married."

Lydia sighed.

"I'm sorry, terribly sorry, but it isn't true."

"And supposing it was, you still wouldn't divorce him?"

There was a pause, then Lydia replied:

9

"Captain Graham, if my husband ever came to me and asked me to set him free, I should do it instantly. As you see, I am a cripple. I had a bad fall out riding over six years ago. You will think, perhaps, when I say that I know that my husband still loves me, that he has a use for me in his life, I am easily deceived. But it is, I assure you, true, and he is, too, devoted to our children."

"Children? I had no idea you had any."

"We have two. Philip is nearly twenty-one and my daughter, Christine, is seventeen-and-a-half. She is returning this week from America. My husband is longing to see her—she is coming out this summer."

Timothy Graham passed a hand across his forehead. He was very young and the whole interview had been a strain.

"This all bewilders me," he said. "It's so . . . unexpected, so unlike anything that I anticipated."

"I know, I understand," Lydia said soothingly. "You see, I have never taken any part in Ivan's public life. When people see him, they expect his background to be wild, Russian and very Oriental.

"I think, too, he likes to pose as something of a mystery to his public. But where his music is concerned he cannot always control or resist the emotions it arouses in others.

"He's a genius, Captain Graham, and geniuses are not like other people."

"I quite believe it is easy to make excuses for him," Timothy Graham said bitterly, "but Mona is young, we haven't been married very long."

"I am sorry, desperately sorry." There was a throb in Lydia's voice.

"Thank you."

"But please do as I suggest and make it up with your wife. Take her back and forget this ever happened. Perhaps in the years to come you will both appreciate each other the more because of it. We learn, Captain Graham, many more things by suffering and pain than we learn from happiness."

"May I, at any rate, think it over?" Timothy Graham said. "And I won't go any further with the proceedings without letting you know what I contemplate."

"Thank you, it is very kind of you." Lydia smiled at him.

Timothy Graham hesitated, then awkwardly, as if unused to paying a compliment, said:

"May I say, Mrs. Stanfield, how wonderful I think you've been about this?"

"It hasn't been easy for either of us, has it?" Lydia said. "But we're sensible people and I hope that together we have found a solution, and one which will bring happiness to everyone concerned."

"I hope you are right," Timothy Graham said fervently.

Lydia stretched out her hands towards the electric bell which stood on a small table beside her.

"And now, won't you have some tea?" she asked, "or would you prefer something long and cool?"

Timothy Graham looked at his watch.

"If you will forgive me," he said, "I will go back to the station right away. There's a train which leaves at 4.15 and I'd rather like to catch it."

"Haven't you even time for a drink?"

"I don't think so, but thank you all the same."

Instinctively Lydia knew that he did not want to drink in her husband's house, so she pressed the bell and held out her hand.

"Good-bye, then, and thank you so very much for coming to see me."

"Good-bye, Mrs. Stanfield. I will write to you; but if you don't hear from me you will know that I am doing what you suggested and trying to forget the whole thing."

He heard the maid open the door behind him, and with another word of farewell he was gone.

A moment or two later Lydia heard the taxi drive

away from the house. Only then did she relax, lying back against her cushions as if exhausted. She closed her eyes, and the lines of pain etched suddenly from nose to mouth seemed to make her immeasurably older.

After a few moments, as if with a tremendous effort she bent forward, took up the receiver and held it to her ear, waiting until the soft buzzing gave way to the operator asking for a number.

"City 33880, please—Fairhurst 92."

Again she waited, her eyes fixed on the gap beneath the sunblinds where they jutted over the open windows. She could see a part of the garden, the grass vivid green and sunflecked, a flower-bed filled with pink roses and edged with purple pansies.

It was a picture, she thought, and smiled at the banality of the idea; then unbidden to her mind came the hackneyed line of the hymn—"Though every prospect pleases, and only man is vile."

She was shocked at herself. Could she really think of Ivan in that way?

There was a sudden click in her ear and a voice said, "Hello."

"Can I speak to Mr. Granger? Mrs. Stanfield speaking."

"Hold on a minute."

A large white butterfly fluttered across the flower-bed. Softly it alighted on the open petals of a rose and then—a man's voice:

"Hello, Lydia, is that you?"

"Yes, Lawrence."

"I've been hoping you'd call me. Well, what news?"

"He's been here, and I think . . . yes, I think it will be all right."

"Thank God for that! I felt certain you'd be able to instil some sense into his head."

Lydia sighed.

"Poor young man, I was terribly sorry for him. He is obviously very fond of his wife."

"I hope he didn't upset you."

12

"No, he was really very restrained; not a very articulate person by nature, I should imagine. Perhaps that's one of the reasons. . . ."

Lydia stopped speaking. In her thoughts she was drawing a comparison between Ivan and the husband of Mona Graham; but somehow she could not say the words, could not force them from her lips.

"Anyway, he won't start proceedings?"

"I think not. And thank you, Lawrence."

"Don't thank me. I do it for you and you only. Do you still hold me to my promise not to mention it to Ivan?"

"Please."

"A pity! I'd be able to tell him for once what I thought of him."

"He'd be very hurt and it would do no good."

"Perhaps not, but it would give me a good deal of satisfaction."

"Please, Lawrence."

"I'm sorry, Lydia. It shall be as you say of course. You're sure you're not too tired or upset?"

"Quite sure."

"Well, I'll telephone if there's any news. Good-bye, and take care of yourself."

"Good-bye, my dear."

Lydia put down the receiver. The butterfly had flown away; the pattern of light and shade on the grass moved slowly as the breeze swayed the boughs of the trees. Impulsively Lydia propelled the wheels of her chair across to the window.

There she reached forward, grasped the cord hidden behind the curtains which controlled the sunblinds, and pulled them up so that the sun poured in on her and the whole of the garden lay revealed. Lydia blinked her eyes a little against the sun.

"Now I am no longer in the shade," she told herself.

Then hid her eyes in her hands. She did not cry, but she felt the chaotic tumult of her own thoughts.

"I have got to keep calm, I have got to be sensible," she kept thinking over and over again.

As she had told Timothy Graham, this was not the first time. During their married life Ivan had had many affairs; she knew about them, expected them and had steeled herself to accept them as she accepted so many other things about him—with forbearance and understanding.

It was only when his security was threatened—his and the children's—that she must play an active part and try to save her husband from the retribution he invited.

If it had not been for Lawrence Granger, Ivan would not have a shred of reputation left. Lawrence loved her, she knew that, although he never presumed to offer her any more than a warm friendship and a kindliness for which she was increasingly grateful.

He had always been Ivan's solicitor—a friend of his father, he had befriended the young musician, and at first Lydia had felt that Lawrence was not over-enthusiastic about their marriage. Perhaps from a common-sense point of view it has appeared rather idiotic.

Ivan, highly strung and impetuous, with very little money and a temperament which was bound to prove extravagant in more ways than one, saddling himself with a wife who had hardly left the schoolroom and who belonged to a very different world from the one he lived in and enjoyed.

Yes, it must have seemed to an outsider an act of madness.

But as the years passed Lawrence Granger had grown to know and understand Lydia and, as he and Lydia alone knew, had learnt to love her—love her so much that he was prepared to do anything in his power for her happiness; and as it happened he was in a position to do a great deal.

Ivan himself never anticipated trouble, he never considered the consequences of his actions and was indeed

14

genuinely surprised if there were any; but Lawrence saved him from himself.

More than once he and Lydia had managed to avert a scandal and to prevent the law case long before Ivan had even realised that such things were looming like a heavy cloud on his horizon.

Once before there had been every likelihood of Ivan being cited as co-respondent in a divorce case, but with Lawrence's advice and help Lydia had been able to settle the whole thing out of court, and Ivan's name had not appeared.

On that occasion the woman herself was at least partially to blame for what had occurred and the marriage had floundered long before Ivan had appeared on the scene.

This time it was different: a young married couple, happy and contented enough, the wife hardly more than a child, pretty, but frivolous and empty-headed; the sort who could easily be carried away by excitement and glamour. How could Ivan have been so blind, so selfishly intent on his own enjoyment of a dangerous flirtation, as not to perceive the inevitable?

They had apparently taken no precautions to avoid being found out and had gone away quite openly for a week-end. Ivan, old enough to be the girl's father, should have had more sense.

Lydia knew that Mona Graham would not have blurted out the whole story to her husband and asked for a divorce had she not felt very certain that Ivan would marry her.

As soon as Lydia heard from Lawrence that a Captain Graham was talking of starting divorce proceedings against his wife she knew exactly when the affair had begun and the very day when it had ended. She had known at the time everything except the woman's name.

While something within herself had cried out in agony and in jealous misery another part of her had scoffed at the whole thing as being ridiculous and part

15

of her imaginings. But she seldom imagined things where Ivan was concerned, she just knew them instinctively.

And she had known that he was in love just as surely as she knew when he had fallen out of it again.

He had come into her room one evening after a concert and had thrown himself down on the bed. He was looking young and jubilant—far younger than his forty-eight years.

His hair was slightly ruffled and he had that puckish, wild expression which made those who hated him describe him as "a handsome devil," and those who loved him picture him as an untamed faun.

"Darling!" He picked her hand off the sheet and kissed it.

She had known at that moment as surely as if he had told her in so many words that he was wholeheartedly hers again.

"What happened?"

"I was a success. Ye gods! What a success I was!"

He was like a boastful small boy, and then he smiled mockingly.

"They clapped until their hands were sore and cheered until their throats were hoarse. And they would have given me anything in the world I asked for—except their money."

Lydia laughed. She knew it was in relief because Ivan was free, because he was hers again.

"You've come straight home?"

"Darling, where else would I have gone?"

He opened his eyes wide and she knew that quite honestly it never struck him that after nearly two months of neglect he might have gone elsewhere.

"Then you must be famished."

"I am. Let's picnic here since you've gone to bed."

There was just the faintest tinge of reproach in his voice. Lydia could have mentioned the nights she had sat up waiting—waiting until after midnight for a husband who was giving supper to younger women.

16

How often had he gone on after a concert without bothering to send a message that the supper which was waiting for him at home would not be required? She could have said many things; she might even have reproached him at that moment.

Instead she smiled.

"I'm sorry, darling, but I was feeling tired."

He wheeled round, his voice anxious.

"You're all right? You're not in pain?"

"No, perfectly all right. But I don't know what there is for your supper. Be an angel and go down to the larder and have a look for yourself. If no one's up you'll have to forage."

"What a homecoming for the breadwinner of the family."

"Nonsense, you enjoy it," Lydia replied.

They had laughed together as he bent to kiss you.

She had been so happy that night, as he had half sat, half lain, beside her on the bed, his tail coat thrown off because he said he was hot, his collar loosened; and they had eaten and talked far into the night.

Because she had said she was tired, Ivan had insisted upon opening a bottle of champagne—an excuse, as she well knew, to have a glass himself. It was the only drink he ever took, and she had drank it feeling that it was an occasion for a celebration.

Ivan was hers again . . . hers.

2

The maid finished arranging the curls at the back of Lydia's head and then fetched the flat leather jewellery-case and set it down in front of her on the dressing-table.

Lydia stared at her own refelection in the mirror. Her hair, newly washed, was shining with soft burnished lights, and the turquoise blue of her chiffon evening dress framed the white grace of her long throat.

She looked—as she well knew—a lovely woman, and then as she caught sight of the back of her invalid chair she threw off with a nervous, irritable gesture the rug which covered her knees.

"Give me the Chinese shawl, Rose," she said, sitting silent while her maid fetched it from the cupboard and placed it over her, the embroidered flowers with their vivid colours adding to the colourful picture she already made.

"That looks lovely, madam," Rose said enthusiastically. "I'm glad you bought that blue dress; it suits you a treat."

"It will go well with my aquamarines," Lydia replied.

But she smiled at the compliment and bending forward opened her jewel-case. She slipped two clips on the front of her dress and put a smaller one on to the lobe of each ear, and then turned to the ring tray. There was a line of rings in it, and as she picked up the big square-cut aquamarine—one of Ivan's last presents to her—her eyes lingered for a moment on a thin narrow ring of coloured enamel which was the first present he had given her after they had been married. It

18

had not cost very much, but in those days it seemed to them a fortune.

Even so, it was in exquisite taste, a ring that anybody would have been proud to own regardless of its monetary value, a Regency piece of white and red enamel made by a clever craftsman and engraved with the words: *My heart is thine.*

Lydia picked up the ring and turned it over in her fingers. How much had happened since then! And yet in some ways it was true that Ivan's heart had been hers.

He had been unfaithful, he had loved other women; and yet she could fearlessly ask herself the question whether he had ever given them anything that was hers?

When she had married him, when she had run away from the quiet, ordered existence of her country home, she had told herself with all the conceit of the very young that she knew exactly what she was facing in the future and was prepared for it.

Perhaps in some ways her very ignorance and inexperience had saved her from much of the agony and heart-burning of anticipation.

Things that happened after marriage had come to her as a shock, but she had not gone through the long misery of waiting for them to happen, of knowing the inevitable before it happened.

No, she could truly say that she had been ecstatically happy with Ivan, especially during those first years of their marriage—the years in which he had been climbing to fame and becoming recognized because his genius compelled attention and could not be ignored.

And then . . . it was difficult for her to put into words even to herself what she had felt when other women first began to play a part in Ivan's life.

She had been jealous, of course—madly, crazily and wildly jealous; and yet somehow she had managed to keep her balance, to keep herself from making scenes and antagonising Ivan as she could so easily have done had she behaved in what anyone else would have called a normal way.

It was not entirely her own cleverness which had prevented her doing this, and it was only now, when she was over forty, that Lydia had begun to understand the strange hold she had over her husband.

She had been brought up to be undemonstrative. All her family were unemotional, calm, and what they called "extremely English" in their outlook. She had learnt it in the nursery that it was "bad form" to show emotion.

When her mother died before Lydia had reached her teens, she had accepted her father's code, which was one of understatement on every possible occasion.

Colonel Windover had brought up his two daughters strictly, but in what he believed was a kindly, decent fashion.

In reality Lydia was starved for affection; but she had no idea of it and only learnt to control her natural instincts and discipline with Puritanical severity a nature which, if left alone, would have been both affectionate and demonstrative.

By the time she was eighteen, when she had blossomed into a sudden and surprising beauty, she had learnt to be ashamed of her own impulses and to be shy and suspicious of her desire to show affection towards those she loved.

"I can't stand this modern exaggerated way of talking," Colonel Windover would grumble, when people talked of things being "too, too marvellous," "topping" and "divine"—using the enthusiastic slang of the post-war period.

Lydia was fond of her father and she had been brought up to admire him.

He had been set up to her as the supreme authority from the very moment of her birth, for in ruling his household with an autocratic benevolence Colonel Windover expected from them in return a willing and unquestioning subservience.

20

He was extremely selfish, although he was quite unconscious of the fact, and consequently filled the house with his own friends, for the idea that his daughters required youthful companions never entered his head.

He had not been a young man when he had married, and by the time Lydia was eighteen his contemporaries were all over fifty and interested only in hunting and shooting.

They had little to say to a pretty girl just leaving the shcoolroom except to kiss her occasionally behind the door in what they assured her was "a fatherly manner," and subject her to a good deal of good-natured chaff about her appearance.

Lydia accepted it all as part of her life because she had known no other; dogs, horses, conversation confined entirely to sport had been, in fact, the main part of her education.

But at times she craved for something different, something less material, something more mystical, desires which seemed to her vaguely reprehensible.

Then like a bombshell came her meeting with Ivan.

She remembered so well being asked to a party at which he was to play. The talented wife of the local M.F.H. had been responsible for it, and Colonel Windover had expressed both his dislike and disgust of musical evenings.

"Why can't the women let us talk, or provide a good game of bridge?" he grumbled. "Sitting about on a hard chair listening to some long-haired gigolo making a hideous noise isn't my idea of enjoyment."

She had so nearly not gone to the party.

Lydia knew afterwards that if her father had definitely refused the invitation, as sometimes he was wont to do, she would have accepted his decision placidly and gone on leading her quiet, even existence without a thought of what might have been hers.

But they had gone, and on entering the crowded room she had seen Ivan. How strange he was, how different from other men she had known in her short life!

21

He was conspicuous, of course, amongst the hard-riding, somewhat boorish country squires and the young men of her own generation who had just missed the war and were looking rather limply into the future, wondering what the devil they were to do with themselves.

There was nothing indecisive, nothing limp, about Ivan. From the moment he stepped into that big chintz-decorated country drawing-room he dominated it.

People listened to him when he was speaking; and even the country squires were hushed into an almost mesmerised silence when he played.

He was not long-haired or exotically dressed, as Colonel Windover anticipated. But he certainly looked un-English.

Also he seemed to Lydia to have very little in common with the other members of his sex in that gathering. He made them all seem coarse and ungainly. Tall and abnormally thin, he moved with a grace which had, however, nothing feminine in it.

He was handsome, but not by any classical or pre-conceived standards. His high cheek-bones, his deep-set eyes, proclaimed his Russian blood, but his hair instead of being dark was a very deep red; his jaw was square and determined, and his mouth in repose was firm too.

One knew at first sight that here was a man who would get what he wanted and that it would be difficult for anything or anybody to stand in his way.

When Ivan smiled he was irresistible; but it was not until he played that Lydia understood that at last here was something that without knowing it she had been waiting for all her life.

His music snatched her up from her mundane normality into an ecstasy which stripped away the superficial veneer which had held her senses prisoner since childhood and which left her trembling, but transformed.

It had all been beyond words; she could only feel and go on feeling her eyes burning in a white face until the vibrations which were emanating from her had met Ivan's and drawn his eyes to hers across the intervening space of the crowded room.

It was then he had strolled across to her, cutting short a voluble woman who was talking to him of her own musical experiences; it was doubtful if the poor lady had even come to the end of her sentence.

He had stood in front of Lydia, not holding out his hand, not touching her, but just looking; and yet she felt as if there and then he took her into his arms.

"You liked it?"

She could only answer him in a monosyllable:

"Yes."

They had stood looking at each other. Somehow it had been a moment when there was no need for words, their eyes said everything that needed to be said.

Both their hearts were beating quickly.

Ivan, of course, had known and understood what was happening. He was already old in experience, and besides his Oriental blood made him fatalistic—this was meant, this had to happen.

To Lydia it was all bewildering.

She was feeling for the first time in her life—feeling not the quiet, well-controlled emotions which she had believed were the utmost of her capability, but something overwhelming and disturbing which threatened to throw her off balance.

She could never remember what happened after that, how it was managed or what she said. But suddenly she found herself alone with Ivan in the garden.

It was midsummer and the darkness had not yet fallen; the trees were darkly silhouetted against a sapphire sky, the bats beginning to swoop and whirl overhead.

They had walked for some minutes in silence, and then as they reached the end of the formal garden with its flagged paths and sunken lily pond Ivan turned and held out both his hands.

"Shall I tell you what I am wanting to say?" he asked.

23

Lydia once again could only answer him with one word:

"Yes."

She could hardly speak for the throbbing in her throat, the suffocating sense of excitement within herself.

He raised both her hands to his lips, and then turning them over kissed the palms.

"I knew the moment I saw you," he said, "that you belonged to me."

She had accepted his statement as a fact. It was only later that night when she was home and in bed that she remembered that at that moment Ivan had no idea of her name, nor whether she was married or not.

She knew then that none of those things mattered. She was Ivan's, as he had so truly seen from the moment their eyes had met.

They had gone away together; for of course Colonel Windover would no more have accepted Ivan as a son-in-law than he would have accepted the devil himself.

They got married, and they found a happiness together which had been quite annoying to those who had predicted that the marriage was bound to be a failure.

It was only gradually that Lydia began to understand just what she had undertaken in marrying Ivan.

At first she was too concerned with studying herself, of being half ashamed of her own passionate emotions and the feelings that he aroused in her by the look in his eyes, by the touch of his hand.

That she who all her life had been taught to disapprove of anything exaggerated, anything even approaching demonstrativeness, should now find herself palpitating and pulsating with a passion of love so great that it was beyond her own comprehension, filled Lydia with something like dismay.

She responded to Ivan, she surrendered herself completely. How could she do otherwise, loving him as she did?

But at the same time some part of her remained inviolate. She could respond, but she could not invite; she could give him what he asked, but in return she would ask nothing.

And Ivan, with his sharpened intuition, his sensitiveness, knew that something was withheld from him.

"Do you love me?" he would ask, and then before she could reply, "I'll make you love me—give me yourself; and if you won't, I'll take you—make you—break you! Oh, my darling, my lovely, you are mine . . ."

He would sweep her into his arms, raining kisses on her lips, her throat, her breasts.

"I want you, I want you, oh God, I want you—all of you! Speak to me . . . tell me that you love me . . . tell me . . . tell me . . ."

Over twenty years were to pass before Lydia really understood that it was her reserve, her very inarticulateness, which kept her husband in love with her.

There was some magic within him, some vibrating attraction which loosened the bonds of conventionality where women were concerned and made them pour out their souls at his feet.

They gave him their hearts before he asked for them. They adored him, they worshipped him, from the moment he entered their drawing-rooms, long before he entered their bedrooms or their intimate lives.

And Ivan, with all his artistry, was essentially a man, and as a man he wanted to do his own hunting, he wanted to choose and pursue the woman he wanted.

Lydia was his wife, but she was never, he felt in his heart of hearts, wholly and completely his.

There was always something hidden from him, some secret, self-controlled part of her that he could not break down, could not charm or conquer into submission.

He never guessed that it was only her shyness, her fear of appearing ridiculous and her inability to express her feelings because ever since she had been a child she had been taught that such feelings were "bad form."

It was strange and in its way a paradox that Colonel

25

Windover's teaching and upbringing should have been instrumental in bringing happiness to the man he most loathed and despised.

It was impossible for the Colonel to forgive his daughter for marrying Ivan Razoumovsky. How could he?

He couldn't understand that anyone could marry such a man and not be degraded. Even when the whole world acknowledged Ivan as one of the greatest geniuses of the century, Colonel Windover was still shaking his head and wondering "what a daughter of mine could see in that mountebank."

What she saw in him could never have been expressed by Lydia in words.

They were happy. It was enough to know that and be grateful for it, and the word itself was so inadequate to express their absorption and feeling of completeness one with the other.

And she grew to understand that Ivan's need of her was much the same need as he had to express himself in music; people, women, herself—everything and everybody with whom he came into contact—were only instruments on which to play.

They made tunes for him and he listened to those tunes, wrote them down, and they became compositions over which critics poured out eulogies of praise.

She was not jealous of his music, she accepted his absorption in it.

But it was harder to tell herself that his absorption in another woman was nothing more or less than the interest any musician would feel in a new and untried instrument.

What woman in love is ever logical? What woman in love can in reality listen to her head and not her heart?

Lydia was at the zenith of her beauty when a fall out riding and a kick from the horse injured her spine so that the doctors said she would be permanently disabled.

She had given Ivan two children. Her life with him

had developed and deepened her beauty, until at thirty-four she was almost breathtakingly lovely.

When Lydia first realised that she would never walk again she wanted only to die.

The Gethsemane into which she went at that moment was all the darker in contrast with the sunshine she had known in the sixteen years she had been married to Ivan.

She prayed to die, and when that had been denied her she faced the act of living with a despair and despondency which in its intensity frightened even herself.

And yet she had said little; once again in the face of an overwhelming emotion she was inarticulate, she had no words with which to express herself, and her despair was too great to allow her even the relief of tears.

She had come home from the hospital to the house which they had only recently purchased with the money that Ivan had been making lately in quite prodigious quantities.

She had loved Fairhurst Manor from the moment she had seen it, and she had begun, just before her accident, to choose the furnishings and furniture which she wanted to be perfect because they were to be the background for Ivan's life and hers.

At first she had felt that she could not bear to see Fairhurst again; she had made so many plans about the house and had dreamed her dreams of its meaning so much to them both.

Then gradually she had understood, just as though it were a play about someone else's life, the role she had to play in the future.

She had begun to realise just a little of the hold that she had over Ivan; and she had seen that after sixteen years his passion and his desire of her had changed and altered almost imperceptibly.

So slowly, as all these things happen, that she had been unaware of it, she had ceased to be entirely dependent upon Ivan and Ivan had become dependent upon her.

She had been brought up without a mother, needing and craving a mother's love, but learning to do without it.

Ivan had been brought up by his mother, and had grown to rely on and expect that maternal love and affection which in a young man's life can mean almost as much as the companionship and passionate love of a wife.

Ivan's mother had died just before he was twenty-one. He had idolised her, and he missed her with that acute sense of empty, aching loneliness which is so much a part of the Russian character.

It was only gradually that Lydia found herself occupying the throne which had belonged to Ivan's mother.

Slowly she filled that empty niche in his heart and watched his fiery, possessive passion change to an adoration almost sacred in its inviolate intensity.

It was not easy for her to accept the transition. How desperately she had prayed during those first years when she had returned to Fairhurst as an invalid:

"Help me, God! Oh, help me, help me!"

Over and over again the prayer would be on her lips. There had been moments when she had felt like screaming, like crying out at the unbearable crucifixion of her body.

She wanted the Ivan she had known—the lover, the man who had taken her devouringly, fiercely, overwhelmingly, and made her his.

She wanted those moments over again when the air between them seemed electric, and something wild and ecstatic fired them both as with a consuming flame and they clung together and became one—the world lost in a maze of vivid, piercing beauty, so that they knew together an indivisible pleasure-pain rising to a crescendo of glory and wonder.

Alone in the darkness of her big bed Lydia would try to move the inanimate, unfeeling heaviness which had once been her legs and would cry out at the inadequacy of her will to act below her waist. "Ivan, Ivan," she would whisper his name into the pillow, wanting him, aching for him, and tortured by the memories of what once had been hers.

She had never been able to speak of what she felt. No one knew, no one guessed, what went on behind that calm, unlined face; no one knew the tumult of emotion which seethed behind her smile and beneath that quiet soft voice which said so little.

Ivan was still hers; but at what a cost!

3

Lydia propelled her chair from her bedroom along the rug-covered passage to the drawing-room.

After her accident a suite had been arranged for her on the ground floor so that she could feel independent and go from room to room without assistance.

She entered the drawing-room to find that her sister Elizabeth who had promised to look in some time between tea and dinner had arrived, and that Ivan was with her shaking a cocktail from the bar which had been cunningly concealed in an old cabinet.

Ivan spoke first.

"Hello, my darling!"

He put down the cocktail-shaker and walking across the room kissed first her hand and then her cheek.

"I've just got back," he said, "and I found Elizabeth on the doorstep."

Lydia smiled at him, and then she moved further into the room to greet Elizabeth, who had risen from a low chair.

"I'm so glad you could come," she said.

Her words were robbed of a formality by her smile and the welcoming way in which she held out both her hands.

"I convinced my conscience that you were definitely on my route," Elizabeth answered.

It was possible for an outsider to see the resemblance between the two sisters, but there was no doubt which was the more beautiful and the more attractive.

Elizabeth was pretty, but her looks lacked all animation. She was, too, slightly prim in her manner, which made Ivan describe her once as a "cross between a New England schoolmistress and a mediaeval nun."

Lydia had enquired curiously:

"Why mediaeval?"

Ivan was as usual ready with his answer. "Because the nuns at that period were always hoping for and expecting ecstasies."

Lydia had looked puzzled.

"Do you really think that Elizabeth is expecting anything so human?"

"You'd be surprised," Ivan answered enigmatically.

Lydia, who could never get him to explain himself, had to be satisfied with that.

But she had not been convinced, although looking at Elizabeth's husband she could well believe that Elizabeth's hopes, if hopes they were, were not likely to be gratified in that direction.

Elizabeth was thirty-two. She had married the Earl of Avon on her twenty-first birthday.

He was a dull man, a contemporary of her father—thirty years older than herself. Lydia had not known her sister at that time, for after she had eloped with Ivan, Colonel Windover had not only ceased to communicate with his eldest daughter but had also refused to allow her to have anything to do with her younger sister.

"He's afraid I shall contaminate her," Lydia had said ruefully to Ivan, and he had added with a puckish grin —"with me."

Elizabeth had been married for five years before she made tentative overtures towards friendship.

But once the sisters had met after such a long separation they had been drawn together by mutual affection. Lydia, while responsive to every advance that Elizabeth made, was determined not to thrust herself in any way upon the Avons.

Despite her utmost resolution, she was in her heart of hearts deeply hurt by the treatment she had received both from her father and her other relations.

It was irritating, to say the least of it, that with the whole civilised world acknowledging Ivan as a genius, the Windovers should sit back smugly in their disapproval still convinced that "poor Lydia had married beneath her."

Thus, although Lydia and Elizabeth had become friends, there was no really intimate confidences exchanged between them.

Lydia anyway would not have thought of discussing Ivan; but she sometimes felt as if it was with an effort that Elizabeth remained reserved, speaking only of her husband vaguely and courteously, as though he was as much a stranger to her as he was to Lydia and Ivan.

They frankly found Arthur Avon extremely dull and it was obvious that he would have little in common with them.

He had always been a friend of Colonel Windover. Lydia could remember his annual visits for the partridge and pheasant shoots, a dull, gaunt man with a drooping moustache and a habit of pausing before he answered a question or made a statement.

It was impossible in many ways to understand how Elizabeth could have brought herself to marry him, and yet Lydia had the idea that she enjoyed her position.

Certainly she played her part admirably, entertaining the right people at the right times in the big family seat of the Avons in Sussex, going north to their grouse moor in the autumn and opening the London house for the season.

A well regulated life, and one which carried on the traditions set by the Dowager Countess both conscientiously and punctiliously.

Lydia always felt when she saw Elizabeth that she wanted to say:

"How well you are doing your duty, dear."

But in one thing—and it seemed to be the only one —Elizabeth had not succeeded in doing her duty, and that was in presenting her husband with an heir. There were no children of the marriage.

But again, Lydia had no idea whether this was a sorrow and regret to her younger sister or whether she accepted it philosophically.

It seemed to Lydia sometimes as if Elizabeth was watching her. She could not quite explain the impression, but she felt as if the younger woman was not only curious, but critical, as if she waited for something to happen where she and Ivan were concerned—watched and waited.

"It's just my imagination," Lydia told herself, and thought how delightful Elizabeth was and how glad she ought to be to have such a nice sister.

This evening Elizabeth certainly looked her best in her Red Cross uniform. It severity suited her, and she ran the family house as a convalescent home, both efficiently and economically.

"What's the news?" Lydia asked.

They were all seated and sipping the cocktails Ivan had mixed.

"I've brought you an evening paper," Ivan answered. "But I haven't had even time to look at it. I've had an exhausting day, the orchestra was excruciating—it must have been the heat—and I had to throw at least two temperaments before they paid any attention to me."

"Were they horrified at the exhibition?" Lydia asked.

He shook his head.

"On the contrary they were relieved. As I've told you so often, my darling, they expect me to be temperamental."

He turned to Elizabeth.

"You must always give people what they expect and they'll be happy. Nothing has annoyed our friends so much as the fact that Lydia and I live together in middle-class respectability."

Lydia had heard Ivan speak in such a strain before and she realised that it meant nothing. He was neither trying to cover up his tracks nor making an effort to convince her of an innocence he did not possess.

He was just talking as it was Ivan's way to talk. But

sensitive after her interview of the afternoon she noticed an expression on Elizabeth's face which perturbed her, and she wondered quickly what Elizabeth could have heard.

Ivan sensed nothing.

"Now you, Elizabeth, for instance," he was saying, "give the public the perfect picture for a grand lady— 'noblesse oblige' in person."

Elizabeth laughed.

"Thank you, I take that as a compliment. Last time I was here you told me there were no great ladies left.

Ivan got up to fetch the cocktail-shaker.

"You must have disappointed me more than usual."

"More than usual?" Elizabeth raised her eyebrows.

"But of course. You are a continual disappointment. I am a cynic. I have always believed that such goodness and such restraints were only a veneer, and that sooner or later they were bound to crack—I'm still hoping!"

Lydia wondered if her own sister really enjoyed being teased in such a manner. She fancied now there was a faint flush in Elizabeth's cheeks and that her tone was half resentful as she replied:

"My dear Ivan, you must not judge everyone by yourself."

"Touché," he laughed. "But all the same, Elizabeth, I get more out of life than you do."

Before Elizabeth could reply the parlourmaid announced that Ivan was wanted on the telephone. Lydia was conscious of a sense of relief at the interruption.

The sisters were alone and for a moment there was a silence between them.

"Christine comes back this week, doesn't she?" Elizabeth asked at length.

Lydia nodded.

"Isn't it exciting? And yet, to tell the truth, I'm rather afraid."

"Afraid?"

"Yes, it's rather frightening not to have seen one's daughter for over four years. She was thirteen when she

34

went away and now she is seventeen-and-a-half. She will have changed from a little girl to a young woman. I wonder what she will think of us all and what we shall think of her?"

"She's been happy in America?"

"Yes, very. Aunt Johanna has been angelic to her. But then, she always was my favourite aunt. I think our mother must have been very like her. Do you remember her?"

"Not really," Elizabeth replied. "I couldn't have been much more than five or six when I saw her last."

"She was the only one of all our relations," Lydia said softly, "who sent me her good wishes when I married Ivan. I have never forgotten it. I cried over that letter and kept it for years."

"Did you mind so much?" Elizabeth asked quickly.

"I didn't mind for myself," Lydia replied, "but I was so proud of Ivan, and I wanted everyone I knew to be proud of him too. I hated his being abused for marrying me. I wanted to justify him . . . oh, I can't explain, I never was good at putting my feelings into words."

There was another silence, then almost abruptly Elizabeth said:

"There's something I want to say, but I'm not good at putting things into words either."

Instantly Lydia became tense. She knew without being told any further that what Elizabeth wanted to say was unpleasant, yet waited, afraid to interrupt or check her sister in case she was wrong.

"It's about Ivan," Elizabeth said hesitatingly.

"Then I would rather you didn't tell me," Lydia said softly.

"But I think you ought to know," Elizabeth insisted. "People are talking. If it's serious, there's Christine to consider."

"It isn't so serious."

"Do you know what I am talking about?" Elizabeth asked. "That Timothy Graham is saying . . ."

"Yes, I know," Lydia interrupted. "But I'm sure ev-

35

erything will be all right. I think you will see that he'll make it up with his wife."

Elizabeth lay back with a sigh of relief.

"Then you do know!" she exclaimed. "Really, Lydia, you're amazing for a woman who can't get about! I've been terrified of trying to tell you about this and you knew all the time."

"Am I so formidable?"

"I thought it would break your heart."

Lydia could not reply for a sudden rush of tears. She choked them back, but she felt as though they must overflow.

"Why hasn't it broken my heart?" she asked herself.

How was it that she was able to go on as usual? It was not self-pity, but the utter simplicity and frankness of Elizabeth's reply which had moved her. She felt a great wave of affection for her sister. She bent across and touched her hand.

"Thank you, darling, for trying to tell me. It was sweet of you."

"I'm sorry about it," Elizabeth said. "That is . . . if it's true?"

She asked the question, but Lydia knew that she knew the answer; and somehow it was impossible for her to lie, to tell Elizabeth that it was untrue. She said nothing.

Quickly, as though they both avoided something dangerous, Elizabeth went on:

"Mona Graham is a little fool anyway. I never liked her. She's pretty, but over-sexed and over-emotional—you know the type."

Lydia still said nothing.

She was staring ahead of her, seeing not the loveliness of the garden where, as the sun sank, the shadows of the trees grew long and pointed and a faint evening wind stirred the flowers.

Instead she looked down the long vista of the years, seeing the many women who had been over-sexed and over-emotional, seeing them with their hungry faces turned towards Ivan, their white arms outstretched towards him.

How little each of them had meant to him; and yet each of them had been a kind of milestone in her own life. Each had left a scar, unhealed, undefaceable, despite the fact that the women who had made them were half forgotten.

She could forgive them. Was it likely that they, being made as they were, could resist Ivan?

There was some magic in him—a magic of personality which drew them as surely as the Pied Piper of Hamelin drew the children of Brunswick.

They had only to look at him, to hear his music, to know that he proffered them some intense delight; and then greedily they would cling to him, demanding that he fulfil the promises he made not by words but in his looks and in his music.

Poor Ivan, more sinned against than sinning! And yet was that true?

He was always hunting, always pursuing some will-of-the-wisp of his own imagination; something—she was not sure what it was—which always remained out of his reach.

But other things were caught and captured, and once they were in the bag how dull they were—how uninteresting, how unimportant! Yet somehow he never seemed to tire.

He had not yet, at any rate, begun to grow old.

Lydia was recalled from her reverie by Elizabeth asking her a question.

"You are happy, aren't you?"

Lydia turned her face towards her sister.

"Terribly, you know that."

Elizabeth looked away now and when she spoke again it was as if the question came from some depth of thought—preconsidered.

"And you never regret marrying as you did?"

"Regret it?" Lydia's voice was light with laughter. "Elizabeth, I've been so wonderfully happy. Whatever

37

happens to me in the future I shall never regret these last twenty-two years. I have had so much, I can almost say—everything."

Elizabeth sighed, and then her lips parted. For a moment Lydia thought she was going to speak, was going to break the reserve that had lain between them—to speak of herself and her own life; but instead, after a moment, Elizabeth got heavily to her feet.

"I must get home," she said. "Arthur doesn't like it if I'm late for dinner."

The moment of confidence was past.

"How is Arthur?" Lydia asked.

"Fairly well," Elizabeth replied. "He has twinges of lumbago every now and then which worry him a great deal. But of course, what with his work on the bench and the estate, he's extremely busy."

"Yes, of course. Well, it's been lovely to see you; come again soon."

"I'll find an excuse to motor over," Elizabeth promised.

She paused a moment and then put her hand on her sister's shoulder.

"You didn't mind my saying what I did?"

Lydia smiled up at her spontaneously.

"Listen, darling, we can say anything to each other—anything, always. Is that clear?"

Elizabeth met her sister's eyes and then looked away. Lydia had the impression there was so much that was left unsaid. Elizabeth's reserve wrapped her about like a garment.

"Good-bye." She kissed her sister perfunctorily. "Say good-bye to Ivan for me."

"I will," Lydia promised.

She watched her sister walk away, tall, slim and graceful, and felt as if she watched a stranger. There was so much she didn't understand about Elizabeth.

She thought of her driving home through the fragrant dusk to Arthur. What did she feel, what did she think about her husband?

Could she really be interested in his lumbago, his everlasting grumble that they were short-handed on the estate, his seasonal enthusiasm for the number of birds killed?

Elizabeth looked older than her thirty-two years, and she behaved like a middle-aged woman. Had she ever been young?

Did she ever want to dance, to sing, to feel alive, to know herself tingling, tense with excitement and joy? Had she ever waited breathless in the dark, throbbing in the anticipation of the happiness and love which was to be hers?

It was impossible to think of Elizabeth like that. And yet one could not be sorry for her; she seemed content, seemed to enjoy the grandeur, the responsibilities and the nobility of her position. The Countess of Avon!

And yet who would change places with her?

Ivan came back and they went in to dinner. It was a short meal, well chosen and well cooked, and when it was over they had coffee on the verandah.

Ivan lay back in his chair, his head vivid and forceful thrown back in sharp relief against a green cushion. He gave expression to his thoughts:

"Poor Elizabeth!"

"Why do you say that?" Lydia questioned.

He smiled at her. "Do you really want me to elaborate the obvious?"

"No . . . poor Elizabeth!"

They were silent. Rose arrived with Lydia's medicine and a book containing the cook's suggestions for tomorrow's meals. While the women were talking Ivan disappeared into the house.

When Rose had gone Lydia was conscious of a vast weariness.

It had been a tiring day; her interview with Timothy Graham repeated itself in her mind. Had she said enough? Would he take her advice?

She had rehearsed herself as carefully and as conscientiously as an actress for the rôle she must play. Now

39

she criticised her own performance. Had it been convincing? Had the response been what she intended?

It was very quiet on the verandah, and after a while Lydia turned her chair and went in through the french windows. She passed through her drawing-room, across the hall and down the passage which led to Ivan's studio. As she neared the big double doors, she could hear him playing.

She stopped for a moment and listened. Ivan's music always expressed what he himself was feeling.

Tonight his fingers seemed as if they were exercising themselves on the keys—a quiet piece, a melody neither strained nor unfinished . . . yet she knew he was waiting for something . . . for somebody. . . .

Lydia waited a moment, and then she opened the door. Ivan wheeled round and when he saw who it was smiled at her invitingly.

"Come in," he said. "I want you."

She did as she was told, pushing the door to, then propelling herself across the polished floor to the piano.

It was a big room and had originally been built as a chapel in the seventeenth century, but it had never been consecrated and had been left empty, used in the succeeding generations sometimes as a barn, sometimes as a ballroom.

Now it was a place of beauty, and to Lydia a fitting shrine for Ivan's music.

The great piano stood at the far end of the room, turned so that when Ivan was playing he could look at the treasures he had collected over a number of years, most of which had been given him by adoring admirers.

There were first of all the pictures, all of them beautiful, many of them worthy of a place in a national art collection.

Beneath them there was Ming pottery, Sèvres china, Waterford glass and strange musical instruments from all parts of Europe, some of them incredibly old, some of them merely amusing in their peasant origin.

There were books on one wall, many of them signed

40

and sent to Ivan by men as famous in their world as he was in his. There was a prayer-mat which had come from Mecca, and an ikon which had been given to Ivan's mother by the Tsar of Russia.

Treasures, some valuable, some valued only for their sentiment; treasures of all sorts and all shapes and sizes in one room and yet perfectly at home and in keeping one with the other because of the taste with which they were arranged.

And for a background there were Madonna-blue curtains falling from ceiling to floor and strangely carved ancient mirrors iridescent with age.

It was a lovely room. And yet Lydia often wondered how much anyone saw of the room when Ivan was in it. It was difficult to look at anything except him. His movements were like quicksilver and he kept one breathless, watchful and alert.

She went to him now and as she drew near he put out his hand. She put hers into it.

"What are you thinking about?" he asked.

She was sharply surprised at his question. She had thought that she had been acting and behaving quite normally. But she might have known that Ivan's perception would have sensed that something was wrong, that something had disturbed her.

"I was thinking of you," she replied quite truthfully.

He looked at her, and then releasing her hand he walked across the room restlessly and yet imperiously, as though he swept through invisible obstacles.

"Shall we go away?" he asked at length.

"Where to?"

"You want a change."

She made no answer, waiting for what was in his mind. And then, walking swiftly back towards her, he said:

"But of course it's impossible. I forgot that Christine is coming home."

He stood looking down at her and then he moved off again, striding round the room like some caged beast.

41

She knew then the tumult within him, knew that he guessed at her knowledge and sought for ways and means to explain himself, to ask her understanding.

"Ivan," she said at last.

Though she spoke softly it was as if she had commanded him for he stood still. Yes, he was troubled, and she knew it. But she could find nothing to say to him save three little words.

"It's all right."

It was then he bounded across the intervening space and knelt beside her chair.

"Oh, darling, I love you."

He whispered the words and put his head down against her shoulder. She felt the sweet heaviness of it, was conscious of the deep, satisfied breath he drew, knew that he closed his eyes in an utter contentment.

His moment of anxiety had passed, the crisis was over; he was like a child, sure of a mother's forgiveness, certain now that he was not to be punished, that his security was unthreatened.

"Darling, I love you," he repeated.

Tenderly, without passion, he kissed the pulse which throbbed in her throat.

4

Elizabeth, driving home through the quiet, twisting lanes, wished she had had the courage to ask the question which had been hovering on her lips.

Yet, could one ask of anyone:

"Am I in love?"

There could be no possible answer save from herself; not even from someone who knew so much about love as Lydia.

It was amazing, Elizabeth thought, the way Lydia contrived to love and to go on loving Ivan, despite his infidelity. And the extraordinary thing was that she appeared happy, in fact, was happy.

There was no doubt, however sceptical one might be, of her contentment and indeed her unity with her husband. What was the secret of it, and how did she manage, in spite even of her physical infirmity, to keep her home together?

Elizabeth thought of all the things she had heard about Ivan—of the women she knew, many of them close friends, who raved about him and who were prepared to hint in more intimate moments of his attentions and his attractions.

Did Lydia mind or did she know nothing of this? And yet she had known about Mona Graham. Elizabeth was astonished.

Never before had she spoken to Lydia of Ivan's affairs, because it had been obvious that while they were the source of much speculation and gossip they were not to be taken seriously.

But this time it was different; everyone with whom she came in contact was talking of the action that Timothy Graham intended to bring against his wife, and she felt in duty bound to say something, at least to warn Lydia.

It had been unnecessary; Lydia knew, and what was more amazing, was taking it quietly and in her stride.

Elizabeth wondered what she herself would have done in like circumstances. It was difficult for her to judge, for such a situation would be impossible in her own married life.

For Arthur to be unfaithful was unthinkable. And yet was there much credit in that?

With a wry twist of her lips Elizabeth remembered someone say of another man—he must, indeed, have been Arthur's prototype—that he rated his wife a little less than his horse, a little higher than his dog.

She remembered, too, a conversation with a witty friend who had been complaining of the dullness of married life when the first passion of youth had passed. In an attempt to console her Elizabeth had said:

"Well, darling, at least your husband is faithful to you."

"That may be so," was the reply, "but it's no credit to him. If women were grouse or salmon he'd have been consistently unfaithful every season."

Elizabeth had laughed at the time, but afterwards she had remembered the remark. Was it, she wondered, worse to be neglected for an estate, for shooting, hunting, or any sport, than for another woman?

It was easy enough for Arthur Avon to speak disparagingly of Ivan.

"A dreadful chap; I'm always hearing stories about him. I can't think how your sister can put up with him. The man's a bounder!"

All her life, Elizabeth thought, she had heard such remarks first from her father, then from her husband; and yet she knew that deep down in her heart of hearts she envied Lydia.

She had only been eight when Lydia had run away from home, and yet the commotion that had been caused was implanted vividly in her mind—the furious anger of her father, the whisperings of the maidservants, the horrified comments made by relations and friends.

From that moment Lydia had been held up to her as an awful example. Hardly a day passed in the ensuing years when she was not reminded of her sister's reprehensible behaviour, and warned not to make such a mess of her own life.

She also was brought up in a cold, undemonstrative way, but unlike Lydia she was satisfied within herself, feeling little desire for warmer or more spontaneous impulses.

When Arthur Avon had proposed to her she had been delighted. She thought him a charming man and accepted him at her father's valuation.

"He's a good chap, my dear," Colonel Windover said, "and a gentleman. I should be happy to think that at any rate one of my daughters had married into a decent family."

She had known when she accepted Arthur that not only was it a solace to her father to know that she was secure in her own future, but that in making "a good marriage" she mitigated a little of the horror and the disgrace of Lydia's.

It was only after she had been married that she found out the truth about Lydia. The first time she had seen her sister it had been unexpectedly, and the impression she received had given her a shock.

She and Arthur had gone to dine with some friends in London. It was a rather smart, intellectual dinner-party, the type that Arthur most abhorred, and Elizabeth saw with amusement the gloom on his face when, as dinner finished, their hostess said with the air of one announcing a pleasant surprise:

"I've got tickets for the concert at the Queen's Hall. They were the last obtainable and we are very lucky to have them."

There was nothing to be done but express their

45

thanks. At the same time Elizabeth, noting Arthur's expression, knew that this was the last time she would be permitted to accept an invitation to dinner from these particular friends.

They reached the Queen's Hall having no idea of the nature of the concert, but as she stepped out of the car Elizabeth saw the posters outside.

She would hardly admit to herself that she was pleased, almost delighted, at the chance of seeing her brother-in-law. She had always been curious about him, and when they were ushered into their seats she looked expectantly at the great orchestra.

There was a roar of applause, and a man stepped on the platform and went to the conductor's rostrum. This then was—Ivan. Elizabeth's first reaction was a statement to herself:

"But of course Lydia married him, I'm not surprised!"

She knew nothing of music and yet as she listened to an orchestra conducted by Ivan she began to understand a little of what she had missed all her life.

It was not until later in the evening that she saw Lydia. Ivan finished the first half of the programme, and turned to face an audience half hysterical with delight and excitement.

Elizabeth noted that he glanced at and included in his very first bow a woman sitting alone in a box. She had not noticed her before as she was sitting far back in the shadows, but now she bent forward to smile and Elizabeth saw who it was.

She stared at Lydia. She was lovely, there was no question about that. She was not clapping, only leaning forward smiling, her eyes fixed on Ivan with an expression of pride and adoration which was indescribable.

Elizabeth felt a catch in her throat. It seemed to make Lydia so vulnerable, so at the mercy of all these people.

And then she realised that none of them except herself was thinking of anyone save Ivan. The tumult of applause rose and fell like waves.

It was Ivan who mattered, Ivan who was the hero, Ivan who had changed a great crowd of quiet, prosaic English folk into an emotional, demonstrative mob.

As they drove home after the concert Elizabeth hardly heard her husband's grumbles:

"A damned waste of an evening I call that," he said over and over again.

But to Elizabeth it was an evening which marked an important moment in her life. For the first time she was questioning her own upbringing, her father's veracity and, indeed, his infallibility.

She was, in truth, far younger in herself than Lydia had been at the same age, and her marriage, while bringing her both position and responsibilities, had not developed her personally.

It had, indeed, been nothing more or less than an extension of the life she had lived with her father—the same conversation at meals, the same interests and the same duties both inside the house and out; only on a vastly bigger scale, for Arthur Avon was a rich man besides being the bearer of an old and distinguished title.

After that memorable concert Elizabeth began to think. She had always rather despised the social life of which she knew nothing and understood less.

And Arthur had not encouraged her to go to dances, to mix with young people of her own age, to become part of that gay Mayfair world which lived for unceasing enjoyment. Now Elizabeth began to wonder what she was missing.

Was it possible that Lydia might be envied in her marriage and not be the outcast Elizabeth had always believed her to be? The idea was revolutionary.

The Countess of Avon made discreet enquiries and everything she heard confirmed the uneasy feeling that was growing within her that she had been deceived.

She was told that the Razoumovskys were a great success; she learnt that Lydia went only to the most select parties where she was a personal friend of the hostess.

Ivan was asked everywhere, but it was very difficult to be sure he would turn up. He was the "lion" of the season, the one person everybody wanted but few were lucky enough to get.

Elizabeth spoke to Arthur about her sister and received the reply she expected: Lydia had "behaved abominably," and had "broken her poor old father's heart." Ivan was "an outsider," one of "these ghastly artistic sort of fellows who thought they could get in anywhere because of their talents!"

Elizabeth sighed, and perhaps for the first time in her life took the initiative. She asked to see Lydia, and the years fell away in that moment so that she was a little girl again, admiring her nearly grown-up elder sister.

All the mothering Elizabeth had ever known had come from Lydia. When she had left home Elizabeth missed her more than she dare confess even to herself. Now she wanted to turn to her again, to ask her advice, to lean on her.

But the years between had created a gulf too wide to be bridged quickly. They were friends, but the barriers were not yet down.

They might have fallen when Lydia was injured and Elizabeth sped to her bedside; but Lydia at that time was too intent on her own misery, too drowned in her own despair to understand that here was the moment when she could have found the real Elizabeth.

By the time Lydia was back at Fairhurst, Elizabeth had donned her mask again. War was declared soon after and the sisters were prevented from seeing very much of each other.

It was only then that Elizabeth began to understand how lonely she was. She had lived quite happily in a world which was almost entirely peopled with a generation older than herself.

Now when the parties and the entertainment that had filled her day ceased and she found herself alone with

48

her husband, Elizabeth for the first time began to question her own happiness.

"What do I want?" she asked herself and knew the answer even though she would not admit it.

It had been hard to watch Lydia and Ivan together, to see the light in Lydia's eyes, to watch the way she became transfigured at Ivan's approach.

And he obviously loved his wife. Elizabeth's imagination developed—she began to see what these two had meant and still meant to each other and why Lydia had preferred to brave their father's anger and cut herself off from all that was familiar for the sake of a half-Russian musician.

"Is love worth any sacrifice?" Elizabeth asked herself. And again the question followed: "Am I in love?"

Was it love when one's heart beat quicker, when one felt breathless and at the same time alive and pulsating simply because some particular person was near?

She was nearly home when, as she turned a corner, she saw a car coming in the opposite direction. The lane was narrow and she braked hard and pulled sharply over to her left for it to pass. Even as she did so she saw who was driving. The man in the other car waved his hand, then passing her he pulled up and switching off his engine walked back.

She turned to watch him come and was conscious of her heart beating quickly.

He moved with the long, easy stride of a man who is used to the open moors. He looked grave, but it was characteristic of him and was an expression which came naturally to his square-jawed, strong Scottish features and deep-set eyes.

"How are you, Lady Avon?" he asked, taking her hand. "I'm glad to see you. They told me you were away for the day."

"I had a meeting in London and stopped at my sister's on the way back. I took Sergeant Cope up with me. You remember, he was to be transferred."

"Oh yes, of course. I've just been seeing that new

49

R.A.F. patient. I'm afraid I shall have to operate, there's no chance for him otherwise."

"I thought you would," Elizabeth replied.

Then, because she wanted it so much, hesitated before extending an invitation.

"There is such a lot I wanted to talk to you about. Won't you turn round and come back for dinner?"

Angus McLeod looked at his watch.

"I ought to say no."

"Say yes instead," Elizabeth begged.

He smiled and suddenly all his gravity was gone. It was the smile of a boy.

"I confess to being hungry and as I wasn't sure what time I should be home I didn't order myself a meal."

"Then come back at once," Elizabeth commanded and started up her car.

She drove it quickly, conscious all the time of the other car following her.

She could not quite remember when she first began to notice Angus McLeod. She had heard of him, of course, before Avon House was turned into a Convalescent Home, and when they had been told they were to have the worst surgical cases there she had been vaguely pleased because she felt it would be more interesting than if they had been allotted patients suffering from nerves or other disabilities.

Nurses had arrived; and then suddenly the name of Angus McLeod seemed to be in the air. "I don't know what Mr. McLeod will think of this." "It would be nice if Mr. McLeod approved of this." "Mr. McLeod always has things done this way."

Elizabeth was half irritated that in her rôle of Commandant she seemed to carry so little weight beside the desires of the great Mr. McLeod. But when she met him she understood.

His patients adored him; it was not what he said—he was a Scot and he said very little—but he gave them confidence and gave them, too, the incentive and the desire to get well.

They strove to improve their condition simply to please him. When she was going round the wards, they would say to her:

"My wound has nearly healed, miss. What do you think the doctor will think about that?"

"He will be pleased," she would answer.

"You bet he will!"

They would chuckle to themselves at the idea of the pleasure they were going to give Mr. McLeod. Elizabeth acknowledged to herself it was a great gift.

The men would be brought in shattered wrecks, and they would go on to the next place of treatment real convalescents both in body and mind.

And then gradually she found herself looking forward to Angus McLeod's visits just as much as the patients and staff.

"Mr. McLeod will be coming today," she would hear one of the nurses say and she would feel the response within herself at his coming; they were all so looking forward to seeing him.

But she seldom had a moment alone with the surgeon until one evening after a particularly severe operation he had entered her sitting-room, and noting how tired he was she had made him have a drink.

They sat down together in front of the fire, and suddenly Angus McLeod looked at her and asked:

"What will you do with yourself after the war?"

Elizabeth had felt startled at the question; it was one she had never even asked herself. She thought of the difference the war had made to her.

She loved having a hospital in the house, it gave her an interest which filled every hour of the day.

Now at Angus McLeod's question a series of pictures sped across her mind. She saw the shooting-parties, the guests coming and going at Avon House.

She saw the parochial calls she must make on the estate, the garden fêtes and bazaars she must open. She saw in each picture herself with her husband beside her —Arthur older, grimmer, a little more querulous, a little more intolerant as each year went by. It was with a shudder she heard her own voice answer:

"I don't know, I haven't thought of it."

"I don't know quite why I asked you," Angus McLeod said, knitting his brows, and yet she felt there was pity in his eyes. "This is a wonderful house."

He was speaking conventionally, and quite suddenly she threw aside all pretence.

"What shall I do with myself?" she asked. "Will there be anything for any of us—our sort of useless people—to do in the brave new world that is so much talked about?"

Then he had laughed, and his laughter dispelled both the gloom and the fear which were closing in upon her.

"Do you know what I am frightened of?" he asked. "All these organising women. Do you realise that we have taught thousands, if not millions of women of all ages, all classes and all types, to use their organising ability? I'm beginning to be afraid that a mere man will have no chance at all."

Elizabeth had laughed with him, and suddenly she had found herself talking as she had not talked for years, telling him a little bit of her life—the mere outline, but somehow she had known that he would be able to fill in so much.

The whole conversation did not take very long, and yet when he had thanked her and gone she felt as though something momentous had happened in her life.

She stood alone in her room with her hands to her cheeks.

That had been the beginning. It had only been a step further to acknowledge to herself that Angus McLeod interested her more than any man she had ever met in her life.

She learnt a little bit about him; that he came from the far north of Scotland, that his parents were poor and that he had made his way by a scholarship to Edinburgh University.

All his life he had had little time to play or to be

52

amused. He had just worked and gone on working, fighting his way by sheer perseverance to the top of his profession.

"I was lucky," he told her once. "The operations I performed when I first came to London were successful. One cannot do without an element of luck in every surgical case."

The sisters and the nurses told her a different story.

"His skill is amazing," they said. "At the same time he inspires his patients, he makes them want to live, and they hate to disappoint him by dying."

Angus McLeod sent all the patients in the Armed Forces in whom he was most interested to Avon House. It was not far from London and he found it easier to operate there where his patients could be at rest in the healing quiet of the country.

He turned up at all hours of the day and night, but usually he would telephone to Matron before he came, and Elizabeth grew adept in finding out what those messages were.

She admitted to herself that she wanted to see him and when she was not quite certain of the time he would arrive found it almost impossible to force herself from the house. She would wait for him, leaving the door of her sitting-room open so that she would hear his footsteps crossing the big, uncarpeted hall.

She wondered in a shame-faced way whether he guessed that many of the questions she asked him were but excuses—some of them seemed so thin even to herself, and yet he, too, seemed glad enough to see her.

But when she saw him smiling at the nurses and the sisters and noted their quickened interest, she told herself bitterly that she meant no more to him than the Commandant of his favourite Home.

Now as she drove home before him she wondered what excuse she could make to talk to him alone when dinner was over.

Arthur would be there at dinner, grumbling no doubt at the Ministry of Agriculture, and keeping up a long monologue about the many difficulties and injustices which he considered should be remedied immediately.

All through her thirty-two years, Elizabeth thought bitterly, she had heard her father and Arthur bewailing the fact that the country was going to the dogs.

"One day it will go," she thought, "and then they will be satisfied."

Nothing was ever right and it seemed to her that they had no sense of gratitude towards life.

Once or twice she had tried to make Arthur see how lucky they were when they compared the conditions in England with the plight of the Occupied Countries in Europe. But she realised as soon as she began to speak that it was impossible for Arthur to compare anything with England, and just as impossible for him to take a broad view of anything.

It was his own small interests that mattered, grievances which presented themselves to him personally.

"How small-minded he is," she told herself once angrily, and then was ashamed that she could critise Arthur so adversely even to herself.

Lately she had found herself fighting a battle to be loyal, and she was afraid because she saw Arthur so clearly and distinctly for what he was—an ageing man.

"I've disappointed him," she told herself. "He married a young wife and I've not been able to give him an heir. I must be kind—I must."

She tried to be particularly loving and considerate, but even while she went out of her way to please him she knew there was no need.

Arthur required so little of her; he had been sufficient unto himself for so long that a wife had made very little difference in his life.

"I'm nothing more or less than a table decoration," Elizabeth thought, and returned to her reflections about Angus—she had got to the stage of calling him Angus to herself.

She wondered what her father would have thought of

him and imagined Colonel Windover saying: "Not a bad fellow for a doctor!"

Oh, the snobbery—the preposterous, unending snobbery—in which she had been brought up! She wondered whimsically to herself whether, if Ivan had been a titled White Russian, that would have exempted him from so much criticism. A foreign title by her father's standard counted as very little; but to be a foreigner without one was completely and absolutely damning.

Those standards at least would die out after this war, there would be no one to keep them up, no one who would care enough, perhaps, even to open the fat red *Debrett* which had always filled a shelf in her father's study.

She thought of what Angus was doing—his work amongst the men who had been wounded on the battlefields, the way he never spared himself, the skill and the brilliance of his operations. And yet to her father and, she was quite sure, to Arthur too, he was "only a doctor."

Arthur was waiting in the hall as she drew up at the front door, and a moment later she heard Angus's car stop behind her. Her husband came out on to the steps and she saw that he held his watch in his hand. He was changed for dinner and was wearing a dinner-jacket with a high, old-fashioned wing collar.

"You're late, my dear."

"I know, Arthur. I'm so sorry, but I stopped to see Lydia on my way home, and look, I've brought Mr. McLeod back for dinner."

Arthur nodded indifferently.

"Evening, McLeod. I didn't think you'd stop or I'd have asked you myself."

"You've seen each other then?" Elizabeth asked.

"Yes, yes," Lord Avon said testily. "Now go and change if you're going to. Dinner should be ready by now."

"I won't be a minute," Elizabeth promised, and ran upstairs quickly like a girl.

55

She was longer than the promised minute, but it did not take her more than ten to change from her uniform into a dinner-dress.

Her maid was surprised when Elizabeth insisted on wearing not the plain black gown which was laid out for her nearly every evening, but a new dress made of soft white chiffon that she had chosen two years ago and had never worn because she felt it was too young and too smart.

She slipped into it now, adding a necklace of emeralds and bracelets to match—family jewels a little old-fashioned in their setting, but very lovely against the white dress.

She looked in the glass and felt the impulse to exclaim at her own good looks, and then realising that Arthur would be furious if dinner was kept waiting any longer she went quickly downstairs.

The men were waiting in the hall. As she approached she heard her husband say:

"News is good tonight, McLeod. It looks as though the war will be over soon and we can all go back to living normal lives."

She felt as though at that moment an icy hand was laid on her heart. "Normal lives" would mean that Avon House would return to its former glory.

The beds would be taken away from the ballroom, and the faint smell of anaesthetic would disappear from converted bedrooms. The nurses would go and Angus would visit them no more.

"I can't bear it," Elizabeth thought.

They looked up at her approach and the old butler, who had been hovering in the background waiting for her, announced stentoriously:

"Dinner is served, my lord."

They went into the small dining-room which they had used since the war. Dinner was served in the big crested silver dishes that Elizabeth remembered thinking very grand and impressive when she had first come to Avon House.

Now at this moment she wondered how she had ever been satisfied with all the pomp and circumstance which Arthur took for granted. At the same time she felt that tonight she couldn't ask herself too many unhappy questions.

She had seen what she believed was a faint expression of admiration in Angus's eyes as he turned to watch her coming down the stairs. Now as he and her husband talked she noted how he tried to include her in the conversation.

She didn't want to talk; she was content for him to be there—content and strangely happy.

She wondered how she was to bring about the chance of being alone with him; but after dinner the opportunity presented itself, for Arthur was told that his agent wanted to see him.

An aeroplane had crashed on one of the farms during the afternoon. No one had been hurt, but there were repairs which had to be seen to at once.

Arthur went to his study and Elizabeth led the way to her own room. She gave Angus a cigarette and refused one herself.

"You don't smoke?" he asked.

"Very seldom."

"I'm glad."

"Why?"

"I like women to be feminine."

"I think we all like to be feminine at heart. I'm very tired of my uniform."

"I like you much better in what you are wearing now."

He spoke gravely, and she realised that what might have sounded flirtatious from another man was merely from him a statement of fact.

"Thank you," Elizabeth smiled at him happily. "I'm so glad that you came back to dinner; but I'm afraid it's been very dull for you. Some time you must let me ask some amusing people to meet you."

"I hate amusing people. I'd so much rather be alone with you and your husband."

Did she imagine it or was there just a faint pause between the last two words?

"All the same," Elizabeth insisted, "I would like you to meet my sister and her husband. I expect you know him by name—Ivan Razoumovsky."

"Is he your brother-in-law?" Angus sounded astonished. "He's amazing. I heard him conduct about three months ago, and at the end of the concert I felt exhausted as though I'd lived through so much."

It was Elizabeth's turn to look astonished.

"Does music have that effect on you?" she asked.

Angus smiled.

"Some music."

"Ivan's an extraordinary man."

"So I believe."

Angus McLeod looked grave now and Elizabeth guessed that he, too, had heard stories.

"And yet my sister and he are tremendously happy," she said quickly. "She is an invalid; she had an accident while out riding six years ago, and the doctors said she could never walk again; but they're still happy, they still love each other."

"Then in that case does anything else matter?" Angus asked.

Elizabeth met his eyes.

"Nothing," she said. "Nothing."

5

"I had forgotten how beautiful England is," Christine said, stretching her arms above her head as she lay full length on the grass beside Lydia's chair.

"Did you miss us at all?" Lydia asked with a smile, speaking half jokingly.

Christine took her seriously. Rolling over on her side and raising her head by supporting it on one hand, she stared up at her mother and answered:

"Terribly at times. But at others you seemed so far away that I wondered if I'd imagined you."

Lydia, looking at her daughter, wondered for the hundredth time since she had returned whom she resembled.

Her oval face and big dark eyes were obviously inherited from her Russian ancestors, who were also doubtless responsible for the grace with which she moved. But her dark hair, almost raven black, owed no allegiance to Ivan's fiery locks nor to her own dark but by no means black ones.

She was not like her father nor would anyone have exclaimed on sight that she was Lydia's daughter; but her smile, which counterbalanced all her more mature charms, giving her at times an engaging frankness, was very English, as was her small, tip-tilted nose.

She was not strictly beautiful, but at the same time she had a piquant, appealing attraction which was distinctive in itself, and Lydia was quite certain that people having looked at her once would look again.

It had been difficult on their first encounter to realise that this was indeed the Christine who had left home four-and-a-half years ago.

The little girl Lydia remembered had gone and in her

place was a grown-up young woman, very poised and sure of herself. An American education, Lydia guessed, was responsible for the latter.

In England girls of Christine's age might be shy, or cocksure with the bouncing, rather noisy quality of over-exuberant youth; but Christine at seventeen-and-a-half seemed the finished product.

She appeared to know instinctively the right thing to do and the right thing to say; and if she suffered from any sort of "nerves" or nervous tension on coming home, she gave no sign of it.

There was no doubt that she was glad to be back. She showed her happiness in innumerable little ways, and Ivan was already entranced by her, watching her and listening to her with an admiration which Lydia could not help but find faintly amusing.

"She has something, that child," he said to Lydia when they were alone.

"What do you mean by that?" Lydia asked, knowing, but wanting to make him explain himself.

"Chic, intelligence, charm and originality," he answered solemnly.

Lydia had laughed outright.

"One might almost think you were a proud father," she said.

"I am," he answered—"very proud. We have made a wonderful job of Christine, you and I."

Lydia had been glad at his enthusiasm. At the same time she could not help a slight pang when she thought of her son. Ivan had never shown as much pleasure over Philip, and Lydia wished, as she had often done before, that he would take a little more interest in his only son.

How she longed for Philip; but he was far away, and with Christine here Lydia rebuked herself for not being content with what she had.

"I want you to enjoy yourself, darling," she told Christine. "It's going to be difficult, of course, to make a whole host of new friends, but we'll invite people here; and besides yourself there's always the swimming-pool as an attraction."

"I'm in no hurry to make friends," Christine said quickly. "I haven't yet decided what I'm going to do."

"Do?" Lydia was startled. "Do you mean you intend to have a career?"

"But of course," Christine answered. "You don't imagine I want to sit about being 'society', do you?"

Lydia who had imagined just that very thing, felt guilty.

"Of course, in war-time . . ." she began. But Christine interrupted her.

"War or no war," she said, "I couldn't bear to be a social butterfly. I'm sorry, Mother. I expect you had visions of my being brought up as you were. How I should loathe it! The daughter of the house, with nothing more strenuous to occupy my mind than choosing the flowers and taking the dogs for a walk! No, I want to work, but in what way I haven't decided."

"You must have some idea of your interests," Lydia said, "or in what direction your talents lie. It seems strange I should know so little about them. Are you musical?"

Christine shook her head.

"One musician in the family is quite enough."

Lydia laughed.

"Thank goodness you feel that way."

"No, I certainly shan't go in for music. And if you don't mind, Mother, I'd like to wait a little until I have sorted out my own ideas."

Lydia did mind, and she felt that she was being barred from her daughter's confidence. At the same time she humbly acknowledged to herself that it was going to take time to get to know this strange young creature who was part of her own flesh and blood.

It was difficult indeed to remember that this was the child who had run to her arms on every possible occasion, who had only to cry out for her in the night to be

61

certain that she would come, who had brought to her knee for so many years all her troubles and her joys.

"It was a mistake to send her away," Lydia thought; she wondered like so many other mothers why she had been foolish enough to be stampeded after Dunkirk into sending her child overseas.

But at that time things had seemed so desperate; there had been the fear of invasion, the threat of air attack; and with herself crippled and—as she told herself ruefully—an incumbrance to everyone, it seemed the sensible thing to accept Aunt Johanna's invitation.

From the child's point of view perhaps she had been right. Lydia had already heard a little of Christine's life in America.

She had been amazingly happy on the big estate in Virginia where Aunt Johanna lived. There had been young people to play with, horses and sports of all kinds to keep them amused.

Aunt Johanna was rich—or rather her American husband was—and there had been periodical trips to New York to buy new clothes and indulge in a perfect riot of entertaining and social interests.

"It would have been dull for Christine here during the war," Lydia thought, "even if I had sent her to a good boarding-school."

At the same time her heart cried out because she had missed those vital years of Christine's adolescence. The years were gone and the friendship they might have enjoyed together was now lost for ever.

It was gratifying in some ways to find how everyone liked Christine and how charming they thought her. Elizabeth came over soon after her arrival and before she left had said to her sister with a sigh:

"Christine makes me feel quite *gauche*; she's so polished and yet there's nothing pretentious or unnatural about it. Could it possibly be true that our upbringing was not the most perfect of its kind?"

She spoke mockingly, but Lydia had answered her almost with violence.

"We were brought up abominably. Think of the ridiculous way when we were in our teens that we were never encouraged to take any interest in ourselves or our appearance, told to keep silent at meals, taught that life would expect nothing from us except that we should get married as quickly as possible."

Elizabeth sighed.

"Poor Father, he thought he was doing his best. Perhaps if Mother had lived things might have been different."

"I doubt it," Lydia said. "They were both of a generation and class and their ideas were hide-bound. They would never have considered us as individuals who should be allowed to make their own choice of what was best for them."

"Well, you certainly did what you wanted to do," Elizabeth reminded her.

"At what a cost!" Lydia said bitterly.

"Not only to yourself," Elizabeth said quietly.

And Lydia looked at her in surprise, waiting for an explanation.

Elizabeth hesitated for words.

"I have often wondered," she said, "if it had not been for you whether I should have married Arthur."

"What do you mean?" Lydia enquired.

"The *mésalliance* that you had made in marrying Ivan was so impressed upon me," Elizabeth said, "spoken of with so much horror, that it made me frightened of anything that was not entirely conventional and absolutely in the tradition of what Father wanted.

"When one is a child I suppose one is very impressionable and the anger and displeasure of grown-ups bites deep into one's consciousness. I was determined that whatever happened I would never make the mistake you had made. You must remember I was brought up to believe it was a terrible mistake.

"Therefore as soon as I grew old enough to think about things I longed for security, for a position where

63

I would impress other people. You can imagine then that Arthur seemed to combine all these things.

"He offered me security in its widest sense—security not only from want, but from being a social outcast as I believed you were, from being the butt of other people's censure."

Lydia stared at her sister.

"I wish you had not told me this," she said. "It's frightening to think of how an action which one believes will only concern one's self reacts on other people. I suppose really I ought to have worried about you far more than I did. It was like abandoning my own child to abandon you to that household. But Ivan wanted me and I forgot everything else."

"Ivan wanted you!" Elizabeth repeated the words almost beneath her breath.

And then quickly, so that it was obvious to Lydia where the line of thought had led, she said:

"I want to bring a friend of mine over next week. Do you mind?"

"Who is it?" Lydia asked.

"The surgeon of whom you've heard me speak. We have all his worst cases at Avon House—Angus McLeod."

"Oh yes, of course," Lydia said. "You know we'd be delighted to see him. Ivan will be interested, too. It always seems to me that there is some link between music and medicine. I have found that most doctors and surgeons spend their spare hours listening to music."

"Yes, Angus McLeod spoke very enthusiastically of Ivan," Elizabeth said.

Lydia waited a moment, and then, greatly daring, proffered a question which in one blow struck at the barriers which had always existed between them.

"Are you interested in him?" she asked.

She saw the wave of scarlet which flooded Elizabeth's cheeks, and for a moment with a feeling of trepidation she thought her sister was going to reply stiffly and in indignation. Then Elizabeth capitulated.

64

"Very interested," she replied. "Are you surprised?"

Lydia smiled up at her in an understanding way.

"I am glad if it makes you happy."

Having made an open confession, Elizabeth now tried to cover her tracks.

"Of course I'm talking jokingly," she said quickly. "There's nothing serious in it, but Angus McLeod is an extraordinarily interesting man and I see a good deal of him. But, to be honest, he doesn't know I exist except as a Commandant."

"I shall look forward to meeting him," Lydia said softly.

She made no effort to press home her advantage after having made Elizabeth at least admit to a human emotion.

They were suddenly interrupted in their talk. Christine came bursting into the room with a telegram in her hand.

"Philip's coming home on leave!" she cried. "Isn't it marvellous?"

Lydia was trembling with excitement as she took the telegram from her daughter.

"At last!" she exclaimed. "I thought he'd never get away. When does he arrive?"

"Of course he doesn't say anything as intelligent as that," Christine scoffed.

"Now let me think," Lydia said. "When I last heard from him his ship was in Scapa Flow. That means if he sent the telegram this morning he should be with us tomorrow evening."

She raised a face alight with anticipation.

"I'm the luckiest woman in the world. Both my children home at the same time. We shall all be together."

She was so intent on her own happiness that she missed the cloud which overshadowed Elizabeth's face and the envy in her eyes.

The next afternoon while sitting in the garden with Christine, Lydia calculated quietly to herself that Philip should be with them in about another half hour.

She had spent some time during the morning looking up trains in *Bradshaw*, and even allowing for delays and missed connections she felt that Philip should manage to catch a train from London late in the afternoon.

Christine interrupted her thoughts.

"What are you thinking about Mummy? We were talking about me."

"I'm sorry, darling," Lydia replied. "I confess I was wondering if Philip would catch the same train as your father or whether I should have to ask the taxi to hang about in case he came later."

"What is Philip like now?"

"Very nice."

"I'm quite sure of that. Anyway, you'd think so. Mothers always love their sons best, don't they?"

"That's not true," Lydia retorted. "It's one of those ridiculous fallacies which people reiterate until they believe them. I honestly believe there's no question of loving any of one's children more than the others; one loves them all, but each in a different way.

"If Philip was killed I shouldn't love you more, and vice versa. I love you both as much as I am capable of loving.

"It always appears to me ridiculous and somewhat blasphemous to believe that we have a limited reserve of love inside us that we dole it out in portions."

"I have never thought of it that way before," Christine said reflectively. "I only remember being jealous of Philip because he was so nice-looking and was able to do things for you that I couldn't do."

"And I remember Philip complaining that you had all the attention after you were born," Lydia said, "especially from your father."

"There's a case in point which absolutely refutes your theory, Mummy. Daddy does like me best, you know that. And shall I tell you why?"

"Why?" Lydia asked.

"Because he's jealous of Philip. He's too young in himself to have a grown-up son. I may be wrong, because I haven't seen them together for four years, but I remember thinking that ages ago, and from one or two things Daddy's let drop since I've come back, I think the old order still standeth."

"You horrify me!" Lydia exclaimed. "I thought you were a sweet little child playing with your dolls and all the time you were watching, criticising and holding views of your own about us."

"I expect all children do the same," Christine said complacently. "But I suppose living in America has taught me to express myself. They all talk so much and they do say what they think. I always feel that over here people only say things you expect them to say."

"Now I wonder if that's true," Lydia questioned, half amused, half astonished at these revelations.

"I know you're wanting me to give you an example," Christine went on. "Very well—Aunt Elizabeth. What she says and what she thinks are two very different things."

"How do you know?" Lydia asked.

Christine laughed.

"I know lots of things. Aunt Johanna said that it must be my Russian blood. When she told me that, I read a great deal of Russian literature and I came to the conclusion there might be something in it.

"If the Russians really are like the books they write about themselves, they are frightfully introspective and incurably curious about the thought behind the action. I'm like that. What was my grandmother like?"

Lydia considered for a moment.

"You will have to ask your father because, of course, I never saw her. But from her photographs she was very beautiful. I expected you to be like her, but you're not, and yet I have a feeling that you doubtless resemble a still older ancestor."

"What has Daddy told you about his mother?" Christine insisted.

"That she was the daughter of a well-known Russian family. They were not of the titled aristocracy, but her

67

father was the librarian in one of the Tsar's palaces, and her mother, I think, had been a teacher or governess to some of the royal children.

"Your grandmother met your grandfather when he was Diplomatic Attaché in Petrograd. They fell very much in love and were married, and she left Russia to travel with him to various appointments all over the world.

"When the Revolution came, her father and mother were both shot. They were old people at that time, but I believe your grandmother grieved so much that it was really responsible for her death."

"Was she musical?" Christine asked.

"Not particularly," Lydia answered. "But I understand that her grandfather was a very fine musician and composed several operas which are still performed in Russia."

Christine was silent for some time and Lydia wished she knew what went on in her young brain. She guessed that the thought of her Russian blood had an appeal for her. It seemed romantic, and she was young enough and, indeed, English enough to want glamour and the excitement of being unusual.

"You must remember," Lydia said softly, "that you are only quarter Russian."

"And yet, as you've just proved yourself, most things seem to skip the succeeding generation," Christine said. "Sometimes I feel that I am very Russian indeed."

"And what does that feel like?" Lydia asked, amused.

Christine stretched herself and got up from the ground.

"I shan't tell you, Mummy, because you're laughing at me. But one day you'll all be surprised."

Lydia felt a slight feeling of dismay. She wished she understood her daughter better, and she told herself that, as about everything else in her life, she must have patience, she must wait.

She remembered the dark days after her accident. She had come through that, need she be afraid of this?

It was then with a bound at her heart that she heard voices coming through the house. She turned her head to see the two men she loved most in her life walking towards her.

Ivan moving swiftly with the evening sun gleaming on his fiery hair, and beside him, seeming heavy in comparison, Philip in his naval uniform, tall, fair and utterly English.

"Hello, Mum, I'm back."

There was no mistaking the gladness in his cry or in Lydia's answer.

"Darling! It's so lovely to see you."

He reached her side, and it was then she gave a little exclamation as she noticed that his arm was in a sling.

Philip answered her question before she could speak.

"Yes, a small 'blighty'," he said. "Isn't it splendid? It means a really decent spot of leave. Are you glad?"

In the conflicting emotions which beset her it was difficult to know which was paramount. Lydia managed to say:

"I'm glad you're back. What happened?"

"Oh, we had a bit of a show," Philip answered carelessly. "You'll be hearing more about it later."

"Who from?" Lydia asked, not understanding. But Christine, who had been listening, broke in with:

"Do you mean you'll get a medal?"

Philip looked at her and held out his uninjured arm.

"Don't tell me this is my little sister home from the land of plenty?" he asked.

"Yes, it is," Christine said, kissing him. "You haven't altered a bit except you've grown."

"Damn it! You've got it in first," Philip exclaimed, "and I'd been planning to say 'How you've grown' ever since I heard from Dad that you were here."

"Well, haven't I?" Christine demanded.

Philip looked at her critically.

"You've done something to yourself," he said; "I'm not sure what it is, but I suppose on the whole it's an improvement."

Ivan bent towards Lydia and kissed her as though he wanted to draw her attention to himself.

"The train was packed to suffocation," he grumbled, "so Philip and I didn't meet until we stepped out on the home platform."

"Poor dear, are you tired?" Lydia said soothingly. "You'll find some ice in the drawing-room. Why don't you make yourself a cool drink?"

Then, turning to Philip as though she could no longer contain herself, she asked:

"Is it true, darling, that you are going to be decorated?"

"There were rumours to that effect flying round," Philip replied. "But don't get excited until I have it on my breast."

"We must have a drink to celebrate this," Ivan said, moving off towards the drawing-room.

He sounded gay enough, but Lydia somehow fancied that something had upset him. She remained talking with Philip and Christine for a little while, and then as Ivan did not return she went into the house. He was sitting in the drawing-room, sunk deep in a big arm-chair. She moved her chair forward quickly.

"What is it, darling?" she asked.

"What is what?"

She knew by the tone of his voice that Ivan was in one of his childish, temperamental moods.

"What's the matter?" she insisted. "Has something upset you?"

"What should upset me?" Ivan enquired. "I have my daughter home from America, my son home on leave, and a wife who adores both her children so much that her whole interest is centred in them. What more should I want?"

Lydia bent forward and put her hand on his.

"Darling, I love you. Our children are only part of ourselves, perhaps that's why I love them so much."

"It's right that you should love them," Ivan said. "But sometimes my children make me feel old."

That, then, was the truth. Lydia knew that she had the key both to his mood and to his jealousy. Christine had been right in some ways—he was jealous of Philip, jealous because he made him feel old.

Ivan, who had always appeared eternally young, was not happy or at his ease in the presence of real youth, the gay, unconscious youth of twenty-one-year-old Philip.

Lydia sought for words to comfort him and found it hard to know what to say.

"We have all got to get old, darling," she said at length.

"I know," Ivan said testily, "but need we pretend we are enjoying it? I hate it—hate it, I tell you!"

He sprang to his feet and started to walk round the room as he always did when emotionally disturbed. "Our bodies will wither and decay, we shall grow flabby and senile, we shall lose the thrill and the joy of living. God! Why was age ever invented save as a torment to mankind?"

Lydia was silent. Here she was powerless to comfort, powerless to help. She felt that Ivan was experiencing in some little degree the rebellion against the inevitable that she had felt after her accident.

Then she had known that all defiance and misery were wasted, that what was unalterable must be accepted.

"What is the point of it all?" Ivan was asking, "the point of living? Is there anything else beyond, and if there is, why should there be so much mystery about it?"

"Darling, no one can answer those questions," Lydia said.

"Of course they can't," Ivan retorted. "And so, poor fools that we are, we must creep on, gradually rotting into decay, helped only by some fairy tale about a better world beyond this. Who wants anything better than this world when one is young and happy and in love?"

Lydia felt her heart contract with pity.

Then, as Ivan ceased speaking and whilst she herself felt for words, there came a burst of laughter from the garden: Philip's laugh, young, wholehearted, unrestrained, and Christine's joined with his, clear and joyful.

Ivan's expression altered, and for a moment it seemed to Lydia that it changed to one of hatred.

Without another word he went from the room, slamming the door behind him so that the sound of it boomed and echoed and the crystal pendants of the chandelier shivered and tinkled.

6

Christine walked down the quiet, rather dingy street in north London glancing at the numbers on the porticoed doorways.

Finally she found the house she sought and walking up the steps rang the bell. It was some time before the door was opened by an old and obviously suspicious retainer.

"Can I see Sir Fraser Wilton, please?" Christine asked.

"Sir Fraser sees no one without an appointment."

"I have an appointment," Christine replied. "Miss Stanfield is the name."

The man let her in reluctantly as if he still suspected that her business was unauthorised. He led the way into a large, gloomy front room and shut the door on her.

Christine looked round.

The room was furnished in Victorian style: heavy portraits were hung against a background of dark red brocade and the windows were draped in the same colour, the betasselled and befringed velvet curtains doing their best to exclude as much light and air as possible.

Christine looked disappointed and then apprehensive. She had expected something so very different, and for a moment she seemed undecided as if she might make up her mind to leave the house at once.

She fingered the letter in her hands, turning it over and over, and then before her decision was made the door opened.

"Will you come this way, please, miss?"

Christine followed the old butler down the long passage which she realised led her away from the front of the house to the back. He opened a door and announced her name.

"Miss Stanfield, sir."

Christine had a quick impression of light and space, and then she saw the man who rose to greet her from behind the desk at the far end of the room.

Sir Fraser Wilton was an old man—that she already knew—but he carried himself superbly; and as he held out his hand with a smile of greeting it was not difficult for her to realise that this was a man whose brains had held the thinking world fascinated and intrigued for over half a century.

Sir Fraser spoke first.

"How do you do, Miss Stanfield? You bring me a letter, I believe, from a very old friend of mind. Won't you sit down?"

He pointed to a deep, comfortable armchair beside his desk.

"Here it is," Christine replied, "and Mr. Vanderfelt asked me to give it to you with his love."

Sir Fraser took the letter, but for a moment he did not open it. Instead he looked at Christine with a twinkle in his eye.

"How is my friend Cowan?" he asked. "Still twisting the tail of New York's intelligentsia?"

"He is very well," Christine replied. "I think he enjoys life more than anyone I have ever met."

Sir Fraser laughed.

"Why shouldn't he? He understands what it's all about, which is more than most of us poor fools are capable of doing. And now, my dear, I will read what our mutual friend has to say."

He slit the envelope with a long ivory paper-knife and drew out the contents.

Christine looked round her. The room in which she sat was certainly in amazing contrast to the one in which she had waited.

It was big—lofty and oblong in shape, and had been converted, Christine guessed shrewdly, by gutting the entire mews buildings which had stood originally at the back of the house.

Now pine-panelled walls were a background for an enormous collection of books, while windows on both sides of the room opened out on to a small flower-filled courtyard on one side and a quiet street on the other.

A big open fireplace which burned logs was the only thing in the room which could be described as of ancient tradition. Everything else was essentially modern, especially the desk at which Sir Fraser sat, which was made of polished wood set in chromium plate.

It was an unusual room and, indeed, a beautiful one; and she wondered at the contrast to the front of the house and realised that this, at least, was the sort of background she would have expected of a great scientist.

Sir Fraser read Cowan Vanderfelt's letter slowly, and when he came to the end of it stared for a moment at the signature as if to make perfectly certain it was genuine.

He then put it down on the table and looked at Christine.

"This is a very extraordinary letter, young woman."

Christine smiled. She was not certain what she should say.

"It's not one of Cowan's little jokes, I suppose?" Sir Fraser asked.

Christine shook her head.

"No," she replied, "it's absolutely true, every word of it."

"Um." Sir Fraser looked down at the letter. "And what advice did our eminent friend give you besides telling you to contact me?"

"He made me promise two things," Christine replied. "The first was that I would tell no one about myself until I had seen you, and the second that I would never at any time make a study of medicine or surgery."

"Why did he ask you that?" Sir Fraser asked interestedly.

"Mr. Vanderfelt said that nothing was more dangerous than the layman with a little knowledge, and that if I tried to use my brains instead of my instinct he was afraid of the consequences."

Sir Fraser chuckled.

"That's so like Cowan. He calls himself a realist, but I doubt if he ever practises his own theories. Suppose we start from the beginning and you tell me your story in your own way and in your own words."

Sir Fraser sat back expectantly in his chair, but his eyes alighted for a moment on one sentence in the letter before him, which read:

I assure you, my dear Fraser, that I have met thousands—I nearly wrote millions—of healers in my life, but they've always attributed their powers to some mumbo-jumbo of spirits, saints or inner voices. Here is the actual thing, unvarnished and presented without any frills. See what you can make of it, it has flummoxed me.

Christine sat hesitating for a moment as if she wondered how to begin, and then quite calmly and without any sign of nervousness she said:

"After Dunkirk I went out to America to stay with my great-aunt in Virginia; she has a big estate there and is a very large landowner. She always had a number of her grandchildren staying with her, and as several of them were about my age I had, as you can imagine, a very enjoyable time.

"I was thrilled with the difference in the life there from what I had known at home, and I was especially interested in the Negro servants.

"Some of them have been in my great-aunt's service for many years, and we often ran into their houses on the estate for some coffee or fruit or merely to call, because the other children knew them so well.

"I talked to them and I liked them.

"I had been in America over two years—I was

76

nearly sixteen—when one day we went down to see an old Negro woman who lived near the river which ran through the estate.

"She had, I believe, originally been cook in my great-aunt's house but had retired owing to old age. We all knew old Sarah and it was an understood thing that the children and the grandchildren of the house called to see her on their birthdays.

"It was not the occasion of a birthday, but my great-aunt had learnt that Sarah's daughter had died in New York and that her child had been sent down to the old woman.

"My great-aunt was unable to visit Sarah herself that particular day, so she sent us to find out all the details.

"We rode there on our ponies and it took us nearly two hours to reach the tiny cottage which my great-aunt had built for Sarah on the estate. There was a small colony of Negroes, houses and cottages making what we would call over here a model village.

"Aunt Johanna had great ideas on raising the standard of living among the Negroes she employed. We jumped off our ponies, calling to Sarah to come and greet us, and we were rather surprised when she didn't come to the door as was usual on our visits.

"We walked up to the door and knocked, and then we heard her voice telling us to come in.

"We entered the tiny kitchen, where a bright fire was burning, and there sitting in front of the stove was Sarah with a baby in her arms.

" 'Come in, missy,' she said to my cousin, 'and shut the door behind you. This babe is powerful sick.'

"Of course we crowded round to have a look at the baby. It was a tiny little thing, a girl of five months old I learned later, and she certainly looked miserable at that moment.

" 'What's the matter with it?' we asked.

" 'This babe is sick to death, missy,' Sarah answered.

" 'That's terrible!' we exclaimed.

" 'Surely you can do something?' I asked.

" 'I will go and tell Granny,' my cousin said. 'Perhaps she'll arrange to have it sent to hospital.'

" 'It's no use,' Sarah repeated mournfully. 'Dis chile will die.'

"She said it in that flat, fatalistic tone which I knew later was characteristic of the Negroes when, as they say themselves, they 'smell death'.

"It was the first time I had come in contact with this attitude and something within me rebelled against giving up the fight and allowing that small, curly-haired child to die.

" 'Oh, let's take her back with us,' I said impulsively. 'Let me hold her, Sarah.'

"Rather to my surprise the old woman put the baby into my arms. I think she was glad of a rest and a stretch. I cuddled the child and sat down beside the fire.

"Then as I held it I suddenly knew exactly what was wrong. I could see its body absolutely clearly as if it were a mathematical problem and where in its small stomach the trouble lay.

"The child was only wrapped in shawls. I pushed them on one side and laid my free hand on its little black stomach. Almost without conscious thought I massaged it slowly.

"The other children went on talking, asking Sarah about the baby and how it had come to her and about the daughter who had died in New York. Sarah was busy making them some coffee to drink and offering them cookies from a big tin.

"As I sat silent, massaging the baby, I could feel a force tingling in my fingers—a kind of vibration passing between me and the child. I knew with an absolute certainty that I was doing it good.

"Nobody took any notice of me and I suppose that I must have sat there for about five minutes when quite suddenly the child opened its eyes and began to cry.

"Sarah started as if she had been shot.

78

" 'For Lawd's sake!' she exclaimed. 'That's the first time that chile has cried since it came here.'

" 'It's hungry,' I said. 'Give it some milk.'

"I still had my hand on its stomach and I thought that Sarah looked at me queerly, but without further question she heated some milk in the bottle and gave it to the baby, who sucked it hungrily.

"One would think a black baby couldn't look ill, but as soon as the poor little thing had taken its bottle her whole face seemed to change; the slight grey tinge disappeared and there was no longer that pinched look round the nose and mouth. When she had finished she smiled, then snuggled down in her shawls as though she would go to sleep.

"It was then Sarah walked across and stood looking down at me.

" 'Missy Christine,' she said, 'what have you been doing to this chile?'

"For the first time I felt slightly embarrassed.

" 'I don't think there was much wrong with her,' I answered lamely. 'I rubbed her "tummy" a little, that was all.'

"The old woman bent over me and took my hand in hers. She turned it over and looked intently at the palm.

" 'It's a healer you are,' she said at length. 'Glory be, but a miracle has been worked in this house! My grandchile will live!'

"And then she threw her apron over her head and started to cry. It was horribly embarrassing and quite frankly I didn't know what it was all about.

"We went home shortly after that and the others teased me, saying if I wasn't careful the Negroes would think I was a sort of god and worship me. It all seemed a tremendous joke at the time.

"Of course we told my great-aunt our exciting, incoherent story, of which she could make neither head nor tail except that Sarah had got her grandchild there and that it was ill.

"She sent for the family doctor, a charming old man

79

who lived in the nearest town, and he went out that very evening to see the baby.

"When he came back—I remember so well it was after dinner and we were all dancing in the big drawing-room—he sent for me and questioned me closely as to what I had done to the child. I told him what was the truth—that I had just rubbed the baby's 'tummy' a little and that she had wakened up and seemed hungry.

"He said very little to me, but talked to my great-aunt alone for a long time.

"When he had gone she called me to her and said that I must be very careful in future not to interfere with the black people and their children.

"They were full of superstition, she said, and while in this instance I had apparently done good, if, on the other hand, the child had died they might conceivably have attributed it to me. I promised her, of course, easily and without thinking much about it, that I would never touch anybody's black baby again.

"I wasn't all that interested anyway, for I had begun by this time to forget—or rather to doubt—what had happened to me when I had held the child in my arms.

"In asking for promises both my great-aunt and the doctor had forgotten the Negro people themselves. Sarah was an old talker, besides which she was known over the length and breadth of the estate. The story obviously spread like wildfire, losing little in the telling.

"The following day we were having tea on the verandah when the old Negro butler announced that there was a young woman at the back door who wanted to see me. Of course I had no idea what it was about; but my great-aunt got up at once and telling me to remain where I was went out to see the woman.

"When she came back she looked rather upset and for her severe. Drawing me aside from the others, she told me that the woman had come five miles to ask me to help her child who had an injured leg.

"My great-aunt had apparently been very stern with her, refusing to allow her to see me, but had told the kitchen staff to give her food before she started her return journey.

"I was rather flattered that my reputation had grown so quickly, but my great-aunt took such a grave view of the whole thing that I was forced to say once again how sorry I was that I had interfered in any way with Sarah's grandchild.

"I then thought no more about the woman till after dinner that evening.

"When it was hot we used to wander through the open windows on to the lawn of the house, sometimes dancing, sometimes impulsively making up our minds to have a last swim in the big swimming-pool.

"Tonight was one of those occasions. The boys suggested a moonlight swim and we all agreed, rushing up to our rooms and tossing off our evening dresses and putting on our bathing-suits. It was an unwritten law that one raced to the pool, the first one in scoring over the others.

"Usually I was pretty quick, and, if not first, I was certainly seldom the last. But that night I broke a fingernail as I was undoing the strap of my evening shoes, and by the time I had straightened it with a pair of scissors the others had got far ahead of me.

"I could hear them shouting and laughing in the pool as I came out of the house.

"There was therefore no hurry and I walked slowly along in the moonlight adjusting my bathing-cap. As I turned from the lawn on to the path bordered by trees which led towards the pool I heard a whisper:

" 'Missy Christine!'

"It frightened me for a moment so that I turned, startled and half afraid.

" 'Who is it?'

"A woman came out from the bushes. She was a Negress and her face was vaguely familiar, although I might have confused her with someone else—so many Negroes look alike to me.

" 'Missy Christine, cure my son.'

81

"She pulled forward a little boy by the hand as she spoke, a child of three or four years. He goggled at me round his mother's skirts, and I saw that he was frightened.

"I shook my head decidedly.

" 'I'm sorry,' I said, 'but my great-aunt will have already told you that she doesn't want me to do this.'

"The woman gave a frightened cry.

" 'Oh, please, missy, please!'

"Quite suddenly she flung herself down on her knees before me. I began to get frightened.

" 'You must go away,' I said. 'You will get into trouble being here.'

"She then clutched my arm and began to sob in the terrifying, heart-rending manners Negroes do. I was horribly frightened lest my cousins should hear. I drew her off the path towards a little summer-house.

" 'Come in here,' I said. 'I will look at your boy, but there is nothing I can do. Do you understand? Nothing!'

" 'Please, missy, please.'

"The woman was now trembling with excitement, and feeling worried and apprehensive of the whole thing I reached the summer-house followed by the woman and the limping boy.

" 'Listen,' I said. 'You don't seem to understand, but what happened yesterday was just chance. There's nothing I can do for any child or anybody. You must go to a doctor and he will help you.'

"The woman looked at me to see if I was speaking honestly, and then patiently as if to a child she said:

" 'Miss Christine, you not understand. You have a healer's hand. Please, you heal my little chile?'

"I had a feeling that nothing I said would make her go away and I thought to myself quickly that the best thing would be to look at the child, to touch him, and then if nothing happened she would realise her mistake. It would be much the best way.

" 'All right, I'll look at him,' I said rather crossly.

"She pushed him forward and I could see that not only did he limp, but one leg seemed more emaciated than the other. I put out my hand and took one of his, and as I touched him the same strange thing happened as had happened the day before.

"I could see him in a different way; I could see his body and I could see where things were wrong. The boy was wearing only a little cotton shirt. I pulled this up and put my hand on his hip. I rubbed him, and instantly I felt that strange vibration passing from myself to him.

"The child stood very still while I rubbed his hip and his leg. He neither whimpered nor spoke. The mother watched me, her eyes very large in the moonlight.

"I don't know how long I rubbed the boy's limb— perhaps it was only five or ten minutes; I only knew it was enough and I stopped.

" 'You had better go,' I said.

"I wanted to add: 'In the morning you will see how ridiculous the whole thing has been,' but somehow I couldn't. I knew it was ridiculous, I knew that the child's leg was going to get well.

"The mother needed no second bidding. She took the child up in her arms and vanished into the shadows of the trees. I wondered why she had gone without saying good-bye, and then I realised that her ears were quicker than mine and that she had heard my cousins returning from the swimming-pool.

"I walked out from the little summer-house to meet them.

" 'What happened to you, Christine?' they called.

" 'I just didn't feel like bathing,' I replied. 'I think I must be tired.'

"They accepted my explanation without comment and we all went back to the house together.

"I thought I should hear no more about the incident, but of course I reckoned on there being no obvious result. Within three days the boy's leg was getting better; the blood was flowing back into it, the lump that he had on his hip had disappeared and already his limp was far less pronounced.

"My great-aunt was informed of what had happened. She sent for me and made me confess. This time she was really angry.

" 'You promised me, Christine,' she said.

" 'Yes, I know.' I replied miserably.

"I was very fond of my great-aunt and I felt that in doing what she expressly asked me not to I had abused her hospitality.

"Two days later we all went to New York. It was usually a month or so later that we made the move, but my cousins, who enjoyed the gaiety and amusements, were delighted at the change of plan, although I knew why it had been made.

"We had a marvellous time and I think I really forgot about the Negroes and their ailments. But when we came home the whole thing started again. If I could forget about it, the Negroes could not.

"They looked on me as something especially sent to help them, and when my great-aunt refused to allow them to see me they lay in wait for me in all sorts of unexpected places.

"It was impossible for me to go out of the grounds without finding some Negress in trouble, begging me to help either herself or her children.

"For a long time I kept my promise, and then at last when I felt I could withstand the pressure of their entreaties no longer I went to my great-aunt and begged her to release me from my given word.

" 'I must help them, I must!' I said.

"She looked at me in surprise.

" 'Do you really believe you can?' she asked.

" 'I know I can.'

"She looked bewildered.

" 'But, Christine, it was just chance. The children whom you touched would have got well anyway. Surely you can see that?'

"I shook my head. 'I don't think they would.'

"She then became quite alarmed, thinking, I suppose, that the episode had affected my mind. She wrote to Cowan Vanderfelt—a very old friend of hers—asking him to come down and stay. Before he arrived she told me why she had invited him.

" 'He is not only one of the most brilliant men in America,' she said, 'but he is one of the most sensible. He has been many things in his life—a doctor, a scientist; he has written many books on psychology; but he is also someone who is eminently full of common sense. Will you promise me, Christine, to tell him the truth and to answer any questions that he puts to you?'

" 'But of course,' I replied.

"To be honest, I was rather flattered that someone so important as Cowan Vanderfelt should be asked down to talk to me. After all, I was only sixteen and I suppose it's not every day that a man who is a household name in America is sent for because some young girl has got ideas.

"That was exactly what my great-aunt believed—that I had 'ideas'. I could imagine her saying in her sensible way:

" 'Of course, all girls about that age have ideas. Christine will grow out of it.'

"And that is how I met Mr. Vanderfelt," Christine smiled. "He's a darling! I think I loved him the first moment I saw him! He didn't tease me, he didn't talk down to me, he didn't make the slightest attempt to belittle me. He just wanted to know; that's what I liked about him, and I told him everything.

"The day after he arrived we went down to see the little boy with the bad leg. It was nearly four months since that night in the summer-house and there was no doubt about it that the child was completely cured.

"He walked just as any other child of his age would walk; in fact, it was difficult for me to remember which had been the bad leg. Mr. Vanderfelt and I went alone to see the child.

"He told my great-aunt that he would rather that she
85

did not come; I believe he thought she would embarrass me.

"We had no sooner appeared amongst the farm dwellings where this particular woman lived than a number of Negroes came running up and surrounded us, begging me to help them.

"After a while, when they realised that I would not, they withdrew, staring at me sulkily, at the same time watching with interest when we came to the home of the little boy with the cured leg. I said very little; it was Mr. Vanderfelt who did all the talking.

"And then when he had joked with the children and got the mother to tell him how the boy had suffered, he said to me:

" 'Don't you think it would have got well anyway?'

"I was rather tired of the whole thing by now. 'Of course it would,' I said. 'I can't think why everybody is making all this fuss about it!'

"He looked at me curiously, and then before he could speak the mother of the child said—I won't attempt to imitate her dialect:

" 'If Missy Christine would only see my sister-in-law. She's been ill for so long now, ever since her baby was born dead. She never speaks, but just lies and looks at the ceiling. She's dying, but if Missy Christine would see her she would get better.'

"I was about to refuse as I had refused so many requests in the last month, but Mr. Vanderfelt silenced me.

" 'Why don't you see her!' he asked.

" 'You know what Aunt Johanna would say,' I retorted.

" 'I will take the responsibility for that.'

"I looked at him and knew exactly that he was determined to prove I was an impostor once and for all. Once again I could hear my aunt's voice saying:

" 'Of course all young girls get ideas. Christine's of that age.'

"I think I hated them all at that moment; the Negroes who had got me into this position, and most of all Mr. Vanderfelt standing there looking at me in his kindly way, but having, I knew, all the years of his study of psychology behind him. I wanted to refuse, but my pride would not let me. I turned to the woman.

" 'All right, I'll see your sister-in-law,' I said.

"She led the way eagerly enough. It wasn't far, and when the other Negroes saw where we were going there was a murmur of excitement and they followed us excitedly. We came to the house—if you could give it such a pretentious name.

"It was a small, very dirty dwelling-place and smelt abominably. With every moment that passed I wished I hadn't come, and when I saw the woman lying on what looked like a bed of rags I almost ran away.

"She was a young woman but dreadfully emaciated, and she lay as we had been told, with her face turned towards the ceiling, just staring. I think Mr. Vanderfelt sensed that I was nervous. He put his hand on my shoulder and said quietly: 'If you'd rather go home, Christine, you say so.'

"I knew exactly what he was thinking, and I believe at that moment I would rather have died than have made no attempt to help that woman.

"I bent forward and took her hands, which were lying limply by her sides, and as soon as I touched them I began to see what was wrong with her.

"Her sister-in-law talked all the time, telling us about the hot fomentations that had been put on her stomach because they were certain the pain was there, and detailing all sorts of gruesome remedies which had been tried.

"As soon as I held that woman's hand I knew that the trouble lay in her head. I laid my hands on her forehead for a moment and felt a slight repugnance at having to touch that thick bushy hair.

"And then I felt that strange tingling in my fingers. I worked on her forehead for a few minutes, but instinctively my hand seemed to go to the back of her neck.

87

"It was very uncomfortable for me as I had to bend over the bed, but still I worked away, forgetting Mr. Vanderfelt watching me and the other Negroes crowding by the door. I went on massaging the back of her neck and then her forehead until my arms ached.

"I stopped from sheer fatigue. I felt I had failed, and stood back with a deep sense of disappointment. Then the woman suddenly opened her eyes, tried to sit up and spoke.

" 'Jem! Jem!'

"She called her husband's name, and at the sound there was a long-drawn breath from the Negroes round the door. They fell on their knees and shouted:

'Glory, Glory, Hallelujah!'

"It was a most extraordinary scene; I don't think anyone could have helped being moved by it. I believe I reached out and grasped Mr. Vanderfelt's hand, I don't know if I said anything. All I remember was looking up into his face and noting with a sense of elation that he believed in me."

Christine took a deep breath. She had spoken so quickly that she was almost breathless.

"He believed in me," she repeated.

"I am not surprised," Sir Fraser said quietly.

Content with the interest she saw in Sir Fraser's face
and the attention he gave her, Christine continued her
story, having first tucked her feet under her in the big
armchair to make herself more comfortable.

"Mr. Vanderfelt," she said, "examined the woman
after she had spoken, and then when she was drinking
some milk—her first nourishment for several days—we
went home. We said very little to each other on the way
back. I was terribly excited by what had occurred, but I
felt shy of expressing my feelings or of asking Mr. Vanderfelt's opinion.

"As soon as we got back to the house he called my
great-aunt on one side and had a long conversation with
her. I was not present and naturally I didn't try to overhear what was said.

"But an hour later, as I came through the hall after a
game of tennis with my cousins, the door of the drawing-room stood open and I heard my great-aunt Johanna say wearily, in the tone of voice people use when
they are repeating something they have said several
times before?

" 'If she was religious I could understand it.'

" 'That's the one thing that makes the case interesting,' was Mr. Vanderfelt's reply.

"I heard no more, but I thought those words over
rather carefully, and perhaps for the first time I began
to wonder very seriously why this power should be in
me. I understood exactly what my great-aunt meant and
I could appreciate her surprise and, indeed, her irritation.

"If I believed that the power came from spirits, angels or saints controlling me, it would have been easier

to explain. But that I, Christine Stanfield, a perfectly ordinary girl, should for no reason at all and without any previous indications find myself able to heal sickness was, to say the least of it, astonishing.

" 'Why had it happened!' I asked my self. At the time I could think of no possible explanation."

"Can you think of one now?" Sir Fraser asked.

Christine hesitated, and then she replied:

"Not exactly an explanation, but I feel there must be a reason for it . . . but shall I finish my story first?"

"Of course. I don't want to interrupt."

"I will make it as short as I can," Christine said, and continued. "The Negroes on the estate were, as you can imagine, wildly excited by what had occurred. There were always one or two asking for me, but on Mr. Vanderfelt's advice my great-aunt did not send them away sternly as she had done before. Instead she talked to them and persuaded them to see a doctor.

"Only in two other cases did I have anything to do with helping them and then Mr. Vanderfelt was with me, and on both occasions I was successful. He took very careful notes of the cases and you will find them here amongst many others."

Christine opened her big white handbag as she spoke and drew out a sheaf of closely typed notes.

"I am not going into the details of these," she said. "Mr. Vanderfelt wanted you to see them and I will leave them with you to read at your leisure, but I want to tell you what happened after that.

"The one thing of which my great-aunt and Mr. Vanderfelt were frightened was that the Press would get to hear of what had happened—you know what the Press in America is like—and apart from the interest in the story itself there was also a certainty that it would be given an added publicity because of my relationship to a very well-known person."

"Your great-aunt," Sir Fraser commented.

Christine had been referring to her father but she did not say so. She did not correct Sir Fraser but went on:

"This necessitated, of course, especial need for secrecy, but Mr. Vanderfelt was anxious to test me out still further. He therefore took me to a hospital for children in which he was particularly interested in New York."

"To a hospital?" Sir Fraser exclaimed.

"Yes, but it was all done very cleverly," Christine replied. "Mr. Vanderfelt knew the Matron very well—I think as a matter of fact she was a cousin of his. He told her the truth, knowing he could count on her cooperation.

"So I was allowed to try to help a dozen cases. When I was to see a patient, the Matron had the case moved into a private room and the only people present were Mr. Vanderfelt, the Matron and myself.

"The nurses were told, I think, that I was just a student of his taking notes, and as he was so well-known and so important you can imagine they didn't take much interest in anyone who accompanied him."

"And you were successful?" Sir Fraser asked.

"In all cases," Christine replied, "except those which needed a definite surgical operation. Where there was a malignant growth, I was able to cure the child after seeing it twice. In the case of a very bad abscess it completely disappeared overnight.

"Where a bone was misplaced I was powerless, and on another occasion where a leg had to be amputated I could do nothing except that the general health of the child seemed to improve. You will find all this recorded in the notes."

"And what did you feel on the occasions when you failed?" Sir Fraser asked.

"I could feel that the effort I was making was not hopeless, but that it was not enough. It was . . . how can I express it? Rather like pushing something very heavy up a hill and knowing that while you can move it a little way your strength will not enable you to reach the top."

Sir Fraser smiled as though he liked the description.

"Good!" he approved. "Go on."

"That is really all," Christine said. "As you can imagine, this was not done in a minute. A month or so would elapse between each case, and I think, too, that Mr. Vanderfelt, although he was extremely interested, made them as few as possible because every time I visited the hospital my great-aunt was so distressed.

"She was really horrified at the whole thing; she felt there was something unwholesome and abnormal about it all. Besides, she was so terrified of my becoming headlines that I hated to distress her.

"Also, naturally, a large amount of my time was spent at school, so I can quite honestly say that for a year I only gave the matter serious thought when Mr. Vanderfelt turned up to present me with a new problem.

"I found, too, that when I was absorbed in other things it was very difficult to remember exactly what the sensation was like in touching someone and trying to heal them. At the time I could understand the case, why I was treating it and what was happening.

"But when it was finished and done with it was hard to recall anything clearly. But I'm not suggesting that I go into a trance or anything like that."

"It is all extremely interesting," Sir Fraser said, "and I shall be most interested to see the notes Cowan has made."

"He was so certain that you would be interested. He told me so much about your investigation and as soon as your last book was published he gave me a copy. I read it very carefully."

"And what did you make of it?" Sir Fraser asked.

"It taught me lots of things I didn't know before about mankind," Christine answered, "but it didn't explain about me."

"Do you expect me to write another book on you?" Sir Fraser asked with a twinkle in his eye.

"I don't want you to write a book about me," Christine replied. "I want you to help me."

"Help you?"

"I want you to advise me as to what I am to do with this . . . well, what shall I call it? . . . talent."

Sir Fraser picked up the letter which was in front of him.

"I see Cowan asked me to advise you, too. You've talked this over with him?"

"Yes, I asked him what I was to do with myself when I got home to England. His advice was to go and see you, and until I had seen you to discuss it with nobody."

"So the onus is on me," Sir Fraser said. "Well, before I pass any judgment tell me a little more about yourself."

"I am seventeen-and-a-half," Christine answered. "My parents are fairly well off and there is no reason for me to work, but I don't want to do nothing. My mother is an invalid, but that doesn't mean that she wants me at home all the time.

"She thinks she does, but she's very happy with my father and I think myself that they are quite sufficient unto themselves. I shall be quite happy to live in the house, of course, but I want something to occupy my mind."

"And you feel, then," Sir Fraser said, "that what you call this talent of yours might be used as part of your career?"

"I had thought of that," Christine confessed.

Sir Fraser hesitated a moment. Then pushing himself a little away from his desk and crossing his legs, he said:

"I am going to be frank with you, Miss Stanfield. I am extremely interested in all that you have told me.

"I believe every word you've said, and I know that my old friend Cowan Vanderfelt besides being one of the most brilliant men of the age is also thorough and conscientious to the nth degree.

"If he has vouched for the truth of the cases in these records which you have given me, every word written there will be true. I am interested, I am intrigued, I would like to investigate further for myself.

"But if you ask me to advise you as to whether there is a career in such things I must answer you frankly and honestly, no.

"Not only is there no possibility of an honest and decent career, but if one word of this gets out to the general public you stand the chance of being a butt not only of sensational journalism, but of every quack, crank and religious maniac who exists in this country.

"There have been two or three occasions lately where we have had an example of public investigations and interest in what is known as the supernatural. The behaviour of the public, incited to action by lurid and often untrue statements in the Press, was to any thinking man or woman fanatical and disgusting.

"You are very young, you have been brought up in a sheltered life by decent people. I tell you quite frankly that you couldn't stand up to that sort of thing."

"But then my . . . results seem such a waste of effort," Christine protested.

"Yes, I know. But I promise you that you must take my word—the word of a man who has lived in this world now for a very long time—when I assure you that not only would the powers you possess be challenged, but the truth about them would be distorted and twisted until you wouldn't know yourself whether you were genuine or not. I am sorry to disappoint you," Sir Fraser added kindly as he saw Christine's crestfallen face; "I wish I could say something different. But you know as well as I do that the medical profession will not support you. If they did, they would be laying themselves open to the encroachment of every quack and hypocrite who thought that spirits were guiding them to heal people."

"But why, why, in that case, should this have happened to me," Christine asked, "if it is to be of no use and I am to stop doing such things? Why should I have been made like this?"

Sir Fraser smiled.

"That opens a long line of questions," he said. "First of all, you are presupposing that you have been specially singled out for particular powers. Singled out by whom, or by what?

"A large number of people will tell you it is far more probable that it was just a freak growth in you, just as one may have a double-yolked egg or a calf with five legs.

"Perhaps you've collected, without the direction of any supermind, an extra amount of life force which by some chemical process within yourself you can transmit to other people, rather like someone being unfortunate enough to become a carrier of disease."

"It still seems a waste if I don't use it," Christine murmured ruefully.

"There I am inclined to agree with you," Sir Fraser replied. "And yet another school of thought would tell us that nothing is wasted; that the artist who stands too close to the picture can see very little, and that the pattern of our lives is not evident until long after we are dead."

"Mr. Vanderfelt was so certain that you would be able to help me," Christine insisted almost childishly.

Sir Fraser smiled at her kindly.

"Shall I tell you what I really think?" he said.

"Please do."

"I think that our dear friend Cowan found you a very interesting phenomenon," he said, "but when it came to being practical he was only too willing—as they say in America—to pass the buck."

There was silence for a few moments and then Sir Fraser added:

"I will tell you what I will do. I will read the papers you've brought me very carefully, and will consider the whole matter really deeply, and then if there is anything I can suggest, I will promise to tell you."

"Oh, thank you!" Christine exclaimed.

"Now mind," Sir Fraser went on, "I am not optimistic about it at the moment. Quite frankly, I can think of no advice to give you except to go home and forget the whole thing. Have a good time and enjoy yourself. You're young and you're pretty; you say that your people are well off.

"The war will be over very shortly now, I think. The world is sick of being serious, of forcing the young to be old before their time. We can do with a little wholesome laughter and music, a little happiness and a little ordinary conscience-free fun. Go and find it!"

"I'm sorry to be a bore," Christine replied, "but I want to be serious."

Sir Fraser sighed.

"The world has altered so much since I was young. Then we were always being told to be serious by grown-ups, while our one idea was to have a good time."

"And yet you have worked, and worked hard," Christine said.

"And enjoyed it," Sir Fraser answered, with one of his quick smiles. "And now don't tell me I'm being Victorian. But I am a man, and I prefer a world in which men work and women enjoy the spoils of their labour."

"You're being dreadfully old-fashioned," Christine said severely.

"I know," Sir Fraser confessed. "And that's a poor thing for a man who has tried to lead world thought since the beginning of the century. Nevertheless I am afraid I mean it. You will hate me for saying it, but I never have been able to prevent myself saying what I think, however unpalatable it may be to others.

"My advice, Miss Stanfield, is for you to forget all these unusual things which have happened and look forward to finding the right young man, to settling down with him and having babies."

"All the same, you will keep your promise to think of an alternative?" Christine begged.

"I will keep my promise," Sir Fraser answered, "but I don't know that I shall alter my opinion."

Walking away from the house down the hot, dusty street, Christine felt lonely and disappointed. She had expected so much from the interview with Sir Fraser and now she realised that he had destroyed to a large extent her belief in her own future.

As if to convince herself she looked at her hands. They were quite ordinary—well-shaped, attractive hands, but not different, so it seemed to her, from thousands of other women's. Could she really have imagined the whole thing? Could each occasion have merely been a fluke?

She knew it was not so. There had been no question either of faith healing; the patients had known nothing of her. There had not been that tremendous buoyed-up exaltation, hope and anticipation which is responsible for so many of the miraculous cures at Lourdes and other places.

No, it was something in her—she had achieved something, she had!

She walked along quickly, feeling as though the mere movement of her body would bring some solution to a brain that felt heavy and dull with disappointment. The street ended and she crossed the Bayswater Road towards the Park.

It was at that moment that Elizabeth saw her.

Elizabeth was bringing up to London from Avon House a patient who had to have an X-ray. She noticed Christine cross the road just in front of the car and turn into the Park.

"I wonder what she's doing here?" she thought.

She noticed how pretty her niece looked in the early summer sunshine. Christine had pulled off her hat, revealing her dark hair and beautifully shaped head. Elizabeth was half inclined to stop, and then she remembered she would be late for her appointment at the hospital and drove on.

She wondered if Christine would like to come and

work at Avon House as a V.A.D., and then dismissed the idea as impractical.

The girl was young, Lydia would want to have her home for some time, and anyway long before she was trained the war would be over. All the same, she wondered if Christine would really be happy living at home permanently.

Living with Ivan could be only Lydia's idea of bliss.

Christine was thinking of her father as she walked across the Park. She had not told Sir Fraser whose daughter she was, and she was now taking herself to task for deliberately withholding the information. She knew only too well the reason for her reticence.

All her life she had been over-shadowed by the fact that she was Ivan's daughter. People either gushed when they heard it, paying fulsome compliments and asking her—a phrase Christine loathed—if she did not feel proud; or else—and these people left there mark —there came a little silence after Ivan's name, a speculative look, and then a remark which carried so much in its implication:

"Your father is very popular, isn't he?"

Christine wondered now what Ivan would say if he could hear the story she had just told Sir Fraser. She had an idea that he would accept it quite naturally. He would be the only one of the family who would; and yet somehow she did not want to tell him.

When she had been a child she had been rather frightened of Ivan. He had been so quick, so brilliant, a comet passing across her small horizon, that she felt when he was near that she must cling to her mother for safety.

But as she had grown older she had been flattered at the attention he commanded; had been pleased when other girls spoke of him with awe and their parents fought for tickets for his concerts.

Then just a short time before Lydia's accident she had overheard a conversation which explained many of

98

the glances and strange remarks which had worried her in the past.

Ivan had taken her as a treat to luncheon at a famous London restaurant. Christine had gone to the cloak-room to wash her hands and tidy her hair, and while she was there two fashionably dressed women came in.

"Did you see Ivan Razoumovsky just now?" one of them asked. "Isn't he good-looking?"

"Not my type," the other replied. "And by the way, who is the child with him? Surely he's not started cra-dle-snatching?"

"Oh, that's his daughter," was the answer. "I saw her at a concert last summer when I was with Gwen, and you know how Gwen always knows the intimate life of the celebrities."

They both laughed.

"A daughter." The words were said reflectively. "One of many, I should imagine. Was this one born on the right side of the blanket?"

Again there was that burst of empty foolish laughter.

Christine had crept from the cloakroom feeling as if the world she knew had been shattered around her. She was just old enough to understand what they meant. She was old enough, too, to piece together so many of the things which had happened in the past—scraps of conversation—they fitted together now and made a complete picture.

This, then, was her father. To all children there comes a time when with a sense of shock they realise that their parents are human. To nearly all children it is a blow of the deadliest sort if they learn that their par-ents are immoral.

Christine was no exception.

She had always thought of Ivan as being different from other people, but different in the way that he was more talented, more brilliant, more marvellous than other children's fathers.

Now she saw him, with the exaggeration of youth, as different, but horribly different.

She remembered occasions when the conversations of grown-ups had ceased abruptly when they had realised that she was there.

She remembered the expression of pain on Lydia's face—a pain that was mental, not physical—when Ivan's visits to his own home were few and far between; and when if they did see him, he was preoccupied and seemingly too busy for them.

She remembered, too, how once when travelling down Piccadilly on a bus with her governess she had seen Ivan coming out of the Ritz Hotel. He had been looking smart and debonair and was smiling.

Several passers-by turned their heads to look at him and Christine had felt a quick thrill of pleasure.

"That's my father!" She had been proud.

Then a woman had run after Ivan. She had slipped her arm into his and it seemed to Christine as though she apologised for something, perhaps for keeping him waiting. He had smiled down at her, and then arm in arm they had turned and walked up Piccadilly out of sight.

Christine had wondered who the woman was. When Ivan came home that evening she told him that she had seen him.

"I saw you today, Daddy," she said gaily. "Did you have a nice luncheon at the Ritz?"

Ivan had not answered for a moment, but his eyes narrowed as they did when he was angry.

"Where were you?" he asked sharply.

"I was going by in a bus," Christine said. "I nearly jumped out but the bus was going too quickly. Besides, you had a friend with you."

She chattered happily, not realising that Ivan was annoyed, and then suddenly he had got up from his chair and walked across the room to light a cigarette.

"If there is anything more boring," he said to Lydia, "than the conversation of stupid little girls when they get to Christine's age, I'd like to know it."

He had walked out of the room leaving Christine

crimson with mortification. Even then she had not understood, thinking in her childish way that Ivan was angry because she had thought of jumping off a bus.

Lydia's quiet:

"Never mind, darling, I expect your father has been working too hard," did nothing to salve her pride.

It was only later, when she chanced to overhear the conversation in the cloakroom, there was revealed much that she had not understood. And Lydia, did she mind?

Christine thought of her mother and felt her heart contract with pity. She must never know, she thought to herself.

More than anything else it was this knowledge that had reconciled Christine to being sent to America to stay with her great-aunt. When Lydia had first told her about it her first instinct had been to say no.

All through the long year when Lydia had lain stricken after her accident there had been at the back of Christine's mind the fear that now her mother was a helpless invalid Ivan would desert her.

Nothing is more pitiably vulnerable than the workings of a child's mind when it fears the actions of grown-ups and is not really adult enough to understand them. Christine was really tortured by the fear lest Lydia, confined to her bed, should find out all those things which she, Christine, suspected went on.

Many of them were, in fact, quite unjust. Ivan had been desperately moved by Lydia's illness. In fact, it was not until long after she had returned to Fairhurst and, indeed, after Christine had left for America, that he had a love affair which meant anything to him.

There were always fascinated and admiring women in his life, the majority of whom meant no more to Ivan than flies on the wall; but Christine, severely censorious, suspected them all.

In America Christine had forgotten much that had perturbed her at home.

101

But even so the things she had learnt poisoned her affection for her father and she came home wary and cautious where Ivan was concerned, watching him critically, ready to notice the slightest slip, waiting for the flaws which she knew were there beneath the charming surface.

No, Ivan might understand better than Lydia, better than anyone else, this strange healing power within herself. His Russian blood, she guessed, would rejoice in it as something unusual, exciting, fundamental.

Yet she was determined not to tell him. She knew then as she made the decision that she had never forgiven her father for the sins she had discovered in him all those years earlier.

Whom, then, should she tell? There seemed to be no answer, and Christine, walking through the Park utterly lonely in the midst of crowds, found herself repeating over and over again:

"Oh, the waste of it, the utter, senseless waste!"

8

Philip lazed away the first ten days after his return home. He seemed content to eat and sleep prodigiously and asked no other entertainment than to be with his mother.

"I had better ask some young people in to play tennis with you," Lydia had suggested once or twice.

But Philip's answer was always the same.

"Don't bother, I'd rather be with you."

While Lydia's heart swelled with pride at his choice, she knew that it was partly due to physical exhaustion.

His hand, badly damaged by a bursting shell, was healing slowly, but the doctor who had examined it had told Lydia that her son was suffering from what he would call—for want of a better term—war weariness.

"He has been tense and alert for a very long time," he said. "If he hasn't been continually in action, he's been prepared and waiting for it. All this reacts just as badly on the young as on the middle-aged, although most of us are inclined to forget it and expect the very young to stand anything.

"Give him plenty of food and let him sleep the clock round. And, what is more important, let him forget that he has to set an example."

The doctor was an old friend and Lydia did her best to carry out his instructions. The weather was perfect, and she would watch Philip bathe in the blue tiled pool at the end of the garden or sit in the shade while he lay beside her on the grass.

Sometimes they would talk, sometimes they sat silent, and as often as not Philip would doze a little and Lydia would watch him and think how young and vulnerable he looked asleep.

Perhaps Christine had been right when she accused Lydia of loving her son more than her daughter.

It would have been difficult indeed not to love Philip; he was so utterly lovable, so completely unsubtle, so frank and honest in every way, that it was hard at times to believe that he was Ivan's son.

He seemed to have nothing of his father in him. But Lydia recognised much that was herself: his difficulty in expressing his feelings for one thing; his method of direct approach to any problem that presented itself; and above all his open, unsophisticated manner.

It was difficult to believe that Philip could hide anything from anyone. To Lydia it was in some ways like looking at her own reflection in a mirror.

Christine was very different. Lydia found herself continually worrying about her daughter. Over and over again she told herself that she must be patient, that she must gain Christine's friendship by first gaining her confidence.

But it was difficult. Christine was like the cat that walked by itself—one was never certain what she was thinking or where she was going. One moment she would be there, the next she had disappeared without explanation or excuse.

From the very moment of her home-coming she had asserted her independence. A few days after her arrival she had come into Lydia's room dressed very smartly in a most attractive little hat and carrying her bag and gloves.

"Are you going anywhere?" Lydia asked in surprise.

"Yes, Mummy, I'm going up to London today. There are some things I need."

Perhaps she had seen by Lydia's face that something was wrong, for she had added half defiantly;

"You don't mind, do you?"

Lydia had wanted to say that she would at least like to be asked, but she felt that she was being old-fashioned and restrictive. So instead she had answered lamely:

"No, darling, of course not. Will you be back for tea?"

"I'm not certain," Christine had replied. "You'd better expect me when you see me."

She had kissed her mother and gone away, leaving Lydia perturbed and conscious of a sense of frustration. Had it been Philip, he would have put things so differently, even though he would still have gone to London.

She had wanted to ask someone else to advise her how she should treat Christine—whether it was wise to let a girl of seventeen-and-a-half do exactly as she liked. But there was no one to whom she felt she could turn, and when she tentatively broached the matter to Ivan he said:

"Oh, let the child do as she wants. After all, she's capable of looking after herself and American girls have a lot of freedom."

Lydia had therefore made no protest to Christine about her continual absences from home, although she wondered about them and about Christine in general.

She tried to find out Philip's opinion of his sister.

"Christine's pretty, isn't she?" Lydia had remarked.

"I suppose so. I never admired brunettes myself."

"How do you two get on together?" Lydia had asked next. "You haven't seen each other for so many years and it must seem strange to try to pick up the threads again."

"Oh, Christine's all right," Philip replied. "She's a nice kid, but one never seems to get to know her."

There was a truth in that which Lydia could not help acknowledging. She also was finding it hard to get to know Christine.

The child seemed preoccupied with her own thoughts; but until she had a clue as to what they were, Lydia could only stand by helpless, feeling instinctively that her daughter was not happy and yet powerless to do anything.

Lydia's happiness at having Philip home was marred

105

not only by her anxiety over Christine, but also by Ivan's strange behaviour.

The latter was obviously suffering from jealousy, which made him in one of his most difficult moods— moods in which he criticised the house and household, when he seemed restless and unsatisfied, when even his music was no solace to him and he felt tormented.

When Ivan was like this he always had the power to hurt Lydia. He could wound her by what he said and by his criticism of the background she had created for him.

Usually such moods were attributable to something that had happened outside the family circle; but now, when the cause lay within, when, as Lydia knew, the presence of his own son was an irritant, she felt both afraid and miserable.

There was no solution, she thought, but to keep Ivan and Philip as much apart as she could; and that she couldn't bear to do without tearing her own heart in two.

One consolation was that neither Philip nor Christine seemed in any way upset by their father. While Lydia trembled and quivered at Ivan's frown and at the first querulous note in his voice, they took it in their stride.

"Dad seems a bit under the weather these days," Philip remarked quite philosophically one morning when Ivan had gone through the house like a whirl-wind, shouting at the servants, grumbling to Lydia and slamming all the doors.

Lydia, who was feeling very near tears, had replied: "I'm sorry, darling."

But Philip, reaching out a large comforting hand to take hers, remarked:

"Oh, it doesn't worry me. He's always been the same, hasn't he? Besides, I expect he feels things more acutely than we ordinary mortals."

Philip's explanation comforted Lydia and she told herself that at least the boy had no idea that he was the cause of his father's temperamental outbreak.

Christine, on the contrary, knew the reason, but

Lydia, without saying anything, somehow trusted her not to hurt Philip by revealing the truth.

For the last few days Ivan had hardly been home at all. Two nights he stayed in London, and another he had returned so late that all the household were asleep and had long given up expecting him.

The previous morning he had come into Lydia's room early. Knowing him as she did, she realised that he had something to say to her that was out of the ordinary and in his own way he was feeling awkward about it.

He kissed her good morning rather more affectionately than usual, then wandered restlessly around her bedroom, humming a tune to himself, playing with the ornaments on the mantelpiece and examining his reflection critically in the tall, gilt-edged mirror on the dressing table.

She waited a little apprehensively, wondering what was coming. And then at last Ivan said what was in his mind.

"I want to bring someone down to stay tomorrow. Is that all right?"

The studied casualness of his question gave it an importance.

"Who is it?" Lydia asked.

"A girl I'm thinking of taking as a pupil," Ivan announced.

Lydia could not have been more surprised if he had sprung a bomb in the room.

"A pupil!" she exclaimed. "But I thought you always said that you would never under any circumstances . . ."

She stopped suddenly. She had seen Ivan's face, she understood.

For a moment her instinct was to cry out:

"Not here, you can't bring her here!"

Never in all the years of their married life had Ivan introduced one of his loves to her. She felt a moment of sheer panic and then with a great effort she controlled herself.

"Tell me about this girl."

"She is a Dane," Ivan replied. "I think you will like her."

With a further effort Lydia asked:

"And her name?"

"Thyra Jörgensen. She is a refugee, as a matter of fact. She escaped to England about a year ago; her father and mother are still in Denmark. She's an extremely fine pianist and is anxious to learn composition. I am determined to do what I can for her, and it would be more convenient for her to stay here."

There was a hard note now in Ivan's voice which told Lydia that he meant to have his own way. For a moment she thought that she would defy him, tell him it was impossible.

There was, if not herself, Christine to be considered. And then something wiser than her own feelings told her to take this quietly.

"I shall be very pleased to see your pupil," she said.

"I will bring her down tomorrow afternoon."

And then swiftly, as if he feared Lydia would change her mind, Ivan was gone. But not before Lydia had seen the glint in his eyes, the smile on his lips. He was in love again. She knew the signs only too well.

Now she understood an incident that had taken place the night before, small enough in itself, but it should have told her what was in the wind.

She was just going to her bedroom when to her surprise she heard the sound of music coming from Ivan's studio. She had no idea that he was in the house. Usually when he returned home he came first to seek her. She had hesitated for a moment, uncertain whether or not to intrude upon him, and then because she felt lonely and a little hurt she went down the long passage to the studio and opened the door softly.

The room was in darkness except for one soft pink glowing light near the piano.

108

Ivan was playing a wild emotional melody which rose and fell disturbingly on the ear. Lydia came softly into the room, pushing the door to behind her, and waited just inside listening, trying to understand what he was attempting to say by his music.

She guessed that the piece was one of his own compositions, it was indeed so obviously a part of himself. And then suddenly he crashed his hands down on the piano in a series of disruptive discords.

"I can't get it right! I can't!" he flashed out angrily. "What's wrong with me? Has even my music deserted me?"

Lydia had wondered miserably what had happened to cause such an outburst. There had been several of them in the past few days. Now she understood.

When Ivan was in love he was always reaching for the stars and always disappointed when he could not grasp them. Love inspired him, made him seek impossible standards to which he could never attain.

He would strive and struggle, driven by a wild mental hunger, until that moment when he was physically satiated and then . . . he would come back to her.

She had been through this too often before not to understand and know the symptoms. But for the first time not only her feelings but those of her children were involved, and fiercely she desired to protect them.

She was haunted now, she had been haunted all day by the horrors of her own imagination. Supposing the woman whom Ivan brought to the house was obviously fast and improper? Supposing she treated them all as interlopers who interfered between her and Ivan's love for each other?

Lydia was frightened; so frightened that she wished at that moment she had never recovered from her accident and had died when she had been able to fight other women with their own weapons.

She thought of the past and pictures of Ivan came crowding back to her.

She remembered how one night in the South of

France the moonlight had attracted him and he had been drawn from their bed to the window, and while he stood there looking out on the almost motionless silver sea she had joined him.

She had worn only the soft transparency of a chiffon nightgown, but when the moon had fallen full on her face she had aroused not his passion, but a love almost worshipful in its intensity.

She remembered how he had stared at her as if trying to absorb her beauty. And then he had knelt at her feet and kissed her instep.

There were other pictures, golden and dazzling in their moments of happiness. She remembered Ivan carrying her in from the sea to the shadow of some quiet rocks on the Cornish shore.

She remembered him flushed and excited one night when they had listened to music exquisitely played in Vienna. That night she had felt herself one with the great lovers of Austria as with Ivan she had known a unity of body and soul beyond expression.

"Why are you looking so sad, Mummy?"

Philip's voice recalled her to the present and she smiled down at him as he lay full length at her feet.

"Was I? I was thinking of the past."

"And it made you sad?"

"Not really. I was remembering happy times."

"Is it nice to have memories?" Philip asked.

"One is told it's a compensation of old age," Lydia replied drily.

"But you're not old," Philip expostulated.

"Sometimes I feel a hundred," Lydia confessed.

"I expect Dad makes you feel like that," Philip said. "Why must he try to be so beastly young?"

"But he doesn't," Lydia rebuked, rising quickly to the defence of Ivan.

"Oh yes, he does," Philip insisted. "You can see all the time he's striving to do things to show how young he is. One wouldn't think about it or notice it if he didn't try so hard."

Lydia was startled. "I think you're being rather cruel," she said at length.

"Sorry, Mummy, if it's upset you. I'm not complaining; I'm just sorry for Dad, that's all. After all, he is still very hale and hearty, but he's not my age and I don't know why he wants to show me all the time that he is more agile and more energetic than I am."

"What have you been saying to each other?" Lydia asked.

"Nothing," Philip answered. "As a matter of fact, it was Christine who mentioned it first."

Lydia stifled an exclamation of impatience. She had felt that such perception was unlike Philip. And yet she could hardly forbid the brother and sister to discuss their father.

"Don't look so worried," Philip begged. "You know I won't say anything, or do anything, for that matter, if I thought it would worry you."

"The only thing that worries me is when we are not all happy together."

"But we are, aren't we?" Philip asked in genuine surprise. And Lydia was comforted.

"By the way," she said at length, "your father is bringing a girl down to stay tomorrow."

"What on earth for?"

"She's a refugee, a musician, and he wants to help her."

"Then I wish to goodness he had waited until after my leave was over. I hate strange women about the house. She'll be arty and intense and will want to play an oboe in the garden after dinner."

"I hope she won't," Lydia said, laughing. "But if we were to wait for your leave to end we should have to wait for some time. The doctor says it will be at least another three weeks before you have the bandages off that hand."

"In one way I'm glad," Philip remarked, "and in another I am terrified the war will end before I have another crack at the Jerries. But anyway, I suppose there are always the Japanese."

Lydia did not like to express her own desire—that all wars would be over before he could go into danger again. She knew that it was hopeless to express such thoughts. Philip would be ashamed of them if she did. So she merely said:

"It's so lovely for me to have you at home, darling," and left it at that.

Christine's reaction to the news that Ivan was bringing home a strange refugee was far more disconcerting. Philip blurted out the information at dinner when the three of them were alone.

Christine's eyes widened with surprise and then she looked at her mother quickly as if for a lead as to what to say.

"Is this true?" she asked.

"Quite true," Lydia replied. "Your father told me this morning. The poor girl is a Dane and her parents are still in Denmark."

"Why does he have to bring her here?" Christine asked.

Lydia had asked herself the same question, but she was not going to allow Ivan to be criticised by Christine.

"Darling, don't you think you're being a little selfish?" she asked. "We have so much, surely we can share it with those who have so little?"

"I rather like to choose the people with whom I'd share anything," Christine said enigmatically.

At the time the conversation lapsed. But later that evening, when Lydia had gone to bed because she was tired, Christine came into her room.

Unlike her father earlier in the day, she came straight to the point, sitting on Lydia's bed and looking, Lydia thought, strangely attractive and ethereal in the pale tulle dress she had worn for dinner.

"What do you know about this woman Daddy's bringing here?" she had asked.

"Only what your father has told me," Lydia replied. "I am sorry if you and Philip feel you don't want her, but if she is busy with her music I don't suppose she will trouble you very much."

"It isn't that," Christine said.

She appeared about to say more and then she changed her mind.

She got off the bed and moved across to the dressing-table. Lydia wondered what was perturbing her and whether the child, who had had a good deal of attention since she had returned home, was jealous.

Christine, however, seemed to have little more to say. She combed her hair and then took hold of her mother's nail scissors to cut a small piece of skin from a cuticle.

It was Lydia who broke the silence.

"Christine," she said, "both you and Philip have asked me not to invite young people here, but I feel that I am neglecting my duty. You, I know, have been up to London quite a lot, but you haven't told me what you do, and I don't know whether you are bored or amused or what you feel about everything."

Christine got up and walked back towards the bed.

"Poor Mummy, I've been treating you rather badly, I know that. But I've been disappointed about something. I don't want to talk about it yet; I don't feel I could talk about it to anyone; but it has been a blow to my hopes and somehow I have wanted to be alone.

"I have done nothing very exciting in London except walk about and look at the people. I visited churches and places that have been bombed, and one afternoon when it was raining I went to a cinema by myself."

"But, my darling!" Lydia's hands went out in comfort.

"I'm sorry if I've worried you," Christine said. "I should hate to do that, but I've felt hurt, resentful and rather angry inside, and that wouldn't have made me good company for any of the nice young people you wanted me to meet.

113

"Besides, quite frankly, I wanted to think. You know I have never had much time to think in my life, I've always been surrounded by people."

"You're not very old as yet."

"No, not in years, but I don't think years always have a lot to do with it, do you?"

"Not always," Lydia agreed.

"I have been thinking so much lately," Christine went on, "that already I feel older."

She smiled as she saw Lydia's uncontrollable smile.

"All right, I know that sounds pompous, but it's true. I'll try to explain myself. There are lots of things in life that I don't understand and I want to. Unless I think about them, I don't see how I shall ever come to a conclusion."

"And have you come to any conclusion?" Lydia asked.

Christine shook her head.

"You wouldn't tell me, I suppose, about the disappointment?" Lydia begged. "I would so love to try and understand."

"I can't," Christine said desperately. "It still hurts rather a lot."

"Do you know, you were like that as a little girl," Lydia said. "When anything went wrong, you couldn't bear to admit it. Philip was so different. If he fell and hurt himself or did badly at school or anything went awry in his life, he would come to me at once for sympathy and encouragement.

"You used to bottle it all up inside yourself. I remember once you had quite a bad fall out riding.

"Nannie found out about it because your clothes were torn and muddy, and I guessed that you must be bruised and perhaps, too, rather frightened. I remember going into the nursery to ask you about it. You were putting your dolls away before going to bed.

" 'I'm afraid you had a tumble this afternoon, darling,' I said.

"I had sent for the groom after what Nannie had told

me and he had explained the whole thing to me. He would have reported it earlier only he felt so certain you'd tell me yourself as soon as you got in.

"For a moment you didn't answer. I can see you now pushing a small fat doll into the doll's house through a door that was too small for it.

" 'Did you hurt yourself?' I asked. 'Jarvis tells me you were very brave.'

" 'I've forgotten all about it,' you said.

"You spoke very distinctly and not another word could we get out of you."

Christine laughed.

"I suppose really it's my pride," she said. "Now you remind me I can remember that incident. I fell on a path and hurt myself a good deal. I remember aching all over that night and yet I wouldn't ask anyone to do anything for me."

"It's a hard way to take life."

"It's my way," Christine answered softly.

"Then we shall just have to accept it."

"I'm afraid so. But thank you, Mummy, for being so understanding."

"You haven't given me much chance to be that," Lydia said reproachfully, and then added quickly: "I'm not trying to pry or be curious, I'm not really. It's just that I feel I've missed so much of your youth that I hate being shut out now."

"You will never miss anything if I can help it," Christine said fiercely.

She bent down and kissed Lydia, and, grateful for her affection, Lydia clung to her for a moment.

"You've put up with too much from all of us."

"I'm a spoiled woman, that's the truth," Lydia said happily, missing the underlying meaning of Christine's words. "I can't think of anything worse than being without children, however tiresome they may be."

Christine kissed her again and went downstairs to find Philip. He was sitting on the sofa with his feet up, reading a detective story.

"Is Mummy in bed?" he asked.

"Yes."

"Then I'd better go up and say good night to her."

"Wait a minute," Christine said, seating herself on the end of the sofa and swinging her legs. "I want to ask you something."

"Ask away," Philip retorted, putting down his novel.

"What do you think of Daddy bringing down this woman tomorrow?"

"Think of it? I think it's a damned nuisance. Why?"

"Don't be silly!" Christine said cooly. "Has he done this before?"

Philip looked at her in surprise.

"Hey! What are you driving at?"

"Let's answer one question at a time. Has he ever brought strange women down before while I've been away?"

"Not that I know of," Philip answered, and added more curiously: "What are you inferring?"

"You must be very stupid," Christine replied, "or peculiarly guileless."

Philip sat up abruptly.

"Good Lord! You're not . . . hinting that . . . But you must be crazy! Look here, I know there are stories about the governor and all that sort of thing, but I've never believed the ones I've heard, and besides, what do you know about it?"

"I've known about him for years," Christine retorted tartly.

"Jehosaphat . . . who told you?" Philip exclaimed. "How dare anyone . . ."

"Don't be so ridiculous! Unless I was stone deaf and blind I couldn't have helped hearing and knowing a certain amount of what went on. Besides, he caused quite a bit of scandal when he was on his last tour in America."

"It's only because he's good-looking," Philip said stubbornly. "Women run after him, it isn't his fault."

"Oh yeah!"

"Look here, Christine," Philip said, assuming very much the tone of an elder brother, "you're much too young to think about things like this."

Christine laughed.

"My dear Philip, if you aren't prepared to look after Mummy, I am. She's put up with a good deal in her life. Of course, we know she dotes on the old boy and all that sort of thing, but at the same time it's getting a bit too much when he brings his women here. Anyway, why should we stand for it?"

Philip scratched his head and looked bewildered.

"I don't know what to say."

"One of us really ought to speak to Daddy."

"Oh, good Lord! You're not suggesting that I should!"

"No, I'm not suggesting it . . . yet," Christine conceded. "For the moment we shall have to wait and see. But for Mummy's sake I am not going to take things lying down. It's bad enough as it is having a father who's a public figure, but if our home is going to be affected by his goings-on, I for one am going to object."

"Don't you like having a famous father?" Philip asked. "I thought girls liked publicity and all that."

Christine looked at him, and for a moment all her sophistication dropped away from her and she was just a child.

"If you want the truth," she said in a very small voice, "I hate it!"

9

Elizabeth stood in the big, old-fashioned bedroom of her husband's house in Belgrave Square and looked at herself in the mirror.

She saw first the reflection of her own eyes, bright and excited, and then the severity of her uniform—the dark blue coat and skirt with its red tabs. She stood for some seconds, then quickly began to undress.

She was dining with Angus, dining with him for the first time alone, and quite suddenly she wanted to be feminine—a woman.

She had come to the house to wash up and tidy herself and was struck as usual on entering the place by its gloomy solemnity.

It had always been an unprepossessing house, but now with many of the wnndows blacked out it had an air of cold austerity which made Elizabeth shudder. When she reached her own bedroom she wondered why she had never changed the decorations.

She had left it as she had found it, and now perhaps for the first time she rebelled against the heavy formality of the ponderous furniture and the dark hangings.

The thought came to her that she had never had any youth.

After Lydia had left home she had been the only child among a number of very much older grown-ups. When she was twenty, long before she had begun to be conscious of the world or of her own feelings towards it, she had married Arthur.

Now she began to realise how much she had missed.

This evening she felt as shy as a young girl preparing for her first dance. She had gone to Angus's consulting-rooms to pick up some things which were needed at the Home. She was standing in the hall with its Hogarth prints and its smell of antiseptic, when Angus came out of his consulting room.

"Hallo, Lady Avon!" he exclaimed on seeing her. "Is anything wrong?"

"No, everything is all right," she replied. "I have only come to fetch some things for Matron."

"Won't you come in for a moment?" he asked. "I'd rather like to speak to you about a patient I'm sending down tomorrow."

She followed him into his own room. The sun was pouring in through a big window and somehow she felt gay and lighthearted. They talked of the patient for some time and then unexpectedly Angus said:

"You're looking tired. You're not doing too much, are you?"

Elizabeth felt the blood rising to her cheeks.

"I always feel I am not doing nearly enough," she replied.

"I'm afraid I have never properly expressed my gratitude for all you do," he said. "I know how much the smooth running of Avon House is your responsibility.

"Both the patients and the nurses are very happy there. and I can't tell you how much that means to a busy surgeon who only too often has to listen to grumbles and complaints which are quite outside his own province."

"I'm glad you're pleased," Elizabeth said simply— words which could not begin to express the pleasure she felt at his praise.

"At the same time you personally are not to do too much," Angus added.

Elizabeth felt at that moment as if nothing could ever be too much.

"When are you coming down again?" she asked to hide her sudden embarrassment.

"Tomorrow," he answered. "Either morning or afternoon. I've got to fit it in with my engagements here."

119

"We shall look forward to seeing you."

Elizabeth spoke the words half shyly. She got to her feet and held out her hand, feeling that the moment had come when she must leave.

Angus hesitated.

"Are you driving straight back?"

"I suppose so. There's not much to tempt one to stay in London these days."

"I was thinking how inhospitable I must appear," Angus said. He looked at his watch. "It's a little late to offer you tea; I suppose you wouldn't care to stay up and have an early dinner?"

Elizabeth felt her heart leap, but she answered him gravely enough.

"I should enjoy it very much, if you are certain you can spare the time."

"Is there anywhere particular you'd like to dine, or may I take you to a small place where I often go myself? It isn't very fashionable, but the food is good."

"I would like that."

"Where shall we meet? Can I pick you up somewhere?"

"Will you come to our house—63 Berkeley Square?"

As Elizabeth pulled off her uniform and kicked aside the sensible low-heeled shoes that went with it, a sudden thought struck her. She rang the bell, pulling at the old-fashioned red bell cord which hung beside the bed. It was some time before she heard the slow footsteps of the housemaid coming up the stairs.

The house was ony partially staffed by three old servants who had been there all their lives and refused determinedly to be evacuated to the country, preferring, as Elizabeth put it to Arthur, "the devil they know to the devil they don't."

"They would far rather face bombs than unfamiliar surroundings," she added. "Do you realise, Arthur, they've been there ever since you were a small boy?"

As it had turned out, their determination had been most convenient for Arthur and Elizabeth. If they had to spend the night in London, the house was there waiting for them.

It suffered during the years of war a certain amount of bomb damage and twice the windows had been blown in. But the old servants remained on, living in the basement and taking the damage done to the house as a personal affront.

"Look at this carpet, my Lady," Grace, the housemaid, had said to Elizabeth when the study windows had burst inwards. "I can't get it better than that and there was years of wear in that carpet. You'd think those Germans would be ashamed of themselves, the damage they're doing to other people's property."

Elizabeth had not dared to laugh, but had agreed quite solemnly that such behaviour was extremely reprehensible.

It was Grace who knocked at her door now.

"Come in," Elizabeth called out. "Listen, Grace. I want you to go down to the cellar and bring up a bottle of his Lordship's best sherry. Mr. McLeod is calling for me and we should both like a glass when he arrives. Open up the morning-room, and don't forget to take the dust-sheets off the chairs, the place looks like a morgue."

"Oh, my Lady, if it wasn't for those sheets you'd have the sofa and chairs ruined by the sunshine. I said to her late Ladyship when she brought the mulberry damask, 'With care, m'lady, those covers will last a lifetime.'"

Elizabeth was on the point of saying she hoped not. She had always thought her mother-in-law's choice of the mulberry damask was extremely ugly, but she bit back the words. Grace would not understand; she thought the place perfect as it was.

"I was content with it until now," Elizabeth admitted honestly.

Now she felt ashamed of the morning-room and, indeed, of all the rooms. She remembered someone once

121

saying a house should be a background for the woman who owned it. This house was certainly not a background for her, and yet until the war she had lived in it continually, thinking of it as more of a home than Avon House.

"Your Ladyship is changing?" Grace asked.

Elizabeth thought there was surprise in her tone.

"Yes, Grace, I'm going out to dinner and I'm tired of my uniform."

The old woman walked slowly across the room to unlock the big wardrobe at the far end.

"I don't know what your Ladyship will find here. Most of your things went down to Avon House."

"Yes, I know," Elizabeth said. "But there's certain to be something."

When Grace had gone to get the morning-room ready, she stood uncertain, looking at her dresses hanging neatly in a row, conscious of the faint smell of moth balls. How dull they were!

She had always wanted pretty things. At the same time she had chosen her clothes with the thought that she must wear what was suitable to her position.

As the wife of a man thirty years older than herself she felt it would have been bad taste for her to be anything but quietly, almost sombrely garbed.

There had been plenty of money for her to spend and yet she had not gone to the best-known or smartest dressmakers. She had somehow been afraid of Molyneux, Hartnell or Worth.

Instead she had bought expensive, but stereotyped, clothes. The cut was good and they were in excellent taste; but they lacked originality, they lacked the smartness which only a great designer can give to his creations.

"Dull! Dull! Dull!" Elizabeth said loud, knowing it was the truth.

She looked at the plain afternoon dresses in good material, the coats and skirts all more or less cut to the

122

same pattern, the neat blouses and ordinary little hats always less exaggerated than the fashion decreed.

"Any typist with a little imagination could have done better," she told herself.

At last, half despairing, she pulled from its coat-hanger a plain black afternoon dress.

When she had put it on and chosen a pair of sheer silk stockings to wear with her highest heeled shoes, she felt she didn't look too bad. She tried on several hats and hated them all. In the end she compromised by tying a velvet ribbon round her head.

She inspected herself in the long mirror; and while not satisfied, she was not too displeased with the result. The dress wanted shortening, and if only she had the sense to have some contrasting colour on it to brighten it a little!

It was the sort of dress which would look well on a woman of forty who wanted to disguise the thickening of her figure.

"And I am only thirty-two!" Elizabeth told herself. "Thirty-two!"

She thought of Arthur and the years they had spent together; of the short, infrequent interludes of passion which had become slightly embarrassing to them both, and which had always seemed somehow unreal.

Elizabeth washed her hands in the bathroom and as she dried them she noted the big, heavily embroidered coronet on the towels.

"That is all I got out of marriage," she thought, "and how little it means!"

She opened the door of the bedroom and heard Angus's voice in the hall. She heard him speak courteously in his own grave, rather charming manner to Grace and then listened to the echo of their footsteps on the un-carpeted marble going towards the morning-room.

Suddenly she was conscious of her own heart beating, and as if in escape from herself she rushed once again to the mirror, powdering her nose, giving a last touch to her hair before forcing herself to walk slowly and with her usual dignity down the stairs.

Angus was standing by the window in the morning-room, looking out on to the little courtyard at the back of the house which had once been filled with flowers and was now dreary desolate waste of rubble and broken bricks.

He turned quickly as Elizabeth came in and she forgot everything but her own gladness.

"I hope I am not late," he said; and then added: "Oh, you've changed! I hope you will excuse my coming just as I am, but I haven't had a moment since I last saw you."

"I was tired of uniform," Elizabeth explained. "Won't you have some sherry? It's pre-war. Thank goodness the cellar hasn't been damaged."

She poured him out a glass and he moved across the room to take it from her.

"I feel quite excited," he said. "It's so seldom I get the chance to go out to dinner, especially with a charming companion."

"Thank you," Elizabeth replied. "I might say the same thing. I believe it's quite two years since I last dined out in London."

"What do you do with your spare time?"

She had the idea that he really wanted to know and without thinking told him the truth.

"I try to read and usually end up by thinking."

"And what do you think about?"

"You will be shocked if I tell you."

She sat down in one of the ugly damask-covered chairs.

"Why? Is it so reprehensible?"

"The answer is—myself. You asked me what I did with my spare time. I don't have an awful lot of it."

"And don't we all think about ourselves when we get the chance?" Angus asked.

Elizabeth looked at him in surprise.

"Somehow I can't imagine you thinking about yourself."

"But I do, I assure you. Although some of my patients seem absolutely convinced that I think of no one but them."

"Are they the worst type?" Elizabeth asked.

"Oh no!" Angus replied. "The worst are the greedy, possessive ones who want not only their money's worth, but a little bit more."

Elizabeth laughed.

"Why don't you tell them the truth?"

"I generally do," Angus replied, "and very sensibly they leave me for another doctor."

They had a second glass of sherry and then drove in Angus's car to dinner at the place of which he had spoken.

It was small and had a charm that was all its own, while the cooking, as Angus had promised, was extremely good. The proprietor, a Frenchman, greeted Angus with enthusiasm and led them to a small table in an alcove apart from the other diners.

"What fun this is," Elizabeth said when they had ordered both food and wine.

"I'm awfully glad you've come."

It seemed to her there was a depth of meaning in his words, and quite suddenly she found her eyes drawn to his. They looked at each other for a long moment.

It was Elizabeth who looked away first and who started talking a little incoherently and quickly of other things.

She knew then that she was afraid . . . afraid of becoming too intimate, of hearing things which had another meaning, which in their implication could make her heart beat, her breath come quickly. And yet she wanted to hear them. . . .

As if he understood, Angus followed her lead and soon they were laughing gaily, and with some feeling of pleasure Elizabeth found that he had a quick sense of humour.

125

Quite small things amused him, and it crossed her mind more than once during the evening that he might have found a subject of laughter in herself, in the pomposity of Avon House and Arthur's patronage.

She was very happy and the time raced past. With a feeling of dismay she realised it was half past nine, and yet she couldn't bear to make the move to go.

"Do you often come here?" she asked, feeling that she would always remember this evening and this cosy intimate little restaurant.

"I don't get much chance," Angus replied. "I usually take a quick meal at my club or my secretary brings me sandwiches. Sometimes, I admit, I forget about meals altogether and only realise how hungry I am when it's long after midnight. There are two coffee-stall keepers round my way who know me well."

"Haven't you got someone who could look after you?"

"My secretary does her best, but she has to go home in the evening and then I am alone in the flat. I have an elderly maid who comes first thing in the morning and makes my breakfast. If I leave instructions she leaves me something cold for supper, but usually I forget."

"What a ridiculous way of living when you're working so hard," Elizabeth said impulsively.

"I manage all right," Angus replied. "Of course I should be horrified if any of my patients were so irregular in their habits, but, after all, what doctor practices what he preaches?"

"I wonder you've never got married."

Elizabeth made the remark which had been hovering on her lips all the evening.

Angus smiled.

"There are two good reasons for that."

Elizabeth waited, curious.

"First, I have never had the time, and secondly, I have never met anyone I have wanted to marry."

He looked at Elizabeth and once again her eyes were held by his. She knew that two words remained unsaid—"until now"; knew, as surely as if he had told her, that Angus loved her.

And yet in her very inexperience she doubted the truth when she met it, and because it hurt her to say it she wounded herself with the remark:

"I shall have to try and find you a nice wife."

Angus shook his head and looked away.

A long silence fell between them, and then at last, quickly because she longed to linger, Elizabeth took up her bag and gloves.

"I suppose I ought to get home," she said.

Angus looked at the clock and gave an exclamation.

"I'd no idea it was so late." He called for the bill and a few moments later they were driving back towards Berkeley Square.

"Won't you come in for a last drink?" Elizabeth asked.

"I won't have a drink, thank you, but I would like to see you off safely."

"I've got my uniform to collect," Elizabeth replied. "Come in for a moment."

She led the way to the morning-room and switched on the lights. The room was not so ugly and austere as in the daylight. Elizabeth noticed that Grace had taken away the sherry and put out a decanter of whisky and a syphon of soda.

"Help yourself to a drink," she invited, "while I get my things."

She went upstairs. Her uniform had been left ready in a small suitcase. Elizabeth looked round her room. Now she was not sure whether the evening had been a success or not. She had enjoyed herself and yet so much had been left unsaid.

She felt uncertain and depressed, even as a child might cry at the end of a party, hardly sure whether she had enjoyed herself because the moment of departure was such agony. She went slowly downstairs.

"I am ready now."

Angus snubbed out the cigarette he had been smoking. Elizabeth noticed he had not helped himself to a drink.

"Let me take your suitcase," he said.

He crossed the room to her side and as she handed it to him their hands met.

It was then they faced each other and knew the full implication of what was meant by the beating in their hearts and the quivering tension passing between their interlocked fingers.

"I'm sorry," Angus said at length. "I ought never to have asked you to come."

"But why?" Elizabeth asked, her voice hardly above a whisper.

"Because I knew—I think almost from the first moment I saw you."

"I didn't know for a long time. And then . . ."

"And then . . .? You fought against it, I suppose? So did I, but it was quite useless. Only I never meant to tell you."

"You haven't told me now," Elizabeth said.

She was conscious that they were still holding the suitcase, his hand over hers on the handle. Now Angus took the case away from her and putting it down walked across the room, standing with his back to her and his hands on the mantelpiece as he looked down at the empty fireplace.

Elizabeth stood very still and waited. She was trembling, and her whole body thrilled with some ecstatic emotion she had never known before.

After a long time Angus turned round to face her and she saw that his face was very white.

"My dear," he said, and his voice was low. "Things have got out of hand. I never meant this to happen. I never meant you to know what I was feeling; I thought it was a secret I could keep to myself."

"And now it is no longer a secret," Elizabeth whispered.

She made no movement, but he knew by the expression on her face that she was asking him . . . begging him . . . to take her into his arms. He drew near to her very slowly as if he fought for his control.

Then he reached out his arms, but merely to place his hands on her shoulders.

"I love you," he said quietly. "I love you as I've never believed I was capable of loving any woman, but after tonight I shall never say so again. I can mean nothing in your life, nothing. You have your husband, your position. Remember this only as a strange dream and try to forget it."

It was then Elizabeth found her voice and knew what she wanted to say. She gave a little laugh and slipped from his grasp.

"Angus," she said, "do you really believe that things can happen like that? I love you; I have loved you for a long time, but I have hardly dared to admit it to myself. I had no idea that you loved me; I only knew that it thrilled me to see you, to know that you were near. Tonight I have been happier than I've ever been in my life before."

Her words seemed in their swiftness to overrun each other. The coldness which had held her captive all her life broke; all dignity and pretension were swept away; she was conscious only of the emotions which possessed her, passionate, intense and demanding. Then she held out her arms to Angus, held them out with a gesture of complete surrender.

"Oh, my darling," she cried, "I love you!"

And at last, unable to prevent himself, Angus took her into his arms.

After a long time, when the world seemed to stand still, they drew apart.

It was Angus who spoke first.

"Elizabeth," he said, his voice deeply moved, "this is madness, you must see that."

"But why?"

They moved towards the sofa and sat down side by side.

"Only this evening," Elizabeth said, "I was thinking

129

how much I had missed in my life, how little youth I'd had, how little happiness. I never knew what happiness was until this moment."

Angus reached out his hand and took hers, holding it tightly. His face was sad and grey, and she knew what he was thinking.

"What is to become of us?" she asked tremulously.

"You know the answer as well as I do," he said wearily. "We have both got our own lives. You are a married woman; I have my profession to consider."

Elizabeth looked at him enquiringly.

"You're the Commandant of a Convalescent Home I have made particularly my own," he explained.

She understood then, and knew that for the sake of the profession to which he belonged and in which he bore an honoured name he could not cause a scandal, any more than for her sake he would countenance one.

Now she was afraid.

"But Angus . . ." she started to say.

He silenced her with a gesture.

"My darling, we've got to be sensible; what's more, we've got to be brave. I love you too much and I honour you far too much to let you take part in a clandestine love affair, however well conducted or discreetly managed."

"But I must see you sometimes!" Elizabeth cried. "I'll be content with that—just to see you and know that you are there."

"Do you think that either of us would be content with that?" he asked.

She knew he spoke the truth, knowing in that moment she was as hungry for him as he for her.

There was so much to learn about each other, there was so much to know apart from the wonder and glory of being close, of knowing that the mere touch of each other's fingers could release that wild thrilling of the senses.

"What then are you suggesting?" Elizabeth asked, and her voice trembled.

"I'll find a solution."

She guessed that he meant to go away. More than once in the past she had heard him say how much he longed to be with the Armies overseas, and how she sensed without words what was in his mind.

"Are we never to meet again?"

She felt in that moment that they had both grown prematurely old.

"That is in the lap of the gods," Angus replied.

She knew they were both thinking that Arthur was an old man.

"But he may live for years," Elizabeth thought, "years and years. I can't bear it! I can't!"

She looked at Angus and the tears welled suddenly in her eyes. He put his arms round her.

"Don't, darling, don't!" he begged. "It's the only way. You must see there's nothing else for us to do. And I've got to protect you, to take care of you."

"Only stay a little longer."

"It will only make it harder. Besides, we have our honour. What else is there left?"

He glanced round the room as he spoke, and Elizabeth guessed that he was thinking it belonged to Arthur.

"Let's go outside," he said. "We'll drive into the Park for a little while."

Elizabeth touched his arm.

"There are people there," she said. "Here at least we are alone. Oh, Angus, are we never to be alone like this again? I'm afraid of the future without you. I have only just begun to live and now you're condemning me to a living hell. Much better to have remained as I was, too stupid to know what I was missing."

Angus drew her head down on to his shoulder.

"Hush, my dear," he said, "saying all these things will do no good. Whatever happens, however much we are crucified, we have to take the right path. There's no other course open for either of us, being as we are."

Elizabeth knew that he was right. She clung to him for one moment longer and then she got to her feet.

"I'm going home," she said.

Angus also rose and without words put his arms around her and held her closely to him.

He did not kiss her, only laid his cheek against hers, and she felt a comfort and happiness beyond anything she had experienced before.

At last she belonged. At last she was no longer alone in the world.

She was part of Angus and he was part of her, whatever happened in the future, whatever separation lay between them.

They were both very white when finally they drew apart. Angus walked across the room to take up Elizabeth's suitcase, and then he opened the door for her.

There was nothing left to do, nothing left to say.

Their footsteps echoed across the hall. Outside dusk had fallen and the shadowed trees in the squares were darkened silhouettes.

Angus put Elizabeth's suitcase into the back of her car and she got in. She made no attempt to touch him; she only looked up at his face, barely visible in the light of the street lamp.

"Good bye, my darling," she whispered.

And then she drove away.

10

Lydia had been conscious all the morning that Philip and Christine were bound together by some tactical understanding, and more than once she intercepted glances and knowing looks between them as if they shared a secret.

They were particularly nice to her and she guessed the reason and was touched by it even while she was half irritated that they should criticise any action of Ivan's.

At lunch-time Christine asked in a voice that was too casual to be natural:

"What time is Daddy bringing home this privileged pupil?"

"I think they will be here in time for tea," Lydia replied.

She noted that Christine glanced at Philip and that both their lips tightened.

"Listen, children," she said at length. "I have a feeling you're hatching something. You've got to be nice to this girl for my sake as well as you father's. This is our home, and if you are inhospitable, it hurts us and our own happiness."

"Darling Mummy," Christine said impulsively, "we're going to behave like angels!"

But Lydia had her doubts. She would not admit even to herself how much she was dreading this stranger's arrival. Why, she kept wondering, had Ivan asked a greater understanding of her now than he had ever demanded before?

She had never failed him in the past, but surely this was asking too much?

More than once she contemplated ringing him up in London to say that she had changed her mind and she could not allow him to bring home this strange woman.

It was doubly hard for her to have to play a part in front of Christine and Philip. She had the feeling that the slightest indication of her feelings in the matter would drive them to open revolt.

More than once lately she had fancied that there was in their manner towards Ivan a pronounced air of criticism.

"All modern children," she told herself, "are openly critical of their parents, saying what they think and being on easy companionable terms with them."

And yet, while she expected it to happen to herself, she could not understand Ivan being viewed in the light of a modern parent. To her his slightest wish had always been law and she supposed that she had spoilt him.

Yet while she was prepared to give all of which she personally was capable to the man she loved, she could not expect the same of her children.

Philip had an uncritical, easy-going nature, and he expected little of the people with whom he came in contact except friendliness and goodwill.

Christine was different. Lydia felt that she would always demand more of those with whom she mixed than they were capable of giving. She would set her standards so high that life was bound to fall short of them and she would be disappointed.

She would perhaps reach greater heights than Philip, but she was also more likely to touch the depths. She was sensitive and also introspective to a degree, traits which, Lydia felt, would at once be attributed by anybody perceptive to the foreign strain in her blood.

At the moment she stood at the cross-roads, hovering not so much between girlhood and womanhood as between the characteristics of her breeding.

The fiery, impulsive, temperamental emotionalism of Ivan warred within her against the quiet reserved depths which characterised Lydia! Which would conquer the other? Lydia knew that only the future held the answer.

She imagined that Christine herself was unaware of the true nature of her instincts, perhaps afraid of what attracted, suspicious even of affection because she could not understand it. What Christine was thinking and feeling now Lydia had no idea.

She only guessed that she had leagued herself with Philip against their father.

Lydia moved her chair from the table. Philip opened the door on to the verandah and they went outside.

"We are very lucky," Lydia said at length.

She looked across the garden where through a gap in the trees the countryside lay beneath them bathed in sunlight.

"Why?" Philip asked.

"I was thinking of this girl who is coming to us," Lydia replied. "Try to imagine what it must be to be a refugee, to be separated not only from the people you love but also from everything that is familiar."

She turned to Christine.

"Weren't you ever homesick in America?" she asked.

Christine did not answer. She looked at her mother and Lydia knew only too well that she understood her reason for appealing to their sentiments at such a moment.

Philip, on the contrary, was moved.

"It must be damnable!" he said "If you only knew, Mother, how often I've thought of being here in the peace and quiet. Once even in the excitement of the battle I suddenly thought of the lilac bushes down by the shrubbery.

"I can't think of what reminded me of them, but they were suddenly clearly vivid, while shells were bursting round us and the noise was pretty deafening."

Lydia put out her hand to touch his arm.

135

"You needn't go on, Mummy, you know," Christine said quietly. "We've promised you we'll behave nicely."

"It would hurt me so much if you didn't," Lydia said severely. "Besides, this house is open to all our friends. I want there to be a welcome not only for your father's and mine, but also for yours."

"That's easy at the moment," Christine retorted. "I haven't got any."

"Then it's about time you set about making some," Lydia told her.

"I have a feeling that the people I would like wouldn't see eye to eye with Daddy," Christine remarked.

"On the contrary," Lydia replied, "there's every likelihood they would be some of his most ardent fans. You will find them everywhere, you know, even in the most unexpected places."

Christine made a grimace.

"I must say that I suspect you both of being rather a disappointment to your father," Lydia said. "There he is, a great musical genius, and neither of you have inherited even an appreciation of music."

"They say it skips a generation," Philip remarked. "I shall very likely produce a couple of young Mozarts, while Christine's brats will compose operas in their cradle."

"I hope they'll do nothing of the sort!" Christine said sharply. "And, Mummy, if you are honest, you know there would be nothing Daddy would dislike more than for either of us to be musical. Can you imagine the feeling there would be if Philip and I both demanded studios in which to work and the strains of our compositions came forth to mingle with Daddy's?"

Lydia knew that Christine was speaking the truth. Ivan would not like it, but she was not going to admit that to his children.

"We should be very proud of you," she said, "whatever you achieved."

"*You* might be," Christine persisted.

136

But Philip suddenly bent forward and gave his sister what he imagined was a surreptitious pinch. Lydia saw Christine wince, and then before she could protest Philip gave her a look which she understood.

Lydia sighed. She hated to think that they were trying not to hurt her feelings where Ivan was concerned. There was nothing she could say or do.

After a while Christine suggested a swim, and although at first Philip said he was too lazy, presently they sauntered away down the garden towards the swimming-pool.

It was difficult for Philip to swim with his bad arm, but he nevertheless managed it; and although Lydia had been afraid that he might retard its recovery, the doctor had told her to let him do what he wanted.

The bandages, of course, had to be changed, and Lydia, fearing he might forget, called after them:

"Don't forget to see Rose as soon as you've finished."

Philip waved his hand from the end of the path.

"I won't forget," he called.

The sun was on his face and hair and Lydia felt a thrill of pride in his good looks. He was so unspoilt, too—only a boy, despite three years at sea.

She heard a step on the verandah behind her and looked round to see Rose.

"Did you call me, madam?"

"No, Rose, I was only reminding Mr. Philip to get you to change his bandages when he had finished swimming."

"He ought not to swim with his hand as bad as that." Rose said disapprovingly.

"The doctor said it wouldn't hurt him," Lydia replied.

"Doctors always say the thing that's easiest," Rose answered tartly. "It's not good for Mr. Philip's hand and he knows it."

Rose had been trained as a nurse and that was the main reason she was engaged as a maid for Lydia. She had given up nursing because she had rebelled against the old-fashioned tyranny that was still exercised in many hospitals, and in consequence she had little patience with or approval of the medical profession as a whole. Lydia was very fond of her.

She was a middle-aged woman with great character and a predilection for speaking her mind which had kept her changing places almost continually until she came to Lydia.

Lydia liked her and enjoyed her frankness, and Rose, though she would never say so, had for her mistress a whole-hearted devotion.

"Now, is there anything you want, madam?" she asked, tidying the cushions on the chairs where Philip and Christine had been sitting.

"No, I am very comfortable, thank you," Lydia said. "But you might just see if the Lilac Room is ready for Miss Jörgensen. See if they've put some flowers on the dressing-table and filled up the ink-pot."

"I've seen to all that already," Rose replied. "Agnes is not best pleased at having a guest, I can tell you. We're short-handed in the house as it is; but there, they'll do it for you madam."

Lydia did not miss the implication and quite suddenly she felt herself flush with anger. First the children, and then Rose, all hinting that there was something reprehensible in Ivan's bringing home a stranger. After all, it was his house.

Without considering her words Lydia said:

"I hope Agnes and everyone else in the house will do things for Mr. Stanfield. After all, he pays their wages."

Rose was quite unperturbed by the outburst, but Lydia was ashamed almost as soon as she had said the words.

"Wages aren't everything," Rose remarked and went quietly into the house.

Lydia leant back against the cushions of her chair and closed her eyes. Here was one of the moments when her composure had been lost.

Actually it did not matter in front of Rose; she alone in the whole world knew how superficial in some ways was that quiet composure which Ivan and other people found so attractive and so admirable. Rose knew the times when Lydia cried out not only in physical pain but in mental pain.

She had witnessed many moments of irritation and anguish when Lydia could not bear the sight of her own immobile legs, when she would fight against the indignity of being lifted in and out of bed and being dressed and even bathed.

More than once she had cried on Rose's friendly shoulder and received both help and comfort from the one person with whom she need not pretend. Whatever her bitterness, Rose had been able to help and cheer her.

"Now it's no use your taking on, madam," she would say in the tone of one speaking to a temperamental child. "What can't be cured must be endured!"

"That's poor comfort."

"Maybe, but what good does it do you, working yourself up and spoiling your looks? If the master sees you with red eyes he'll wonder what's the matter!"

Somehow her half-scolding admonition was more comforting than any amount of sentimental sympathy.

Once, after a particularly miserable time, Lydia had reached out her hand and taken Rose's.

"Thank you Rose," she had said. "I don't know what I'd do without you."

"Well, you may have to one day," Rose had said cheerily. "It's no use relying on anyone except yourself, that's what I've always said. Half the troubles of the world would soon be over if we were self-sufficient."

Lydia had laughed. It was no use expecting tenderness from Rose. She was somehow like a strong breeze of clean fresh air.

Rose was also the one person who dared to speak her mind to Ivan. If she thought Lydia wanted him particularly, she had no compunction about marching into

139

his studio even when he was composing and fetching him to Lydia's bedside.

The other servants were frightened of him. They grumbled about his irregular hours; at the same time, when he wanted anything, they flew obsequiously to obey him. Rose was frightened of nothing and nobody.

"The mistress wants you, sir," she said once, walking into the studio while Ivan was sitting at the piano where he had been for the last three hours grappling with a difficult passage in a symphony he was composing.

Ivan had looked up furious.

"Get out!" he said. "Can't you see I'm working?"

"The mistress is waiting for you," Rose had said determinedly. "It's time she went to sleep, and she won't go until you've said good night to her, you know that. Come along now. Your music won't run away, sir."

"Damn you!" Ivan had shouted.

Then suddenly he had begun to laugh. He threw his score on the floor and went upstairs obediently to Lydia's bedside.

"Rose has ordered me here," he said. "I've an uneasy feeling, darling, that she doesn't consider a musical career is of real importance. A dilettante's pastime! Not the sort of work a man should do!"

"Has she disturbed you?" Lydia said. "I am so sorry. I've told her not to."

"Disturbed me?" Ivan laughed at the question. "I believe Rose would disturb God Himself if she thought you wanted Him."

"I'm sorry," Lydia had said again.

"Did you really want me?" he asked, sitting down on the bed beside her.

It was typical of their relationship that he had to ask the question.

"I always want you," Lydia replied.

Ivan bent to kiss her.

"Then I'll forgive Rose."

"And me?" Lydia asked.

"There's nothing to forgive you for," he replied. "Rose is right; music can wait, we can't."

He had bent to kiss her again, and when he had left her Lydia had fallen into an easy dreamless sleep.

"How lucky I am to have Rose," she thought now when she was left alone on the verandah, and half jokingly she began to count her blessings.

Ivan, Philip, Christine, Rose; Lawrence Granger— like a kind watchdog always in the background and always there when wanted; Elizabeth, and lastly, this house, their home, undamaged and intact through all the dangerous years of war.

"I am lucky, terribly lucky," Lydia told herself.

She looked up to see Ivan and a young woman approaching towards her through the garden.

Ivan called out a greeting as soon as he was within earshot.

"Hello, are you surprised to see us?"

"Very surprised," Lydia replied.

She was conscious of a moment of panic as they approached. She could not bring herself to look at the girl and kept her eyes on Ivan's face as he came nearer.

"It was so hot in London," he said. "We couldn't stand it another moment so we took an early train. We walked up and left our luggage at the station. This is Thyra."

He indicated the girl who by now was a few paces behind him, and at last Lydia had to look at her. She was very pretty, there was no denying that, which was, indeed, what Lydia had expected, but she had not expected to see someone quite so young.

"It's so kind of you to have me."

Lydia heard the words spoken in a low, rather sweet voice with just the faintest touch of an accent.

"You must be hot after your walk," Lydia said. "Won't you sit down?"

"Thank you."

Thyra sat down on a comfortable chair and stretched

141

out her legs—lovely legs, Lydia noticed, with absurdly small feet. Ivan threw down his hat.

"I'm going to find a drink," he said, "and lots and lots of ice."

He walked across the verandah and in through the dining-room door.

For a moment there was a silence between the two women. Lydia with an effort turned towards the girl.

"My daughter and my son are both having a swim. They also found it very hot."

"I didn't know you had any children," Thyra replied. "Ivan told me about you but not the family."

Lydia was not surprised and she said:

"My son is in the Navy, he's home on sick leave, and my daughter has recently returned from America."

"They're grown up, then?" Thyra's eyes widened.

"Oh yes, quite," Lydia replied.

"I have no brothers or sisters," Thyra volunteered. "It is very sad. My father and mother would have liked a big family, but unfortunately I was the only one."

"Your father and mother are still in Denmark?" Lydia asked.

"Yes. I only left them three months ago. I had the opportunity of escaping to England and they made me take it. You see, it was important that I should go on with my musical career."

"It was difficult, I suppose, in Denmark?"

Thyra shook her head.

"Not difficult—impossible. You do not understand what it is like to have the Germans occupying your country. My father was—what do you call it?—a farmer; he had hundreds of cattle, sheep and hens. Now he has none, the Germans have taken them all. They have made a pretence of paying, of course, but they have paid us with marks. What will those be worth after the war?"

The girls's voice deepened as she spoke of her parents. Lydia told herself that she must feel sorry, must be sympathetic.

142

At the same time she was acutely conscious of the girl's attractions: the young face with its clear pink-and-white complexion and wide blue eyes, the white-gold hair—characteristic of the Scandinavian countries—falling in heavy waves on to the small well-set shoulders.

She was neatly and attractively dressed, but Lydia knew that her clothes were not expensive, and she had the idea that anything the girl put on was bound to seem charming. And she was young, so young!

Ivan came out on to the verandah carrying a tray in his hand.

"Here's a nectar of the gods," he said gaily.

Lydia saw the quick turn of Thyra's head and the lithe movement with which she sprang to her feet.

"Let me help you," she said to Ivan.

But he shook his head and carried the tray to the table by Lydia.

"It's for me to wait on you," he said. "You are our honoured guest."

Two dimples showed in Thyra's cheeks when she smiled.

"Now you are making fun of me. It's I who am honoured and so very excited at being able to come here. After those horrible lodgings in London this is like Heaven."

"They were certainly peculiarly nasty," Ivan said, pouring a sparkling mixture into the long, coloured glasses.

Thyra turned to Lydia.

"The landlady was very old-fashioned and if a gentleman called for me she thought—well, terrible things."

Lydia found it difficult to know what to say, but Ivan, raising his glass, said:

"Forget the past. I give you a toast to the music you are going to compose here in liberty and in freedom."

He bent across the table to touch the rim of Thyra's glass with his, and then he drank deeply.

143

Lydia was silent and it was with a sense of relief that she heard voices in the distance and saw Philip and Christine returning from the swimming-pool. They were still in their bathing-dresses.

Christine was pulling off her cap as she walked, very slim and very lovely in a close-fitting suit of scarlet satin which she had brought back with her from America.

"Here are my children," Lydia said to Thyra.

She fancied Ivan looked towards them with a slight scowl on his face.

Christine came sauntering up the verandah steps.

"Hello, Daddy," she said. "We didn't expect to see you so early."

"It was hot in London," Ivan said shortly.

"Miss Jörgensen, may I introduce my daugher Christine," Lydia said, "and my son Philip."

Christine and Philip said, "How do you do?" and then sat down on the floor of the verandah.

"What about your hand?" Lydia asked at once.

"I'm going in again in a few moments," Philip answered. "That's why we didn't dress. The water is like a hot bath anyway."

"Would you like a swim?" Lydia asked Thyra.

"I'd love it," the girl answered, "but I'm afraid I haven't got a bathing-dress with me. I was only able to bring a small suitcase away with me when I left home."

There was silence for a moment while Lydia waited for Christine to speak and, as she did not, gave her a reproving look.

"I am sure my daughter can lend you one."

"I expect I can find something that will fit you," Christine said without much enthusiasm. "Would you like to come upstairs?"

"Miss Jörgensen is in the Lilac Room," Lydia said.

Thyra got to her feet and then looked at Ivan beseechingly.

"Aren't you going to swim?" she asked.

"Oh, you don't want me."

"But please, we do," Thyra said quickly.

144

He smiled at her, his good-humour restored.

"Then of course I'll come," he said. "I'll show you how to do a swallow dive."

"That would be lovely," Thyra enthused.

She followed Christine into the house, and Ivan, having finished his drink, went after them.

Philip looked up at his mother.

"I didn't know Daddy liked bathing; Christine and I never thought of asking him to come with us."

"Oh, he enjoys it at times," Lydia replied, trying not to remember that it was only a month or so ago, when they talked of filling the pool, that Ivan said he did not intend to swim at all this summer.

"I say, she's pretty, isn't she?" Philip said.

"Who, Miss Jörgensen?" Lydia asked. "Yes, very."

"I've never seen such pale hair. If she'd had pink eyes, she'd have been an albino."

There was silence for a time and then he added:

"She doesn't look musical."

"How do people look musical?" Lydia asked, amused.

"Oh, rather arty-crafty and peculiar."

"Well, our guest certainly looks neither of those things."

"Who doesn't look what?" Christine asked, appearing suddenly.

"Did you find Miss Jörgensen a bathing-dress?" Lydia asked.

"I gave her a pale green one which I have never liked," Christine said. "And I regret to say that she looks extremely attractive in it."

"Christine!" Lydia ejaculated sharply.

Christine bent down and kissed her mother.

"Sorry, darling. I'm a cat, and all cats scratch at times."

At that moment Thyra came out on to the verandah followed by Ivan.

"I'm so excited," she said. "This is my first swim this

145

summer and I'm very grateful for the lovely suit, which fits me perfectly."

It certainly did, and the green silk was in startling contrast to her very white skin.

"You look like a sea nymph," Ivan told her, and then holding out a hand to help her down the verandah steps, he added: "I'll show you the way to the swimming-pool. But you must promise me you won't vanish as soon as the water touches you."

"I promise," Thyra smiled. "I don't want to vanish, I'm enjoying myself far too much."

She stood for a moment at the foot of the verandah, blinking in the sunshine.

"The swimming-pool is down there?" she asked, pointing in the direction from which Philip and Christine had come.

"That's right," Ivan answered.

"I'll race you to the water," Thyra suggested.

"All right," he answered.

They sprang across the grass, running side by side.

Lydia looked after them and then looked away.

Christine sat down in a chair.

"So young, so very, very young!" she said in an affected voice. "Really, Mummy. I feel quite middle-aged."

11

Lydia heard the telephone ring and went through into the drawing-room to answer it. She had not expected the caller to be Elizabeth, who seldom rang up during the day.

"Can I come over and see you?" Elizabeth asked.

"Now?" Lydia exclaimed in surprise.

"Yes, now—as soon as I can get away. I want to see you. I can't explain on the telephone."

"Yes, of course, dear. Will you be staying the night?"

"Yes, please. I'll try and be with you within an hour."

Elizabeth rang off and Lydia put down the receiver, vaguely perturbed at her tone. She sounded agitated. Lydia wondered what could have happened, but could find no possible answers to the questions which presented themselves. Also she found it hard to concentrate on Elizabeth while she was beset by her own troubles.

"How I loathe jealous women!" she told herself, and knew that she was indeed possessed and torn by all the aching anguish of a physical jealousy.

It was hard to watch Thyra, young and slim, moving pliantly and gracefully beside Ivan, while she must now sit back and watch them—only a spectator.

She was sensible enought to realise that even had she not been tied to an invalid's chair she might have been experiencing just the same feelings, but that did not soothe her pain at this moment. In some ways it made it worse.

She hated to remember that she was forty; what someone had called "the old age of youth and the youth of old age."

She sighed and hid her face in her hands.

It was hard to grow old, hard to adjust oneself to the thought of a future when one's passage through life would not be helped by facial beauty, when one must try to believe that character and personality counted more than the easy, conquering charm of mere prettiness.

With an effort Lydia controlled her tears and wheeling her chair across the room rang the bell. When Rose came in, she gave her instructions to prepare a room for Elizabeth and then went back on to the verandah to await the return of the bathers from the pool.

Ivan came first—and alone.

"Did you enjoy your swim, darling?"

"I hate fresh water," he grumbled. "If one's got to bathe, one should do it in the sea. I didn't stay in too long as it was my first dip this summer."

"Very sensible," Lydia agreed.

Although she noticed that his fingers were slightly blue at the tips and that he shivered a little, she made no mention of it. She guessed that it had been an effort for him to come away and leave the young people still disporting themselves.

"Go and dress," she suggested.

"I will," Ivan said, and went into the house.

A few moments later Lydia heard from Ivan's bathroom which overlooked the verandah the sound of running water and guessed that he was having a hot bath.

The others came sauntering back some twenty minutes later. The girls had wrapped themselves in the big multi-coloured towelling cloaks which were always kept down at the swimming-pool, and Lydia noticed how absurdly young Thyra looked with her shining head emerging from the folds of a bright blue cloak.

"She is only a baby," she thought.

Then remembered that though she might be young in age Thyra threatened her peace and the peace of her home.

"I am ravenously hungry," Philip announced. "Do

148

hurry up tea, Mummy, and ask them to give us something pretty substantial."

"You've eaten us out of house and home already," Lydia replied. "I don't think there is anything substantial left."

"I shall go and make love to Cook myself," Philip replied, "and I bet you I'll get something delicious."

"I wouldn't like to bet on a certainty," Lydia replied.

She knew that the old cook, who had been with her ever since Philip was born, adored him and that anything he asked for he was certain to get.

Sure enough Philip had a newly laid egg for his tea, while Christine made rude remarks about his appetite and the favouritism which existed in the household.

Ivan came down in good spirits. He had put on a pair of grey flannel trousers and a sky-blue short-sleeved tennis shirt which made him look absurdly handsome.

He had obviously recovered both from his swim and from his irritation earlier in the day. He was at his gayest and most charming and Lydia, watching him talking animatedly to Thyra, told herself it was understandable that she or any other girl should fall in love with Ivan.

"They haven't a chance," she thought sadly;

She knew that whatever he did, however he behaved, she would love him until she died.

They were half-way through tea when Elizabeth arrived. She came out on to the verandah in her usual slow, dignified manner, looking, Lydia thought with a sense of relief, her calm, imperturbable self.

"What a surprise!" Ivan exclaimed, jumping to his feet. "To what do we owe this unexpected honour?"

"Nothing more sensational than the fact that I wanted to see Lydia," Elizabeth replied.

She kissed her sister and Christine, shook hands with Philip and was introduced to Thyra by Ivan.

"My protégée and pupil," he explained grandiosely.

Lyda guessed that he wanted Elizabeth to be surprised; perhaps perversely he even wished to shock her a little. Elizabeth's face registered only a polite indifference.

She shook hands, then sat down beside Lydia, taking a cup of tea and a sandwich absent-mindedly as though her thoughts were elsewhere.

Her entrance had broken the thread of conversation and Philip and Christine fell silent, finishing their tea rather hurriedly and then escaping into the garden with the same sort of relief they had shown when they were children.

"Would you like to see the estate," Ivan asked Thyra, "or would it bore you?"

"I'd love to see it," Thyra replied, "and I couldn't be bored here."

"You can't say that so positively as yet," he said.

"But I can," she argued. "It's all so wonderful and you are so kind."

Ivan held out his hand to help her up from the table.

"Come along, then, you shall see all the beauties of Fairhurst."

They walked away together and Lydia returned to Elizabeth, anticipating apprehensively the questions she felt were bound to be asked about the stranger.

But Elizabeth, after glancing round to see that they were not overheard, put her hand on her sister's arm with an impulsive gesture.

"Oh, Lydia, I had to see you. I am terribly unhappy!"

"Unhappy!" Lydia exclaimed in surprise. "What has happened? Has Arthur . . .?"

"Oh no," Elizabeth said quickly. "It's nothing to do with Arthur. It's Angus. We . . . love each other."

"Oh, Elizabeth!"

Lydia was both surprised and astonished; but she had only to look at Elizabeth's face to realise how much must have happened since she had last seen her sister.

The Elizabeth she knew so well—cold, unemotional, reserved—had vanished, and in her place was a woman fraught with emotion.

150

"Tell me everything," Lydia commanded.

Elizabeth pulled off her hat and threw it down in a chair, then she opened her bag and took out her cigarette-case. Lydia noticed that her hands were trembling as she struck a match.

"I have told you a little about Angus, haven't I?" she said.

Her voice lingered on his name with a new, strange and throbbing note.

"Yes, you have mentioned him."

"Last night I dined with him, and he told me he loved me—has loved me since the first moment he saw me."

"And you?"

"I knew then that I loved him, that I have loved him for a long time without knowing it. And then we said . . . good-bye."

Lydia waited. After a moment Elizabeth went on:

"I will be honest with you, Lydia. For the first time in my life I understand why you ran away with Ivan; why, whatever you suffered and whatever happened, it was worth while."

Her voice broke and Lydia put out her arm to place it round her sister's shoulder.

"Poor, poor Elizabeth."

"Not really," Elizabeth replied. "I am really very lucky in some ways. I am so happy because I realise that I have never lived before, never understood what life meant: and then when I remember that I shan't see Angus again I feel I can't bear it, that I can't go on without him."

"I don't quite understand," Lydia said.

"I didn't at first," Elizabeth admitted. "But now at last I do see that there is no other course open to us. He has his profession to think of. The scandal would not only ruin him, but do immeasurable harm. I am the Commandant of the Convalescent Home he has made exclusively his own.

"If he were not a professional man, I think things might be very different. As it is . . ."

Elizabeth made a gesture of helplessness.

"What is he going to do?" Lydia asked. "He must see you when he visits his patients."

"I telephoned him this morning," Elizabeth said tonelessly. "I felt I had to speak to him, had to ask him so many questions which had kept me awake all night. I could not get hold of him for some time, he was in conference. When finally he came to the telephone he told me that with great difficulty he had got permission to give up his work here in England and go overseas. He had tried to go over since the war started, but each time he broached the subject the Medical Council had persuaded him to stay.

"Now, having made up his mind that nothing or nobody should stop him, he has got his own way."

"When does he go?" Lydia asked.

"He wouldn't even tell me that." Elizabeth replied. "I think he thought it would upset me. Instead he told me that he loved me and he would always be thinking of me, but that it was good-bye."

Elizabeth's voice broke and Lydia realised that in some ways the tears were a relief. She let her sister cry, only occasionally murmuring words of comfort.

After a few minutes Elizabeth regained control of herself.

"I'm sorry to be such a fool," she said, "but I felt if I didn't tell someone I should go mad, and there was no one but you who could possibly understand. Oh, Lydia, I had no idea that love was like this!"

Lydia reached out her hand and took Elizabeth's.

"You've got to be brave, darling."

"I know, but I can't bear to think of the future without Angus. I think we were meant for each other always, and who knows if we shall ever be together?"

"Perhaps something will happen," Lydia said vaguely.

"Perhaps it will."

152

Neither would put into words what they were thinking, but each understood the other's thoughts.

The parlourmaid came on to the verandah to clear the tea and Elizabeth got to her feet.

"I will go up and change," she said. "Which room am I in?"

"The Pink Room," Lydia answered. "If you don't find everything you want, ask Rose."

"I will," Elizabeth promised, and went upstairs.

Alone, Lydia considered her sister's problem, and thought how strange it was that at the first touch of love Elizabeth would change so much. She was suffering, but Lydia knew that she would be immensely more human and more understanding because of such suffering.

No one can love and not grow and develop. And she knew instinctively that—swiftly though that love had come to her—Elizabeth did love Angus deeply and with every fibre of her being.

When Elizabeth came down again she was looking more composed, but even so there seemed to be some subtle change in her; she was less certain of herself, less assertive even in the way she walked and in the way she spoke.

"I am glad to be here," she told Lydia simply, as she sat down in a comfortable armchair beside her sister.

"And you know we are glad to have you," Lydia replied.

Then came the question that she had been dreading.

"Who is the pretty girl?"

"Thyra Jörgensen."

"Ivan said she was a pupil. What is he teaching her?"

"She wants to compose."

"I thought Ivan couldn't be bothered with pupils?"

"This is the first one he has ever had," Lydia said lightly. "I suppose one has to start some time."

Elizabeth looked at her and Lydia knew that she had not been convincing.

"I'm sorry, darling. Do you mind?"

"Of course I don't," Lydia lied.

Elizabeth was silent for a moment and then she said: "Do we all suffer when we love?"

Lydia dropped all pretence and answered her honestly:

"I think so. I don't believe that it is possible in this life to have the ecstasy without paying for it."

Elizabeth nodded her head.

"I suppose that's true, and it is worth it, isn't it?"

"Always. It's always worth it."

Lydia spoke fiercely and Elizabeth bent forward.

"How blind I've been," she said. "I never understood before—about you, I mean, and Ivan; and about your accident . . . there are so many things . . . I feel now that I have been asleep for years and years and just woken up. I am terribly ashamed of having been so stupid."

"You weren't," Lydia said gently.

"Oh yes, I was," Elizabeth contradicted, "but now I understand. Only, Lydia dear, I can't be sorry for you whatever happens now. You've had Ivan for so long—all those years together."

There was nothing Lydia could say and for some moments they sat in silence until Philip and Christine came through the garden, Philip carrying a big cabbage leaf covered with raspberries.

"We've brought you these, Mummy," Philip said, putting them down in Lydia's lap. "There would have been more if Christine had not eaten most of them."

"I like that!" Christine retorted sharply. "He only thought of bringing you some when he was so stuffed himself that he couldn't eat any more."

"I am very grateful for small mercies," Lydia said, with a smile, "and thank you for thinking of me."

"We were just wondering what we would do this evening," Christine said, pulling a cushion off a chair and sitting on it at her mother's feet. "Philip thought of going down the river in a canoe, but I'm frightened—(a) that he'll upset me and (b) that there will be mosquitoes; I loathe being bitten."

154

"Why must you do anything?" Lydia asked, and knew the answer even before Christine and Philip glanced at each other.

"Well, we just thought we'd like to enjoy ourselves," Philip said casually. "It's the river or the local dance-hall. You don't mind, Mummy, do you?"

"Of course not," Lydia answered. "You can do whatever you think most amusing."

"Who can?" Ivan asked, coming on to the verandah.

"The children," Lydia replied. "They were considering going down the river in a canoe after dinner."

"A good idea," Ivan said, "but Thyra and I have got a better one, so for tonight they must stay at home."

"What's your idea?" Lydia asked.

Ivan pulled out a chair for Thyra, who had followed him on to the verandah, and then sat down himself.

"I have shown Thyra the whole estate," he said. "She admired everything with all the right and most conventional phrases until she came to my studio, and there she made a really original remark. It shocked me at first, but I see her point."

"And what did she say?" Lydia asked.

"She said: 'What a room for a concert!' I had never thought of it before from that point of view, but it's true, you know, and on summer nights if we pull back the curtains and open the windows we can let the moonlight—provided there is a moon—stream through on to the player. What a setting!"

"It sounds very attractive," Lydia said, trying to make her voice enthusiastic.

"That's what Thyra and I thought," Ivan replied. "And so tonight, ladies and gentlemen, you are formally invited to a concert given by two famous star performers."

"One, please," Thyra interrupted, "only one. If I play at all, it will be just an overture while the audience take their seats. Once they are settled, it will be you they will want to hear."

"You're too modest, my dear," Ivan told her. "The

world takes you at your own valuation, never forget that. Well, what do you say to our plan?"

"I think it sounds lovely," Lydia said, "and we shall look forward to hearing Miss Jörgensen play."

"I do hope you won't be disappointed," Thyra said shyly;

But Ivan refused to allow her to depreciate herself, and a few minutes later, full of enthusiasm, he carried her and Philip and Christine off to the studio to get things ready.

"Is she really good?" Elizabeth asked curiously when she and Lydia were alone again.

"I have no idea," Lydia answered; then added: "But if Ivan says so, she must be."

All the same, she wondered as, when dinner was over, they went down the long passage to Ivan's studio. There was no doubt that Ivan had been right in saying it was a perfect room for a concert.

Ivan and Philip had moved the piano into the big alcove at the end of the room and Christine and Thyra had arranged great vases of flowers beside it.

The windows were all wide open; it was already turning dark outside, and the audience sitting in the shadows of the room could see a vista of trees silhouetted against a sable sky and the first evening stars twinkling above.

The peace and beauty were shattered only occasionally by the noise of an aeroplane passing overhead, a reminder that the savagery and brutality of war were still paramount in the world.

There were big armchairs arranged for Elizabeth, Christine and Philip; and Lydia, pushing her own chair beside them, wondered a little at the enthusiasm that Ivan had shown in arranging this little impromptu concert.

Usually he disliked playing at home even to her, and she thought that the times when Philip had heard his father perform except in public could be counted on the fingers of one hand.

156

"Ladies and gentlemen," Ivan said, stepping on to the improvised stage, "it gives me great pleasure to present on her first appearance in England the lovely Danish artist, Miss Thyra Jörgensen."

Obediently the little audience clapped. Then with a courtly gesture Ivan led Thyra to the piano.

The girl was wearing a simple dress of white lace; it gave her an ethereal, fragile appearance very much in keeping with the setting and the background.

But Lydia saw that she was nervous; her face was pale and she rubbed her fingers together as if they were cold.

"What am I to play?" she asked Ivan, her eyes fixed on him.

"What do you like best?" he asked.

She gave him a little smile and then, as if with an effort to echo his mock formality, she rose to her feet.

"My first piece tonight, ladies and gentlemen," she said, "will be *Rhapsody in F Sharp* by Ivan Razoumovsky."

Lydia knew the piece well. It was one of Ivan's early compositions which had brought him fame all over the world.

Thyra turned to the piano and, lifting her hands, struck the opening chord. For the first few bars she was obviously nervous and then gradually she began to play smoothly and well.

"She's good," Lydia said to herself, "very good."

The piece was one of her favourites and she gave herself up to listening; she could understand Ivan's feelings when he had written it.

The surging, yearning not which was to be found in all his best compositions rose to a paean of joy and exhilaration. It was a pagan zest for living translated into music, ever pleasing in its magic.

It was a lovely piece, but exacting on the performer, and when it was finished Thyra dropped her hands with a little gesture of relief and exhaustion.

They clapped enthusiastically.

"Good! Bravo!" Ivan exclaimed.

"And now must I play again?" Thyra asked.

"But of course," he replied. "We've encored you, don't you realise that?"

"Thank you. This, then, is my own work. It is a composition made up of a medley of Danish folk songs, the songs every Danish child has known from its cradle."

She played it charmingly, with a freshness which Lydia knew would captivate any concert audience.

There was no doubt about it, the girl was definitely good and unusually promising; but Lydia knew that something more was required if she was to achieve success in the difficult, critical musical world.

Thyra finished and Ivan with a flourish handed her from the piano to a seat beside Philip which had been unoccupied.

"Now we shall hear you?" Thyra asked with shining eyes.

"I do hope you won't be disappointed," Ivan said, mocking her own original statement.

Lydia saw the child flush.

Ivan sat down at the piano. For a moment he ran his hands up and down the keys. He had originally started his career as a pianist and only when he had become a conductor had he given up playing, though he still performed on very rare occasions.

Lydia knew that it had been said that nowadays it was easier to get Ivan Razoumovsky to play the piano for love than for money.

He had gained this reputation, she had learnt, because sometimes, though rarely, he could be persuaded to play in the drawing-room of some *bonne amie*, but she guessed that he often played alone to someone who held his fancy.

Now, having run his fingers with a flourish over the keys, he turned to his audience.

"I will start my programme," he said, "with *Rhapsody in F Sharp*."

Lydia heard Thyra give a little gasp, but no one else

158

made any movement as Ivan started to play. It was a cruelty which no one there had expected of him. Thyra had played the *Rhapsody* very well indeed, but in comparison with the man who had composed it she might have been a high-school girl grinding out her examination piece.

Under Ivan's skilful fingers the music rose into a crescendo of emotion; one became aware of subtle tones, of an undercurrent one had not realised was there, of the expression in music of the difficult, complex personality of the composer.

He conveyed to his listeners an understanding of all that the young Ivan had wanted and required of life, all that he had found, all that he had experienced, and all that had remained uncaputred—out of reach.

When Ivan played, it was difficult to think of anything but him. It was only when the last chord crashed in a triumphant finale that Lydia could take her eyes from him and look at Thyra. The girl was very pale and her eyes brimmed with tears.

She knew without words the lesson that Ivan had taught her; taught her, Lydia thought grimly, with unnecessary harshness. It was as if he had said openly to the world:

"You're good, but not good enough!"

Yet, knowing Ivan as she did, Lydia wondered if that was what he had intended. She could not help but feel that perhaps in his own childishness he wanted merely to show off—to proclaim to Thyra and to them all his own vast superiority.

That this was indeed the true explanation she knew as the piece finished and Ivan rose from the piano. Seeing that Thyra was distressed, he walked across and, picking up her hand, raised it to his lips.

"Forgive me," he said.

There was nothing theatrical for the moment either in his action or in his words.

No one said anything and he went back to the piano

and, looking out the open window, seemed for a moment to seek inspiration.

Then he started to play. He played something new, a work Lydia had never heard before and which, she guessed, was part of a new symphony he was composing.

It started quietly and then into the peace and serenity of the melody came again that hungry yearning which Lydia understood so well. Unsatisfied, unrequited, Ivan was crying for that which he had been seeking all his life.

The agony of wanting was almost painful to listen to, and yet there was a glory and an ecstasy within it too. The melody rose higher and higher, seeking, longing, always just within reach of attainment and never quite finding it.

Its very poignancy made those who listened tense and still; it keyed them up almost to breaking point until Lydia felt she could bear it no longer.

"This is what Ivan is suffering, this is what he craves for," she told herself; and over and over again she repeated, "it's out of reach! Out of reach!"

The words seemed to mock her. She was powerless to help him.

Then suddenly Ivan stopped playing. There was no ending, no finale, he just took his hands from the piano and rose to his feet. He looked strange and wild at that moment, exhausted, too, as if he had given all of himself into the music.

He wiped his forehead with a silk handkerchief; then without a word to those sitting still and quiet in the shadows of the great room he moved towards the open window and putting his long legs over the sill slipped out into the garden.

It was almost dark now and they heard rather than saw him go, listening to the scrunch of his feet on the gravel.

There was a long, long silence. Elizabeth was surreptitiously wiping her eyes.

160

Then Philip broke the tension by getting to his feet and holding out his hands to help Thyra from her chair.

"We've got a radiogram in the drawing-room," he announced causally. "What about a dance?"

12

"You seem pleased with yourself," Philip said. "What happened?"

Christine looked at him and smiled.

"How do you know anything's happened?" she asked.

"Well, I haven't seen you in such a good mood for a long time," he replied. "Besides, no one but a lunatic would want to go to London on a day like this unless there was someting pretty exciting to be gained by it."

"What a little Sherlock Holmes!" Christine mocked; and added more seriously: "Yes, something pretty exciting has happened, but I can't tell you about it yet; perhaps when I come back—I don't know."

Philip looked at her face and then he looked ahead to where down the narrow, dusty road the roofs of the station could just be seen.

He was silent for a few moments before in a tone half apologetic, half embarrassed, he said:

"I say, Christine, you're not letting yourself get mixed up with someone the family doesn't know? It's nothing to do with me and all that, but . . . well . . . you are my sister and I've seen a good bit of the world one way or another . . . and . . . damn it all, you're not very old yet!"

Christine stared at him as he first began to speak, then as he continued she gave a little gurgle of laughter and slipped her arm into his.

"Philip," she said, "I love you! You're the nicest brother any girl ever had! But just now you're on the wrong track. There isn't a man in the case, I promise you that; but if there ever is one, I'll come and tell you first. That's a promise."

Philip looked relieved. It was obvious that his attempt at being the big brother had been an effort.

"That's all right then," he said. "You got me worried for the moment; you were so cheerful . . . and, well, you've changed from what you've been lately."

"I know," Christine said. "I have been rather a pig because I've been depressed. But now . . . no, I don't want to say anything yet in case it doesn't come off . . . all the same, Philip, I like having you look after me."

Five minutes later, as Christine was leaning out of the crowded carriage waving her hand to Philip as the train slid out of the station, she thought how lucky she was to have a brother who really seemed to care for her.

She remembered some of the girls she had known in America who had got themselves tangled up with boys while they were still at school.

She thought of one particular friend who had run away to get married when she was only a few days over sixteen. Christine despised their foolishness, and yet somehow she could understand the excitement and thrill of having love affairs.

The girls didn't want to be in love with one particular person but in love with love; they wanted to be sought after and made a fuss of, and to extract greedily every ounce of pleasure that there was to be had from the experience.

There had been boys who had been interested in her too. But Christine found them callow and unattractive.

She had wanted something better, more sophisticated, and at times had felt immeasurably older than her contemporaries who giggled happily in corners over what "he" had said last night.

"What sort of man do I want eventually?" Christine asked herself; and the consideration of this question kept her oblivious of the discomfort and heat of the journey till the train slid into Waterloo.

She looked at her watch and saw that it was on time. There was no need to hurry and yet she felt unable to stop her feet carrying her swiftly down the platform in search of a taxi.

It had been hard enough to wait forty-eight hours after that telephone call which had changed her mood of depression to one of elation!

Sir Fraser Wilton had telephoned her, and at first Christine had been so surprised to hear his voice that she could hardly concentrate on what he was saying.

She had told herself so definitely that she would never hear from him again. He had promised, it was true, but that, she felt, meant little. Why should he in his eminent position be concerned with the hopes and disappointments of a young girl?

Christine had been sensible enought to realise that everything Sir Fraser had said to her was the unvarnished truth. Her gift, or talent, whichever she liked to call it, would have no chance to survive or be of use in a world of noisy publicity.

"The best thing I can do," she told herself severely, "is to forget all about it and start living afresh now I have come home."

There was a certain pathos in the effort she made—a pathos of the very young who must through circumstances throw away the few roots they have already acquired.

Then when indecision and the effort of controlling her own thoughts made her moody and depressed so that she felt herself in a deep valley through which she must pass but never raise her head to the mountains, Sir Fraser telephone.

"I want you to help me," he said.

"Help you?" Christine stammered.

"Yes," he replied. "I have been consulted regarding a very difficult case and one in which I believe your peculiar powers might be of tremendous assistance. Will you—in modern parlance—co-operate?"

"You know I will," Christine said. "But when and where?"

She guessed he smiled a little at her words and at the eagerness of her tone.

"Come up to London on Thursday," he said. "If you will be at my consulting-room at three o'clock we will go along together and see the patient."

Christine felt a glow of excitement. He believed in her then. That indeed was sufficient to make her feel extremely proud.

"I will be there," she promised.

Travelling towards Sir Fraser's house, Christine knew that she was nervous. Suppose she failed? The question presented itself and commanded her attention. If she did, what would it prove? That she had been misguided in the past, misled into believing herself better than she was?

Supposing that her powers—if powers they were—should be affected by a different climate, a different atmosphere, a different people?

Christine tried to shake herself free of the fears that beset her, which whispered round her like evil sprites, tantalising, irritating and upsetting her so that by the time she reached Sir Fraser's house she half wished she had never come, that he had never reawakened within her all her old questioning.

The old butler, who had been so suspicious of her on her first visit, welcomed her with what was intended to be a smile.

"Sir Fraser is expecting you, miss. Will you come this way?"

He led her down the long passage to Sir Fraser's room at the back of the house. Christine was glad to escape the gloomy solemnity of the Victorian waiting-room. She wondered what Lady Wilton was like. Was that her taste?

Sir Fraser, rising as she entered, looked, it seemed to Christine, taller and more impressive than ever.

165

"So you decided to come," he said as Christine sat down in the chair to which he motioned her.

Christine looked surprised at the question and then guessed he was perceptive enough to realise the battle which had been taking place within her.

"I'm rather frightened," she confessed honestly.

"Of course you are," he said. "You're frightened that you may fail and a little apprehensive of what the future will be if you succeed. My dear, I understand perfectly.

"At the same time, as you told me at our first meeting, you really believe that there is some reason in all that happens, some pattern in which we all take our allotted place here, what a very good example of it!"

He paused, and studied for a moment some papers on the desk in front of him.

Christine sat silent and still waiting for him to continue.

"About a fortnight ago," Sir Fraser said, "I was called into consultation by a very old friend of mine who is extremely interested in nervous diseases. He admitted to me that after handling a case for two years he had failed utterly to obtain any result whatsoever.

"The patient is a young woman suffering from the results of an accident. To be frank with you, Miss Stanfield, it has been announced by her relations that her injuries were sustained during an air raid. This, I understand, is untrue.

"You will, of course, appreciate that I am being completely honest with you, speaking in confidence because at the moment I am treating you as one of ourselves."

"Thank you," Christine said softly.

"There is no need to go deeply into whether the injuries were caused by an accident or by a bomb. What is important is the fact that the patient at the time was suffering from great mental distress. It happened nearly three years ago.

"She was operated on and her bones were set by one

166

of our most distinguished surgeons who later pronounced her completely and absolutely cured—physically.

"It was after that my friend and colleague was called in, for, although there was nothing physically wrong with the patient, her mental reaction was very much at fault. To put it in the language of the layman, she would not make an effort of any sort to come back to life.

"In fact, from the reports I have read and from what I have been told she made up her mind not to live.

"That she didn't die by sheer will power was due, I imagine, entirely to the fact that her relations could afford the best nurses and the best treatment in an effort to keep her alive.

"I went to see this young woman and I realise that from a psychological point of view I am as powerless as my friend has been. You can't reason with what appears to be a living corpse."

"Her mind is all right?" Christine supposed.

"That we don't know," Sir Fraser replied. "She lies in what—for want of a better word—we call a coma. She is fed artificially, washed and looked after by her nurses.

"She appears to be quite inanimate and oblivious to what goes on around her; but my friend, who is an extremely astute man, is certain that she could, if required, make the effort to become normal."

"And you think that I . . .?" Christine asked.

"Might be able to enthuse some form of interest into her, some form of life," Sir Fraser said. "In a way it will be like raising someone from the dead. Anyway, we can but try. You can do no harm and may do good. I am presenting the case to you, Miss Stanfield, in all honesty."

"I should like to try, of course," Christine said in a low voice; "but if your friend is right and she has some knowledge of what is going on around her, she may be able to resist me as well as the doctors."

"Perhaps your power is stronger than theirs," Sir Fraser suggested, and he spoke quite seriously.

Christine smiled at him.

"Whatever happens," she said, "thank you for believing in me enough to give me an opportunity to prove myself."

"Shall we go then?" Sir Fraser asked.

They walked from the house to Sir Fraser's car which was waiting outside.

"What is the patient's name?" Christine asked as the car drove off towards the Park.

"Hampden—Stella Hampden, and her brother in whose house she lives is an extremely clever young man who was well known before the war in civil aviation."

"What is he doing now?" Christine asked. "Building aeroplanes?"

"Not building them, flying them," Sir Fraser corrected. "Or at least he was—at the moment he is at home after having been shot down in Normandy, taken prisoner by the Germans and later released by our advancing armies.

"I think, between ourselves, it is due to his insistence that something more has to be tried. He is impatient of doctors who accept the inevitable. One can hardly blame him."

The car stopped at a big house in a quiet square.

The chauffeur got out and rang the bell, and a few minutes later Christine and Sir Fraser were ushered into a large library where a young man stood waiting for them. Christine saw that his foot was swathed in bandages and that he walked with the aid of a stick.

He was tall and rather good-looking, with a square-chinned, level-eyed type of face; but as they entered he was scowling, and Christine had a quick impression that either he disliked the medical profession as a whole or resented Sir Fraser and herself personally.

Sir Fraser introduced them: "Wing Commander Hampden, Miss Stanfield."

"Is this the young lady you were telling me about?"

the Wing Commander asked in what Christine thought was a somewhat rude tone.

"It is," Sir Fraser replied. "Miss Stanfield has been good enough to come here to see if there is anything she can do for your sister."

Wing Commander Hampden did not say in so many words that he thought she was ridiculously young and inexperienced, but Christine knew he was thinking it as he turned to her abruptly and asked:

"Do you think you can help my sister?"

"I hope I can," Christine replied.

Her words seemed to cause some annoyance.

"Hope! Hope!" ejaculated the Wing Commander, gesticulating with his stick. "That's what every doctor says who comes here! They 'hope' to do something! When I see the miracles they have performed on our men who have been injured in this war, when I see what can be done with those who are burnt or practically broken into small pieces.

"I say something has got to be done for Stella! I'm sick to death of hopes! I want action, and I want it quickly!"

Christine stood staring at this outburst, but Sir Fraser took it quite calmly.

"I couldn't agree with you more," he said. "For years I have been saying that doctors are fools and don't know their job. But you must understand that the human will is one of the strongest ingredients in medicine: and whatever a doctor may say, if a human being says he won't live, it is a ninety-nine chance to one that he doesn't."

"Stella has got to be made to live then," Wing Commander Hampden said authoritatively.

Christine thought he was the type of young man who was used to giving orders and having them carried out implicitly.

"Supposing instead of talking so much," Sir Fraser said calmly, "Miss Stanfield and I go up and see your sister? Will you stay here?"

169

Without waiting for their host to agree Sir Fraser turned towards the door. Christine had the impression the young man they left behind watched them go without much confidence in the result of their mission.

As they went up the broad stairs, Sir Fraser said:

"I believe Hampden and his sister were devoted to each other. It is a rather sad story. They were orphaned when they were both quite young. Their father and mother were killed in a motor smash and the boy came into an immense fortune.

"He was the individual type of boy who remains alone even in a crowd, and he concentrated all his affection on his young sister. She is a number of years younger than he is."

"How old is she?" Christine asked.

"About twenty-four, I believe," Sir Fraser replied. "She was twenty-one when the accident occurred."

They reached the landing on the first floor and a nurse came out to meet them. She greeted Sir Fraser respectfully, but Christine imagined that even her starched apron rustled her disapproval when she saw who had been brought in on the case, and there was no disguising her surprise and almost horror when Sir Fraser announced:

"Miss Stanfield and I would like to see the patient alone,"

"Dr. Dearman is not here yet, Sir Fraser," she said reproachfully.

"Then we won't wait for him."

They went into the room. The blinds were lowered and shut out the afternoon sun, and it took a moment for Christine's eyes to grow used to the dimness.

The bedroom had originally been the drawing-room of the house. It was exquisitely furnished and arranged so that the invalid should have everything that was lovely and most attractive round her.

The room was left as a sitting-room and nearly every table held great bowls of flowers—roses, carnations, lilies—their fragrance scenting the room and making it slightly exotic in its luxury and beauty.

The bed, set in an alcove, was of carved wood, gilded and coloured by Italian craftsmen, and the figure that lay still and inanimate against lace pillows was covered by an exquisite bedspread of old Chinese embroidery.

Sir Fraser approached the bed with the assurance of one who is used to the sick, but Christine held back a little, afraid of what she was about to see.

When finally she came to Sir Fraser's side, she found herself looking at an extremely pretty face; indeed, it might have been beautiful had not it resembled a death mask. The skin was magnolia white and tightly stretched across the sharpness of jaw and cheekbones.

The fair hair was brushed tightly back from the square forehead, while Stella Hampden's eyes, deeply fringed with dark eyelashes, were closed beneath exquisitely marked eyebrows.

Was she breathing? Christine held her own breath to be sure.

There was something uncanny in the utter inanimate stillness of the invalid. Involuntarily Christine made a slight exclamation.

"She seldom moves," Sir Fraser said, speaking in a quite natural voice. "She might almost be in a trance."

"Can she hear what we are saying?" Christine asked, lowering her own tones.

"No one knows," Sir Fraser answered.

Christine looked at Stella.

"I feel as if she were dead already," she said.

Then quite suddenly, as she said the words, some instinct within her rose to contradict it. She felt that strange familiar sensation which told her that she was about to see and understand what was wrong.

As if he knew what was happening, Sir Fraser stepped aside.

Christine did not move; instead she stood looking down at the sick girl. It was very quiet in the room. A taxi passed outside. There was an insistent flutter

171

against a windowpane, as if a butterfly had got caught inside and was trying to make its escape.

And then after a long pause Christine moved.

She put one hand against Stella's forehead and slipped the other one behind her neck, cupping it upwards so that she held the small head between the palms of her hands.

She remained like this for some minutes before she slowly moved her hands to massage the neck and touch the closed eyes.

There was a slight convulsive movement beneath the bedclothes and then Christine spoke urgently:

"Wake up! Wake up!"

Again there was that convulsive movement as if someone struggled. Christine took her hands from Stella's eyes and slowly, very slowly, as if an immeasurable weight was being cast away, they opened.

"Wake up!" Christine spoke again.

The eyes looked at her unseeingly, then focused themselves as if with a tremendous effort.

Now Christine moved the bedclothes and took both Stella's hands in hers. She held them tightly, seeming to pour through them strength and vitality.

She felt the throbbing sensation in her own arms, heard the beating of her own heart. Stella's lips, dry and faintly blue, opened.

She tried to speak, but it appeared impossible.

At last her voice, so low and cracked that it was almost impossible to understand, came from between her lips.

"Don't! Don't!"

"I must," Christine replied. "You've got to wake up and get well."

"I won't!"

Again the words were almost intelligible.

Christine bent forward again, putting the tip of her fingers beneath the girl's neck and placing her other hand on the forehead.

172

It was then that the patient screamed—screamed with a horrible, strident sound.

"Go away! Go away! Leave me alone!"

The nurse came hurrying into the room. Sir Fraser moved forward, but not before Christine had relinquished her hold to stand trembling by the bedside.

Stella Hampden screamed again and then her voice subsided into an unintelligible gurgling and she moved her head restlessly from side to side. Sir Fraser had his hand on her pulse.

It was at that moment that Christine was aware of someone else in the room, someone standing by the door. She turned her head and saw it was the Wing Commander. Sir Fraser looked across at the nurse.

"Dr. Dearman ought to be here," he said. "Telephone him."

"I am here," Dr. Dearman said in a quiet voice.

He moved past the Wing Commander without apology and reached the bedside.

Stella was still moving restlessly, turning her head from side to side as if she wished to escape. Her eyes were closed again, but there was a faint flush in her cheeks.

The doctor took her pulse and her respiration. Then he looked at Sir Fraser.

"So it worked," he said.

Sir Fraser put his hand as if in approval on Christine's shoulder.

"I think that's enough for today," he said quietly.

It was then that Stella Hampden opened her eyes. She looked straight at Christine.

For a moment she lay still, breathing deeply, before her lips moved and in a voice hoarse and hard with suffering she said:

"Leave me alone!"

13

Christine, arriving at the Hampden's house on the following day, was conscious of a sense of reluctance to enter it.

The excitement and elation of the day before had passed, and during the night she had lain awake wondering whether she was right to be instrumental in bringing Stella Hampden back to life, when it was obvious that her sole desire was to remain in a merciful oblivion

Christine wondered how much the coma in which she had lain for so long had been self-induced.

Sir Fraser Wilton had been frankly delighted by the events of the day before, but Christine was well aware that Dr. Dearman had not been so pleased, while the nurse had been openly hostile.

It was not going to be easy, she thought, to visit this house daily and know that at least half the people within it were opposed to her.

The Wing Commander had said little.

Christine thought at first that he was ungracious, and then she had understood that his apparent lack of gratitude was only a lack of words. He had been emotionally upset and stirred by what he had seen and had found it impossible to say anything.

At the same time Christine sensed that there was some bitterness within him which she did not entirely understand.

She had the impression that he could not think or speak about his sister's illness wthout it arousing some savagery within him so strong that Christine felt it was a hatred almost fanatical in its intensity.

They had talked for a long time after they had come down from Stella's bedroom and all the time Christine had been acutely conscious of the Wing Commander's feelings.

They were obvious even while he sat silent, and she wondered what exactly was the secret behind Stella's so-called accident.

More than once Dr. Dearman had referred to Stella's physical injuries and on each occasion Christine noticed the expression on the Wing Commander's face. "Murderous" was the only adjective which seemed sufficiently expressive.

When Christine arrived at the house she was shown immediately up the stairs and met by the nurse, more frigid and starchy than ever.

"Dr. Dearman is with Miss Hampden," she said. "I'll tell him you are here."

"Has she had a good night?" Christine asked.

"Extremely restless," the nurse replied.

Christine would have expressed her regret if she had not suddenly thought that this was all to the good. She looked at the nurse with a smile.

"You must be pleased!" she exclaimed, and for once that worthy person had no reply, as Christine passed her and entered the room.

Dr. Dearman was sitting beside Stella. He rose and crossed the room and held out his hand to Christine, and then drew her to the window as far away as possible from his patient.

"I am a little worried about Miss Hampden," he said in a low voice. "I am wondering whether it would be better to leave her alone for at least twenty-four hours."

He looked worried, but Christine was not particularly concerned with Dr. Dearman's feelings. She had not liked him very much on first acquaintance.

It had struck her that he was the type of doctor who disliked experiments, and that only Sir Fraser's repu-

175

tation and insistence had made him agree to a continuance of treatment by a layman.

The neurologist who was Sir Fraser's friend and who had called him in to the case was unfortunately away at this moment, and Christine summed Dr. Dearman up as a fussy, unimaginative G.P. who hated anything out of the ordinary."

"What does Sir Fraser advise?" she asked him.

"I did speak to Sir Fraser this morning," Dr. Dearman replied. "As a matter of fact he telephoned me to hear what sort of night Miss Hampden has had. He hopes to get in to see her later this afernoon. Perhaps we should wait until he comes."

"May I look at her?" Christine asked.

She moved across the softly carpeted bedroom towards the bed. Stella was lying with her face half buried in the pillows. Stella was very still—as still as she had been the day before, and yet Christine knew instinctively there was a difference.

Today Stella knew what was going on around her; Christine was as sure of that as she was sure of anything, although there was nothing to tell her the truth save her own sharpened senses.

She stood looking down at Stella and then suddenly made up her mind. Turning to Dr. Dearman she said:

"Would you mind very much if I talked with Miss Hampden alone?"

She saw both surprise and hesitation on his face and added quickly:

"I won't touch her, I won't treat her in any way without your being present, but I want to talk to her."

Dr. Dearman smiled patronisingly.

"My dear young lady, Miss Hampden won't answer you. She has lain like this, as you know, for a very long time; in fact, it is doubtful if she will hear what you say."

"I quite understand that," Christine said gravely, "but I would like to try if you don't mind."

Dr. Dearman shrugged his shoulders.

176

"I presume it can do no harm," he said ungraciously. "I will wait outside the door. If you want me perhaps you will call."

He turned away, muttering as he moved towards the door:

"This is all very unprofessional, you know."

Christine did not answer him. She waited until she heard the door shut quietly behind him and then sat down on the edge of the bed. Stella lay very still, but Christine was certain that she was listening.

"What do you want me to do about this?" Christine asked in a low voice. "Shall I go away and leave you?"

Very slowly Stella's eyes opened and gradually, as if it was an immense effort, she twisted herself round on the pillows so that she could see Christine.

"Yes, go away," she whispered.

"Isn't it too late?" Christine asked. "I mean, you're awake now; it won't be so easy to slip back again, to drift away as you've done in the past."

There was a long silence while Stella seemed to consider this. At length she said:

"Why couldn't you have left me alone?"

"What was the use?" Christine asked. "They won't let you die, not as long as your brother can afford to pay all these nurses and doctors."

Stella closed her eyes wearily, and then after a pause while Christine wondered whether she had indeed slipped away out of reach she opened them again.

"What am I to do?" she asked.

Christine sensed rather than heard the words, they were so faint and weak. Without thinking of her promise to Dr. Dearman she bent forward and took Stella's hands in both her own.

"You're going to come to life," she said. "There's lots to do, exciting things, thrilling things. Besides, there's someone who wants you and needs you."

For a moment Christine thought there was a sudden expression of eagerness on Stella's face.

"Your brother has been wounded," Christine said. "He is lonely."

The expression faded—if, indeed, it had been there. Stella closed her eyes again.

Christine, still holding her hands, gave them a little shake.

"Help me," she said. "You've got to go forward, it's too late to go back."

Stella opened her eyes and for the first time there was an expression of humour in them.

"All right," she said in that weak, choked voice. "Do your damnedest."

Christine was aware that someone had entered the room. She expected Dr. Dearman, and then realised that the person who approached the bed was limping and knew who it was. She made no attempt to relinquish Stella's hands; instead she held them tightly as if forcing the girl's attention. The Wing Commander drew near and stood beside the bed looking down at his sister.

"Stella," he said.

There was an appeal as well as wonderment in his voice.

"Hello, Harry," Stella said, as if, Christine told herself, she had come back from a long voyage.

The Wing Commander sank down on to the chair which stood beside the bed and bending forward put his hand on his sister's arm.

"Thank God, you can speak to me," he said. "Oh, Stella, get well. I want you to so much."

Stella's lips gave a little twitch as if she tried to smile, and then she said hoarsely:

"I'm thirsty."

Christine relinquished her hands and slipping off the bed went to the door. The nurse was outside, but there was no sign of Dr. Dearman.

"Miss Hampden is thirsty," Christine told her, not without satisfaction.

"How do you know?" the nurse asked swiftly.

178

"She said so," Christine replied, well aware that the remark was sensational and deliberately stating it simply.

"She said so?" the nurse exclaimed. And added: "Good gracious!" before she hurried into the room.

As she vanished, Dr. Dearman came up the stairs.

"Oh, there you are, Miss Stanfield. I've just been speaking to Sir Fraser on the telephone. He agrees with me that if there is no particular response from the patient it would be wiser to let her rest for at least twenty-four hours."

"Miss Hampden has just asked for a drink," Christine said demurely.

"A drink!" Dr. Dearman exclaimed. "God bless my soul!" And he, too, went into the bedroom.

Christine went slowly down the stairs. There was no reason for her to go back. Her work, at any rate for the moment, was done. She was not certain that it was not completed and finished.

She knew with that strange sixth sense, which was always there when she helped someone who was suffering, that Stella would not be able to sink back into the coma again or to hypnotise herself into being oblivious of what went on around her.

It would take time for her to crawl back to life, but crawl back she must whether she wished it or not.

Christine picked up the parcel which she had left in the hall on her arrival, and was just moving towards the door when she heard her voice called from the top of the stairs.

"Miss Stanfield."

She waited while the Wing Commander came slowly down the staircase, supporting himself heavily on the banister and swinging his bandaged leg from stair to stair. When he reached the hall he turned aside to open the door into the library.

"Won't you come in a moment?" he said. "I want to talk to you."

Christine did as she was asked, at the same time combating a feeling of embarrassment.

The room seemed bathed in sunshine. She walked across to where a sofa and chairs were arranged somewhat stiffly before the fireplace, but she did not sit down.

Instead she stood and waited until the Wing Commander reached her side.

"I want to thank you," he said.

"Please don't," Christine spoke quickly.

"When Sir Fraser asked me if he might bring you here I thought he was crazy. I didn't believe in faith healing, and when I saw you I am ashamed to say that I felt he was insulting me by bringing anyone so young and—may I say it—pretty.

"I felt not only that it was improbable you would help Stella, but that it was literally impossible. I had consulted so many doctors and all of them had eventually come to the same conclusion—that there was nothing to be done. And now . . ."

The Wing Commander made an expressive gesture.

"Please don't say all this," Christine said. "I might have failed too. To be frank, I don't understand what has happened, or why. Your sister is better; I think that now she will get well quickly."

"You will come and see her tomorrow?" the Wing Commander asked.

"If there is any need," Christine said. "But I feel that Dr. Dearman . . ."

"Oh, damn Dr. Dearman!" the Wing Commander exclaimed. "He's an old fool and always has been. But he's our family doctor and has treated all of us since we were children. We haven't got to consider him, or anyone else for that matter—only Stella. You will come to see her?"

Christine smiled at his impetuosity.

"If she wants me," she said simply.

The Wing Commander hesitated and looked embarrassed.

"There is one thing more, Miss Stanfield. How can I show my gratitude, mine and Stella's?"

Christine knew what he meant.

"You can't. Let's be frank. I should not be allowed to take fees for this sort of thing even if I wanted to. This is all very unprofessional, you know that."

"Of course I know it," the Wing Commander replied. "Sir Fraser swore us all to secrecy before he brought you here. Dr. Dearman and the nurses didn't like it; in fact, to be honest, they were very opposed to your coming."

"I guessed that," Christine said softly.

"But Sir Fraser had his own way. I expect he usually gets it, he's that type of chap. But I can't let things just rest there."

Christine looked at him and smiled.

"I suppose I should feel the same," she said. "But don't let's bother about it until your sister is really well and on her feet again. The day she comes downstairs and goes for a walk—well, we'll throw a party, shall we?"

The Wing Commander threw back his head and laughed.

"Thank you," he said.

Then he held out his hand.

"One day I will think of a way to say it more adequately.

"We are only over the first fence, you know," Christine said gravely. "Your sister is unhappy, you realise that?"

The Wing Commander's face darkened.

"I've been thinking of that for three years," he said.

Abruptly he turned towards the window, his back to Christine. He stood there for a moment, then he turned again to face her. She was half astonished by the expression on his face.

"Shall I tell you something?" he said grimly. "Whenever I shot a Jerry down in the sky I thought of my sister. Whenever I've watched one of their planes go

181

swirling down towards the earth I thought of her. I felt in some way I was avenging her.

"You may think it's silly, but those thoughts have been with me for nearly three years. I don't feel quite sane when I think of her. She was so pretty, so gay, and we meant a tremendous lot to each other until . . ." He stopped abruptly.

"I don't want to bore you with this," he said. "I am rather fanatical on the subject."

"You aren't boring me," Christine said quickly, but she realised that the Wing Commander intended to say no more. With an effort he controlled himself.

"I never offered you a cigarette," he said. "Do you smoke?"

Christine shook her head and looked at her watch.

"I had better be going," she said. "If I hurry, I shall be home in time for tea."

"You live in the country, don't you?" the Wing Commander asked. "I thought I heard Sir Fraser say so."

"Yes, in Surrey," Christine answered.

"What do you do? I mean apart from this sort of thing?"

"I don't do 'this sort of thing' as a rule," Christine smiled. "As a matter of fact it's the first time I have done it in this country. I have only recently arrived from America; I was evacuated there."

"How sensible," the Wing Commander said.

"On the contrary. I resented it a good deal at the time," Christine replied. "I think all older children should have remained in England."

"War isn't for children, whatever their age," the Wing Commander said.

"It's a quick educator, though," Christine argued. "At the moment I feel very ignorant. And now I really must go. I will come again tomorrow unless I hear from you or Dr. Dearman in the meantime."

"You certainly won't hear from me," he answered. "As for Dearman, don't listen to the old gasbag."

182

Christine laughed. She was still smiling as she hurried away down the road in search of a taxi.

"He's nice," she told herself: "I like him." She found it easy to imagine him riding in the sky.

She could even imagine the cold, calculating fury with which he would shoot down an enemy, feeling in some personal way he was identified with his sister stricken and still, lying so utterly alone in the luxury of their home.

Loneliness! That indeed was the key word, Christine thought.

She knew then that she had always suffered from loneliness—during those long years when she had been away from home; during her childhood, when she had felt alien from her father; and now when, as she put it to herself, she was neither one thing nor the other, but suspended, as it were, between Heaven and earth without a place in either.

Loneliness! Yes, Stella must have been lonely, and she imagined Harry Hampden being lonely too when he had come home to that quiet, empty house filled only with the impersonal attentions of doctors and nurses.

So that was his name—Harry.

It suited him, she thought. Despite his reputation for brains and intelligence, there was about him something slightly debonair and spirited which had always been associated in Christine's mind with the name Harry.

When at school she and her friends had often picked out the men's names they most liked, and "Harry" had been a popular choice.

"Harry Hampden!" She would see him tomorrow.

That in itself was a pleasant thought. She thought of him all the way down in the train, until she saw Philip waiting for her on the station. Christine jumped out of the carriage to kiss him.

"It's sweet of you to come and meet me," she said, "but rather rash; I might easily have missed this train."

"Oh, I thought the walk would do me good," Philip said. "Besides, to tell the honest truth, I missed you."

"Did you really?" Christine's heart warmed towards her brother. "What are the others doing?"

"Mother had a bit of a headache and went and lay down after lunch, and I had just persuaded Thyra to play tennis with me when Daddy carried her off to his studio and they've been there ever since."

Christine said nothing for a moment, matching her strides to Philip's as they moved up the road side by side.

"What do you think of her?" she asked at length; and there was no need to ask to whom she referred.

"I like her," Philip said firmly.

"So do I," Christine agreed. "I thought at first I should hate her. I felt it was terrible of Daddy to bring her here. But—well, she's not what we expected, is she?"

"Not a bit."

"In fact," Christine went on, "while I feel it's almost disloyal of us for Mother's sake not to hate her, it's impossible; she's such a baby and so ingenuously pleased with everything. Do you think she loves Daddy?"

"I don't know," Philip said. "I feel as puzzled as you are."

"Of course she adores his music. It's to be expected that she should look on him as one of the great masters and all that sort of thing. But as a man—surely she must realise how much older he is!"

Philip said nothing as they left the road and climbed the five-barred gate into the Park.

"I don't believe Mummy minds as much as she thought she would," Christine said. "At the same time it must be infuriating to watch Daddy pandering to a younger woman and making all that fuss about swimming with her and playing games—you know how he goes on."

"All the same, he can be pretty nasty at times."

"Yes, he can," Christine agreed. "Thyra was talking

184

about music last night. She didn't hear him come in and suddenly he snubbed her. She went crimson. Did you notice?"

"I did," Philip replied, "and I wish to Heaven he wouldn't behave like that. It makes me feel so damned sorry for his victims, whoever they may be."

"I don't believe he means to be unkind," Christine said, with more preception than she knew. "I think he just wants us to realise how awfully clever he is."

"It merely makes me think he's a bit of a cad."

Christine sighed. "I suppose it would have been much simpler to have had an ordinary sort of father."

"The huntin', shootin' and fishin' sort?" Philip suggested.

"That's right. One who'd have been proud of our progress in the school sports and taken us out and given us a good feed at the tuck-shop. Oh, Philip, can you imagine Daddy being like that?"

They both laughed rather helplessly and then continued to talk of the imaginary parents they might have had, until Lydia, coming out on the verandah, heard their voices high and rounded with laughter as they crossed the lawn.

Her heart leaped as it always did when she saw Philip.

"Hello, Mummy, are you better?" he called.

"Much; I'm sorry I was so mouldy at lunch. How are you, Christine? Did you have a good day in London?"

She asked the question warmly enough and yet there was a hint of reserve in it. Lydia had longed to know what was this mysterious business which took Christine to London but she could not bring herself to question her daughter even though it was hard to wait patiently for Christine to choose her own time in which to tell her the truth.

"Yes, a very good day, thank you," Christine answered.

Just for a moment her secret trembled on her lips.

Should she tell them and tell them now—pour out to her mother and Philip all that had occurred?

She was tempted—almost the words came. And then it was too late.

"Is tea ready? We're starving!" Ivan called gaily from the door of the verandah.

Arm in arm with Thyra he advanced towards them.

14

Lydia lay in bed and let her breakfast grow cold. She had passed a bad night and felt overwhelmingly miserable and depressed.

"I am being ridiculous," she told herself, and forced her mind to acknowledge that her depression was, in part at any rate, due to the fact that she was feeling resentful at being "left out in the cold" by her family.

Once she had known that she was the centre, the hub round which her whole household revolved. In those days she had by her beauty and vitality been able to hold Ivan to her both physically and mentally.

True, their relationship had been strained at times and always the fear had been there that he might be attracted by someone else, that the emotional side of him, so strong and virile, might lead him astray;

Nevertheless Lydia had known that his love for her was a very real and a very live thing.

Now, while she sought to readjust herself to their new intimacy—a union one-sided and in many ways unnatural to them both—it was hard actually to watch him obsessed by a younger woman.

"It means nothing; it is only a passing fancy," Lydia told herself over and over again, and yet the jealousy in her heart gave her no rest.

Every time she saw Ivan look at Thyra, every time he touched the girl or even engaged her in interested conversation, Lydia felt stabbed and wounded.

However strongly she could hold her mind in control, she had not yet the power to subdue and conquer her heart.

"He's mine! Mine!" she longed to scream at Thyra. "Leave him alone!"

When she went to her bedroom at night to lie alone in the darkness, memories of the past rose to haunt her, while her suspicions of the present jeered and taunted her through the wakeful hours.

She found herself listening for the sound of Thyra's voice, to the shutting of doors, for movements in the passages and overhead; and she loathed herself for listening because, she told herself proudly, she would never play the spy.

Ivan was courteous and considerate as always, but with Thyra present only Lydia knew how much was missing from their relationship.

The quick understanding which had always bound them together in other people's presence, his eagerness to be with her as soon as he had returned home, the caresses of affection which had started her day and ended it—these had ceased for the moment.

As in everything he did, Ivan loved too well and not wisely. He made no secret of the fact that he was wildly attracted to Thyra.

When she was not present, he would discuss her charms with Lydia quite openly and naturally—rather like a son who talks frankly with a beloved mother—not knowing that every word he said hurt her until she must bite her lips so as not to cry out in pain.

She tried so hard with a bravery of which she was quite unconscious to play the rôle allotted to her.

"How is your pupil progressing, Ivan?" she would ask.

Then lean back with a forced smile to listen to the praise which came so eagerly to his lips.

"She's lovely! She has a presence that will make itself felt on any stage—the public will adore her, how could they help it?"

"And musically?" Lydia asked once. "Is she good enough?"

Ivan hesitated.

"She'll be good enough," he answered at length.

Despite his infatuation he made Thyra work hard.

188

The hours they spent in the studio were no subterfuge to be alone together; for although Ivan thought her amazingly attractive he could be a hard taskmaster where music was concerned.

More than once Lydia saw that the girl had been crying after she had been with Ivan for her lessons.

"What a mixture he is," Lydia thought, as yet another side of her husband's complex personality was revealed.

Ivan had few principles, but anything to do with music was to him sacred.

He would rather cut off his right hand than lie or prevaricate where that was concerned, and Lydia could understand that while he taught Thyra, all thought of self would be put aside.

When they were free of their self-imposed hours of work it was very different.

Once when Lydia was resting in the summer-house at the end of the garden she heard them talking as they passed by to the swimming-pool.

"You're very lovely," Ivan was saying. "But I suppose you've been told that a thousnad times?"

"No, no one has told me," Thyra replied; and Lydia heard the girl's voice quiver.

"Are they all blind in Denmark?"

"No, but there are a lot of pretty girls there."

"As pretty as you?" Ivan asked. "I don't believe it! There could only be one Thyra—at least as far as I am concerned."

They passed out of earshot, while Lydia sat alone suffering, and sighing a little, too, for Thyra. This was a heady draught when one was so young!

As though Ivan's interest in Thyra was not enough to bear, there were also new and disturbing barriers between herself and the children which were hard to explain. She felt as though both of them shut her out.

She had somehow expected it from Christine. When the girl first came back from America, Lydia had realised that the little daughter she had loved had gone and

189

in her place was a cool, poised, sophisticated young stranger with whom it was going to take time and patience to be friends.

What Lydia had not expected, though, was that Christine would continue her reserve and complete independence for so long.

"She will settle down in a few weeks," Lydia had told herself happily, "I won't force her confidence, I will try to be friendly and unpossessive."

But the weeks had passed and other weeks had followed them and still Christine remained a stranger to her mother.

Sometimes she would seem about to become intimate, to surrender to the affection which was so obviously waiting for her, and then like an animal which has been startled she would rush away, remaining more aloof, more unapproachable than she had been before.

Lydia at times felt near to despair when she thought of her relationship with Christine.

Now, lying alone in her bed, she told herself:

"I am a failure both as a wife and as a mother."

"As a mother." The words stabbed her and brought to her the realisation of at least the major part of her present misery—Philip.

Next to Ivan, who had for so long filled her life, Lydia was honest enough to admit to herself she loved Philip best in all the world.

There seemed to her to be a particularly close emotional tie between all mothers and their sons and this had been very true where Philip was concerned. She loved him and he loved her, and his open-hearted frankness had been a solace and a joy all through the years of his life.

His placid and good-humoured personality had been a perfect antidote for the storms and exaggerations of Ivan; he had in fact to Lydia been a harbour in which she could find peace and rest when she most needed it.

And new, astonishingly and unexpectedly, Philip eluded her.

It had only been very recently, during the last week or so, that she had felt him withdrawn from her and waited for his confidence in vain.

At first she though his arm was troubling him, but the doctor's delight at the way it was healing made that explanation improbable. Then she had wondered if he was jealous of Christine being at home, but had dismissed this explanation as too unlike Philip to be possible.

She had pondered and waited and finally asked Philip himself but had gained nothing by her questions.

"What's wrong, darling?"

"Wrong? Why should you think anything's wrong?"

"I just thought you seemed a bit under the weather."

"Oh, I'm all right."

Was it her imagination, Lydia wondered, or did he colour a little as if in embarrassment?

"If there's anything I can do, darling, you know I would."

"There isn't anything. I've told you there's nothing the matter."

What more could she say? And yet her instinct told her far better than words that something was wrong. Philip was different, very different from what he had been when he first came home on leave, and Lydia could find no explanation for it.

It was little wonder that she found it difficult to sleep at night and lay awake hearing the hours strike and longing, with an intensity which seemed to possess her whole being, to be free of the mazes, the obstacles and difficulties which seemed to isolate her into a loneliness which was almost unbearable.

"You haven't touched your breakfast and it's stone cold!"

Rose's reproachful tones roused Lydia. She pushed back the hair from her forehead and looked at the tray beside her as if she was surprised to see it there.

"I forgot it," she said weakly.

"I'll get you some fresh tea, and the toast is a bit of leather by this time."

She picked up the tray.

"It doesn't matter, really," Lydia expostulated.

Rose took no notice. She fired her parting shot only as she reached the door.

"You'll make yourself ill if you go on like this, and then where will you be?"

Lydia wanted to say, "Not much worse off"; but she knew from experience that it was no use arguing with Rose, who always had the last word.

The door had hardly shut behind her when it opened again for Ivan. Lydia saw at once that he was in a bad temper.

"I've got to go up to London," he stated without any preliminary greeting.

"I wondered why you were dressed like that," Lydia replied, raising herself a little on her pillows.

"I've got a rehearsal at eleven o'clock, and Heaven knows it's necessary if we are to give this concert next Thursday."

Lydia felt guilty. She had forgotten that Ivan was conducting a famous orchestra at the Albert Hall the following week.

Ivan looked at his watch.

"I hope I shall be back on the 4.30," he said, "but don't wait tea for me."

"We won't," Lydia answered quietly.

He hesitated a moment and she guessed that he was coming to the real point of what he wanted to say.

"By the way," he started, "you might have a talk with Thyra, will you? She's got some damn fool idea of leaving here. I can't make head or tail of the matter myself. I suppose you haven't been saying anything to her?"

He looked at Lydia accusingly and for a moment she felt a surge of anger rising inside her. How dare he accuse her after all she had stood for, after the welcome

192

she had given this girl brought here at his invitation! And then as quickly as the anger had arisen it died again. She realised almost with pity that Ivan was perturbed and anxious, perhaps even a little unhappy.

He wanted Thyra to stay, he loved her—yes, in his own way he loved her; and Lydia admitted it even while the truth seemed to tear her into small pieces and leave her weak, vulnerable and trembling.

"I've said nothing that could in any way upset Thyra," she replied with that quiet dignity which she knew always calmed Ivan at a crucial moment and kept him steady.

"Then what could have upset her?" he asked sharply. "The children?"

Lydia made herself smile.

"Leave it to me, Ivan; I'll talk to Thyra when you've gone."

"Thank you," Ivan said.

Then suddenly he softened and as if he realised his own irresponsible behaviour walked across to the bed.

"Thank you, darling," he said, this time in a gentler tone;

Reaching out he took one of Lydia's hands in his.

"She is so young and so lovely," he said. "She gives me something. Since I've known her I have felt revivified—no, that's the wrong word—but what I have done is good. I know that."

"I'm glad," Lydia forced herself to say.

"Wait until you hear it," Ivan said with a sudden cry of elation, his eyes shining. He bent and kissed Lydia on the forehead. "Bless you, darling, you never fail me!"

He turned and left the room, and when he was gone Lydia closed her eyes against a sudden overwhelming weakness. She was past tears, almost past any feeling save that of submission. That was the right word.

She must submit herself to Ivan, accept him as he was and try somehow to mould her own will to his.

193

Rose came back with the breakfast tray and put it down on the table by her with a little bang.

"You're looking pale," she said uncompromisingly. "You'd better stay in bed today."

"I'd rather get up," Lydia replied. "There are such a lot of things I want to do."

"They will wait."

Lydia shook her head.

She had finished her breakfast and was looking at the morning papers when there came a knock on her door.

"Come in," she called and looked up to see Thyra standing in the doorway.

She had not been expecting the girl and for the moment felt almost embarrassed at the sight of her.

She had been thinking of her and of Ivan's words, and now Thyra stood there slim and lovely in a dress of pale green linen, looking absurdly young and at the moment shy and uncertain of herself.

"May I come in, Mrs. Stanfield?"

"Yes, of course, my dear."

Thyra called all the rest of the family by their Christian names, but to Lydia she was invariably formal. She crossed the room towards the bed and Lydia with a gesture indicated a chair beside her.

"Won't you sit down?"

Thyra sat on the edge of the chair and then clasping her hands together nervously she said:

"I'm sorry to bother you like this, I should have waited until you came downstairs. But please, Mrs. Stanfield, I want to leave today—this morning."

There was no pretence about her agitation, it was very real.

"But Thyra," Lydia expostulated, "I don't understand. I thought you were so happy here with us."

"But I was—I mean, I am. All the same, I have to go away. I can't explain. Please, Mrs. Stanfield, don't ask me why, but I must go."

Lydia felt a sudden icy hand grip her heart. Was this Ivan's fault? What had he done to reduce the girl to such a state? For a moment she did not know what to say, then with an effort she asked:

"But have you anywhere to go?"

"I will find somewhere."

"And your music, what about that?"

"Your husband has been so kind, I can never be sufficiently grateful. Perhaps he will still be kind and help me so that soon—very soon—I shall begin to make money."

Lydia felt bewildered.

"But if my husband can still help you," she asked, "why can't you stay here?"

"I can't explain," Thyra replied.

"But surely you must realise," Lydia insisted, "that it's unfair to us—to me—if you run away like this so suddenly without an explanation. Have any of us offended you in any way?"

Thyra bent her head still lower and Lydia could see her lips were trembling. She felt ashamed that she must bully the girl with her questions and yet she knew that for Ivan's sake she must try and keep her in the house.

"Won't you tell me?" Lydia asked gently.

"Please, please, Mrs. Stanfield."

Now Thyra raised her eyes to hers and Lydia saw they were full of tears.

"You've been so kind to me, so wonderful. I could never possibly tell you what it has meant to me to stay here in your beautiful home, to be one of your family. But something has happened, I must go."

"Something has happened?" Lydia repeated. "But, Thyra . . ."

The girl suddenly jumped to her feet and went to the window. Her shoulders moved and Lydia knew she was fighting for control.

"Won't you tell me?" Lydia asked again.

"It can do no good."

"That is for me to judge."

Quickly Thyra turned and came to the bedside. She stood there looking at Lydia, her face almost distorted

195

by the anguish she was suffering. And then at last she spoke, the words seemingly dragged from her lips.

"I love him, Mrs. Stanfield. I love him. You must see that it's impossible."

Lydia had known this was the explanation and one she had to hear. Slowly, deliberately, she held out her hands to the girl.

"Now listen," Lydia said. "You must not upset yourself, dear. I want to hear everything, your whole story. Sit down here and talk to me. Let us try to understand each other and face this thing together."

Thyra stood looking at Lydia and then suddenly she collapsed utterly.

She knelt down by the bed and hiding her face against Lydia's hands sobbed as if her heart would break. Lydia let her cry. She understood that the tempest within must find relief and expression.

The girl's sobs seemed to fill the room, the heart-rending tears of the very young experiencing emotional intensity for the first time.

Lydia looked back over her own life. She remembered how she, too, had cried when she thought that she must love Ivan for ever.

She remembered one terrible night when she realised how much she loved him and knew clearly, too, the opposition she was up against.

Her father's dislike and distrust of all artistes had risen before her like a great cloud to deaden her mind and fill her heart with a kind of terrible helplessness on the one hand, while on the other Ivan offered her a wonder and a glory she had never known existed before.

The combat between Ivan and all the traditions of her childhood and the life of which she had been a part all her thinking years was fierce and bitter. It was then that she had broken down and cried even as Thyra was crying now.

She had sobbed until she could sob no more, until it seemed to her as if she had cried a part of her very lifeblood away. Never before and never since had she given such rein to her feelings.

And she had known afterwards that her love for Ivan had surmounted everything, that nothing was worth while or of value if she must lose him.

She could understand now what Thyra was feeling. Ivan had come into her life seeming to carry in his hands the whole essence of loving and of happiness—even her career would seem of little importance beside the fact that she must lose him.

Lydia supposed that the girl had only just become aware of the depth and import of love, having in her innocence believed that Ivan was really interested in her from a musical point of view and that it was sheer generosity and kindness of heart which had caused him to invite her to stay.

Perhaps, Lydia mused, she had only gradually become aware of her own feelings and now at last had awakened to the full realisation of her love. That was why she was afraid, why she must go.

She was afraid of herself, afraid of becoming entangled irrevocably in Ivan's charming, sophisticated love-making.

Lydia sighed. There had been few women in Ivan's life who would not have taken all that Ivan offered and been glad of it. But Thyra was so honest and decent.

She would not understand a world where unfaithfulness was tolerated, where a wife could sit back and condone her husband making love to another woman and try only to understand it. The child was afraid, afraid and unhappy.

This was Ivan's doing, yet another crime to be laid at his door. But somehow even now she could not blame him for it; he was not as other men. If he could create beauty, he must have some source from which to draw it.

Love to him was an unfailing source, stimulating and invigorating, which each time inspired him to further and more wonderful heights.

Thyra's sobs were a little quieter. Lydia bent forward and withdrawing one of her hands, wet with tears, from Thyra's hold stroked her head.

"Stop now," she said. "If you cry any more you will hurt your eyes."

Thyra did not respond for a moment or two though her weeping was less violent. Finally she raised her face.

"I'm sorry," she stammered, "terribly sorry."

"Don't be sorry," Lydia replied. "I understand so well. I have cried just as you have and things seemed clearer afterwards."

"How can they ever be clear for me?" Thyra cried. "Even when the war is over my father and mother will be very poor. I must support them. I've got to have money, do you understand?"

'Of course I do," Lydia said soothingly.

At the same time she wondered as to the connection of Thyra's speech. What had this urge for money to do with Thyra leaving the house?

"Supposing you get up," she suggested, "and sit down on the bed. You must be tired of kneeling. That's better; now we can talk. Let us start from the beginning."

"But you know all the beginning," Thyra said quickly. "You know that I came to England to make money to help my father and mother. I don't care for myself; I was happy enough in Denmark, and to be honest, really honest, Mrs. Stanfield, I am not ambitious.

"Oh, I know it's wrong to say that in this house, but I am not. I want a home of my own, a garden, perhaps a farm and why should I not say it?—babies, lots of nice, fat babies. That is what I really want out of life.

"I like playing, I love music, but the idea of having to sell myself to the public, of making them pay to listen to me, frightens me; indeed, at times it terrifies me, and yet I know I have got to do it, for my parents' sake I have got to do it."

"And so you came here," Lydia prompted, "so that my husband could teach you?"

"Yes, and I realise how lucky I am that he wanted to," Thyra said. "And I've been happy, so terribly happy. You have all been so wonderful to me."

"Until now?"

Thyra's face clouded.

"How can I explain?" she asked. "When I told Ivan that I must go away he was angry, very angry. He didn't understand and I couldn't explain to him, could I? That would have made him more angry. I know that.

"He says he likes me; I expect he has said charming things to many women, but I am flattered—very flattered. And you're so wonderful, you understand!

"I've watched you, Mrs. Stanfield. I have said to myself that one day I will try to be a good wife like you. I will try to understand by husband's needs, to find him in many ways but a little boy."

Lydia was astonished at the girl's perception and for a moment it was difficult to know what to say to her. But then as she paused Thyra said with childlike enthusiasm:

"I think you're marvellous!"

"Thank you, my dear," Lydia answered softly. "It is very sweet of you to say so. Sometimes I feel I am only a failure. But, you see, I love my husband very much; I want him to be happy, I want him to have the things which make him happy, although, unfortunately, as you have seen so cleverly, just like a greedy little boy the things he wants sometimes bring unhappiness to others."

Thyra gave a little laugh.

"He is so handsome, so clever, so Ivanish, but he is also a little greedy." She laughed again and then added: "And sometimes he is a little jealous of those who are young."

"Naturally, we all are," Lydia replied. "That is one of the penalties of growing old."

"All the same," Thyra said, speaking seriously, "with

the jealousy there—and it is there, I know that—how could I tell him?"

"Tell him what?"

"Of my love," Thyra said simply.

"I expect he knows of that already. Don't you think perhaps you are thinking about it too much, making it seem too important? Ivan wants you to stay here and so do I. There are a lot more things for you to do. I shouldn't worry too much, my dear, but take things easily and happily."

Even as Lydia spoke she wondered if she was right in saying the words. Was she putting the girl in temptation's way and, what was more important still, jeopardising her own hopes of happiness?

It would have been difficult not to remember how sweet a nature Thyra had and that she was extremely pretty. Ivan was grasping at youth, for youth, he felt, was slipping out of his reach.

"Perhaps I am being foolish," Lydia thought, but she forced herself once again to smile at Thyra.

"I shouldn't worry," she repeated.

"How can I help it?" Thyra asked. "No, Mrs. Stanfield, you don't understand. We love each other, both of us, with all our heart and soul. It is not possible for us to pretend. We want to belong to each other, we want to be married; and because it is impossible, how could I stay here, seeing him and hearing him and knowing that he needs me?"

Lydia felt as if an artificial world she had built round her was crashing to the ground. This was real, this was serious, this was far worse than anything she had visualised.

"Has Ivan said that he wants . . . marriage?" she asked, and her voice trembled.

"Ivan?" Thyra's eyes opened wide in surprise. "But he doesn't know. If he did, he'd be angry, very angry, and jealous. Surely you understand that?"

"Then whom are you talking about?" Lydia asked; and the question was a cry.

"Why, about Philip, of course," Thyra replied. "Oh, I thought you understood that we love each other—Philip and I!"

15

There came a knock at the door and mechanically, her mind occupied with the shock of what she had just heard, Lydia said: "Come in."

"Is Thyra here?" Philip's voice asked.

He came into the room, saw the two women staring at him and realised by the expression on their faces that something had occurred.

"Good morning, Mummy," he said; and then as Thyra moved towards him he asked her:

"What have you been saying?"

"I have told your mother everything," Thyra replied. "But, oh, Philip, I thought I understood from you that she already knew about us?"

Philip slipped his arm round her shoulder in a protective gesture and then smiled across at his mother with an apologetic smile.

"I rather thought you might have guessed already Mummy, that something was up—but anyway, you know now."

"Yes, I know now," Lydia echoed.

Thyra looked up at Philip.

"It's difficult for your poor mother. You see, I didn't explain properly and she thought for a moment that I was in love with . . . with Ivan."

A look of deep understanding and affection crossed Philip's face. He moved to his mother's side and bending down kissed her. There was something so simple and natural in the caress that Lydia felt the tears spring to her eyes.

"I'm sorry, Mums," he said. "This all seems to be a terrible muddle, but I didn't know that Thyra cared for me until yesterday and now she has complicated things by saying she must go away. You'll persuade her not to, won't you?"

"No one can persuade me not to!" Thyra asserted. "I've got to go."

"But why?" Lydia asked.

Thyra made an expressive little foreign gesture denoting despair.

"That is what I have been trying to tell you. But wait—you are bewildered and I am not surprised. May I start from the beginning?"

"Yes, please do," Lydia said, and reached out her hand for Philip's.

She felt as if she had passed through a deep, devastating experience. What she feared and anticipated had not materialised, but she had not remained unscathed.

She could not for the moment comprehend that her happiness was unthreatened, that Ivan, as far as Thyra was concerned, remained her own.

Thyra took a deep breath.

"You'll forgive me if I am very frank?" she asked.

"But of course," Lydia replied.

"You're so understanding. No one could understand things as well as you. But . . ." She hesitated.

"Mummy doesn't mind the truth," Philip prompted.

Thyra looked at him and smiled, and Lydia saw that the girl was genuinely in love. There was a sudden radiance in her eyes as she looked at Philip, a radiance which gave her beauty something new, something which had not been there before.

"When I met Ivan," Thyra began, "I was thrilled and counted myself very lucky—to be honest, I knew just how much he could help me if he wished.

"That he thought I was pretty and very nice was obvious, and I thought that he might get me some concert engagements, or at least give me an entrée into the musical world of which he is the acknowledged king.

"When he offered to teach me himself I felt I was dreaming, it was all too wonderful, too marvellous; and when he asked me to come and stay here I was excited beyond words. I came and you were so kind to me.

"I was grateful for that, but I was not at that time thinking of anything except my own interests, my own ambitions. I have told you that I want to make money. I must make money.

"My parents are getting old; all that they had has been stripped from them by the Germans. My mother is in constant ill health, she requires the best doctors and the best treatment.

"To make money was my object in coming to England, and I knew that I could make it only by utilising to its fullest extent the small talent I have for music. You can imagine what Ivan Razoumovsky's offer meant to me.

"I wasn't so stupid as not to realise that his interest in me lay mainly in the fact that he thought me pretty.

"There are hundreds, maybe thousands, of young musicians far more talented than I am, but I had been lucky enough to attract his attention. Well, I was prepared to make the most of it.

"Then I began to know Ivan better. He is—you will forgive my saying it—a very attractive person but in some ways very childish.

"When he plays, he is a god; no one could help worshipping him for that wonderful power which lies within him. But when he ceases to play he becomes not a man, but a little boy who has never grown up.

"He is greedy, possessive, and I know, too, he can be very jealous."

Lydia stirred slightly. Gently Thyra bent forward to touch her hand.

"You don't mind my saying this?" she asked. "I want to explain—oh, so many things, and it is difficult unless I put it clearly—not only to you but to myself."

"I want you to tell me everything that is in your heart," Lydia answered simply; and satisfied, Thyra went on:

"Ivan made love to me. That, of course, I think you

realise. But I knew, young and inexperienced though I am, that it was the sort of love he makes to any pretty woman who takes his fancy.

"His heart is yours, Mrs. Stanfield; oh yes, all yours; but he is just like a small boy who, seeing a box of chocolates, must steal a few here and there—and when they are eaten forgets all about them.

"He has said very beautiful things to me and many times he has asked me to love him. But I have been brought up by my parents to be straight-forward and direct and so I ask him:

" 'You say you love me and you want me to love you. Does that mean you want to marry me?'

"The first time I said this, if I had not been so frightened at my own bravery, I should have laughed at his expression.

"The last thing that Ivan wants is anything permanent. As I said before, he wants only to gobble up the sweets which attract him—and forget them.

"Because I have refused to do what he wants, it naturally makes him want me all the more—or he thinks he does.

"We talk together and we argue; but all the time I manage to have my lessons, to go on working and, thank goodness! to keep him interested in those. But then a terrible thing happens . . . ."

Thyra stopped, looked at Philip and smiled.

"A terrible thing?" Philip questioned, knowing the answer.

"A terrible thing," Thyra repeated firmly, the softness of her voice belying her words. "I fell in love, really in love—with Philip."

Philip relinquished Lydia's hand and held out both of his to Thyra. For a moment she hesitated, then put her fingers into his and he raised them to his lips.

Lydia, watching, felt a pain she had never experienced before—the pain of knowing that the child which had been hers now belonged to another woman.

"But why is it so terrible?" she asked. Her voice

205

broke across the spell which seemed to hold the two young people oblivious to everything except themselves.

"Because," Thyra answered tragically, "Philip wants me to marry him and give up my music."

Lydia looked enquiringly at her son. Philip answered firmly—in that moment she knew him for a grown man, the boy had vanished.

"I think one musical member of the family, Mummy, is enough."

"And if I give it up altogether, how would my father and mother live?"

"We'll manage somehow," he said.

"And you think they would consent to live on the very small earnings of their son-in-law?" Thyra asked scornfully.

Philip looked unhappy, but Lydia saw that his jaw was set in a manner which told her all too clearly how determined he was on his point. Easy-going and good-natured, he had at certain times a streak of insurmountable obstinacy.

He had been the same ever since he was a small boy, when he used to dig in his toes and his Nannie would exclaim:

"There's no moving Master Philip."

"When I marry," Philip said quietly, "I want a home for myself and for my children. I don't want a wife who has to rush off to play at a concert just when I come home; I want her with me. I don't intend to stay in the Navy after the War; I want to have a farm. I've always wanted one and I believe I could make a success of it."

Lydia looked at him helplessly.

"Darling, I had no idea you cared for anything like that."

"I hadn't much chance to say so," he answered, "before the War—I was too young. I have been very happy in the Navy. At the same time, Mummy, I want a home life, and as things have worked out it couldn't be better.

Thyra knows all about farming, she has always lived on one."

"I am a musician," Thyra flashed at him.

"Through necessity," Philip countered, "not by choice."

Lydia looked at Thyra.

"Would you mind very much giving up your career, my dear?"

"I won't ask my parents to live on Philip," Thyra answered fiercely.

It seemed to Lydia that they were at a deadlock, but while she considered their problem Thyra spoke again.

"You must see why I must go away," she said miserably. "I love Philip, but I can't marry him. And if Ivan finds out he will help me no longer."

Lydia started. She had almost forgotten the part that Ivan must play in all this. She longed to contradict the girl, to say that Ivan would not sink to anything so petty or so mean, but she knew him too well. He was already jealous of his son. What would he feel when he knew that youth had turned to youth and he was left outside—unwanted?"

Anxiously she looked for a solution and found little comfort anywhere. Ivan had appealed to her that very morning. He wanted Thyra to remain in the house, but would he want it when he knew where her real interests lay?

"What are we to do?" she murmured. And instantly Philip turned to her.

"We're brutes to worry you," he exclaimed. "We ought to fight our battles by ourselves; but, Mummy, you have always been there to help, almost before one knew something was wrong—that's why, I suppose, I expected you to guess what was the matter with me this last week or so."

Lydia laughed, and felt it was a relief.

"I couldn't make up my mind," she said, "whether it was indigestion or boredom."

"I didn't know love could be so upsetting," Philip murmured, his eyes on Thyra.

The girl got up and walked towards the window, then she walked back again; and Lydia saw that her expression was desperate.

"What are we to do?" she asked. "I see now that it is no solution if I go away. We love each other, we want to be together. How could I pretend day after day, even supposing that Ivan would go on teaching me?"

"Listen," Lydia said, trying to break the tension which held them all unhappy and disturbed. "Supposing we do nothing for the time being and let things take their course. Philip has got to get well and then he must go back to his ship. Thyra remains here and for the moment she can think about her musical career.

"Perhaps when the War is really over and the Germans have left Denmark, her parents may not be so badly off as she anticipates. Let us take the line of least resistance, at any rate for the moment."

As she spoke Lydia thought her words sounded middle-aged, the kind of advice that youth would never heed, being impatient and hot-headed and wanting things decided all at once.

Then Thyra refuted her suggestion quickly in two words.

"And Ivan?"

Lydia knew that there lay the difficulty. Ivan did not as yet know why Thyra had wished to go. But however hard they tried to pretend, would they be clever enough to deceive him—and if so, for how long?

There was no use in blinding her eyes to the fact that Ivan was jealous, very jealous, of Philip. He was also desperately afraid of losing his own youth.

Already he was conscious that it was slipping away from him, and this would be paramount to a knock-out blow.

"What else can I suggest?" she asked.

Thyra shrugged her shoulders as she said in a tone of utter despondency:

"I'd better go. It is I who have caused all this, it is for me to leave."

"If you leave, I leave with you," Philip said.

He moved forward to place his arms round Thyra's shoulders, holding her closely to him.

Once again Lydia felt that strange, unfamiliar pain. All these years Philip had been hers, and now at the bidding of a stranger—a girl he had known only a few weeks—he was ready to relinquish her and his home, everything familiar and sure.

Thyra leant her head back against Philip's shoulder as if thankful for the moment of his protection.

"Thyra darling," Philip said to her urgently, "let's get married—now, at once. What is the point of waiting? The War is still on, I may even be killed. Let's take what we can for the moment and forget the future. Somehow or other the future will look after itself."

"You might be killed . . . ." Thyra repeated the words almost beneath her breath. "I had forgotten that."

She moved away from his arms and looked up at him. For a long second they stared into each other's eyes and then she surrendered, subservient to his will.

"I'll do anything you want," she said.

Lydia saw that Philip's face whitened for a moment with emotion. Then, his eyes very bright, he turned towards his mother.

"It's settled, Mummy."

"But, darling . . ."

Philip interrupted her.

"I know it's the only way," he said. "I'll get a special licence or whatever is necessary. We'll be married very quietly and come back here. There will be nothing Daddy or anybody else can do then. Thyra will be my wife."

There was a world of pride in the way he said the words.

"You're glad, Mummy?"

"Very glad," Lydia forced the words between her lips.

She raised her face to his and then, having kissed him, held out her arms to Thyra.

"I only want your happiness," she said.

"You can be sure of that," Philip said confidently.

"I'm happy, so happy, Mrs. Stanfield," Thyra whispered, "that I am afraid."

"It's a secret, then," Philip insisted. "Nothing must be said to Daddy until it's all over and done with."

"I feel we are behaving rather badly to him," Thyra said. "He's been so kind to me. But at the same time . . ."

She made a little gesture eloquent of her feelings.

"I would like to have seen you married," Lydia sighed.

Philip hesitated, but before he could speak Lydia continued quickly:

"Of course it's impossible really. Ivan will be hurt anyway, we have to realise that, but at least I shall have taken no active part in deceiving him."

"I'm going to London now to see about ways and means," Philip cried, slipping his arm through Thyra's. "Are you coming to help me get ready?"

"Of course I will, and I'll walk to the station with you."

Once again Philip bent to kiss his mother.

"Thank you, Mummy, for being so understanding. You've never failed us."

His words remained with Lydia when she lay alone after they had both gone. It was strange the ways things worked out. The woman she had dreaded Ivan bringing to the house, the girl she had resented and been jealous of, was now to be her daughter-in-law.

And she liked her, yes, that was the truth. She liked Thyra and knew deep within herself that she would make Philip happy. She felt that ultimately he would have his way and Thyra would give up her music professionally and settle down to be a good wife and bear him children.

Grandchildren! How would Ivan bear the thought of himself a grandfather? Ivan, always Ivan! It was impossible to escape from the thought of him; of his reactions and feelings, his surprise and his anger!

Was this the first time, Lydia wondered, that the woman he desired had eluded him? She had the feeling that perhaps it was.

Always in the past Ivan's love affairs had quickly come to an end—finished because he became satiated and bored once he had conquered and possessed.

Thyra had eluded him, and Lydia knew, although the girl had been too polite to put it into words, that she thought of Ivan as "an attractive man, but old!"

How terribly, terribly old middle-age appears to the very young! Lydia herself had learnt that lesson bitterly, a lesson that all men and women must learn sooner or later.

Ivan would not face the truth; he was blinding himself, seeking by pretence and illusion to spin out the time before he must face his old age and the years ahead.

When he had to face the reality, Lydia wondered, what then?

Somehow she felt that he would always need her. Had Thyra been right in saying she was the only person he really loved? Men had strange ways of showing their love and Ivan was no exception. But if he loved her, what did anything else matter?

There was a knock on her door and Christine came in. Lydia saw that she was dressed ready to go to London, and knew that Christine was off on one more of her mysterious outings.

"I came to say good-bye, Mummy."

Lydia roused herself to speak normally.

"Are you going up to London again?" she asked unnecessarily. "Must you go today, dear? I think it's going to be hot."

211

"Yes, I must," Christine answered. "Is there anything you want?"

"Nothing, thank you. I think Philip's going up too."

"Oh, is he?" Christine said. "I thought something must be up. He and Thyra have just walked down the passage so intent on gazing into each other's eyes that they almost knocked me down."

Christine spoke aggressively, and Lydia guessed that she was feeling hurt at being excluded from what she had guessed to be the truth.

"There is something up darling," Lydia said quietly, "but I expect Philip and Thyra will want to tell you themselves."

"Do you mean they're in love with each other?" Christine asked. "Good Lord! What is Daddy going to say?"

Lydia felt wearily that that was just what she was wondering herself, but she tried to answer lightly.

"It is to be a secret from him at the moment."

"I think it's rather ridiculous, don't you?" Christine asked. "Philip's awfully young."

"Being in love has nothing to do with age," Lydia replied in an amused voice.

"All the same, this complicates matters, and you know that as well as I do, Mummy. Are they going to tell Daddy? He'll guess, anyway."

"Darling, you're making it difficult for me," Lydia remarked. "As I have said, it is Philip's and Thyra's secret and they want to manage things in their own way. I think we had better let them do so."

"I still think it complicates things," Christine remarked in a hard voice, and then suddenly she capitulated.

"I'm sorry, Mummy. I'm being rather a beast about it. I expect really I mind losing Philip. I was just beginning to know him and to like him."

"Must we lose him?" Lydia asked, voicing the question which was in her own heart.

"It's worse for you, of course," Christine went on.

"He's always been your blue-eyed boy, hasn't he? Poor Mummy, are we both being a disappointment to you?"

"Neither of you is being anything of the sort," Lydia retorted almost angrily.

"Are you so sure about me?"

"Quite sure," Lydia said against an innermost conviction.

"Oh, Mummy, you're sweet!" Christine exclaimed. "Listen, I'm going to tell you everything now, even if I miss the train to do it."

She sat down on her mother's bed and started her story even as she had told it to Sir Fraser Wilton. As Christine proceeded, Lydia stared at her incredulously. Could she really be hearing this? she wondered. Could it be true?

Yet it was hard to disbelieve the tale as it flowed smoothly from Christine's lips, sounding so utterly convincing and credible. It was only when one looked deeper below the surface that one realised the thousand doubts, difficulties and problems which it presented.

Christine had pulled off her hat as she talked and now, as she sat on the end of the bed telling her story animatedly with expressive little gestures of her hands.

Lydia could only watch her in bewilderment, her own thoughts chaotic with the surprise of the whole thing.

"And Stella Hampden is getting well," Christine finished dramatically. "Yesterday she talked normally just like you and me. She is weak, of course, but every day she seems to get stronger. There's really no reason for me to go there except that they like having me and I think in some ways she clings to me. When she is better, Mummy, may I bring her down here?"

"Of course," Lydia said, and then added: "But I can't believe it, darling! The whole thing is so fantastic, so extraordinary!"

Christine laughed.

"Everybody says that; but it's just one of those things that happen and prove that truth really is stranger than fiction. That's what I told Aunt Johanna, but she never got over the surprise of it."

"Why didn't she write and tell me?"

"Between ourselves, I think she was rather ashamed of the whole thing. I believe she felt that some sort of black magic had got into me and that you would blame her for it. To be honest, I wasn't sure myself at times whether that wasn't what had happened.

"That is why it's been so exciting that I have been able to save Stella Hampden—because I have saved her from what Sir Fraser calles 'a living death'."

Lydia sighed.

"You will have to give me time to get used to the idea. I want to think about it and then there are such a lot of questions I want to ask you."

"I'm quite certain I won't be able to answer them," Christine said. "Quite seriously, Mummy, I don't quite understand it all myself. I have no explanation of it whatever. I feel like Aunt Johanna—if I was religious, it would be easier to account for."

"But you do think that it is due to some power outside yourself?" Lydia asked.

"Of course," Christine replied. "But what power I don't know. When I am treating anyone, I don't feel any more holy or good than I do now. I just feel much more alive, more vital—that's the only way I can express it, and the power seems to flow through me just as if someone had turned it on with a tap."

"And who is that someone?" Lydia asked.

Christine spread out her hands.

"If only I knew," she said, "perhaps then we should know the answer to all our questions."

16

Elizabeth cut the roses carefully, moving from tree to tree.

She hardly saw the red and yellow beauty of their second blooming, nor was she aware of the formal loveliness of the box-hedged garden which was one of the famous sights of the neighbourhood.

Instead her thoughts were far away—thoughts which brought a soft smile to her lips and an expression of gentle brooding to her whole face.

This morning she had received a postcard. At first she had stared at it in surprise for there was no writing on it. She had opened the envelope in which it was enclosed automatically and without looking at the address.

It was only when she found inside nothing but a picture postcard that she examined the envelope and with a leap of her heart recognised the handwriting and the signature scrawled in the left-hand corner.

Angus had not forgotten her then; but why, she wondered for a moment, had he sent her a copy of one of Ruben' famous pictures?

And then slowly and with that strange pulsating excitement with which one gradually sees the inner meaning of what at first appears commonplace, Elizabeth began to understand.

The postcard was the usual good but cheap reproduction which before the War one could buy in any Catholic church abroad. The picture was "The Virgin and Saints," which Elizabeth knew hung in a church in Antwerp.

Here was her first clue—Antwerp. Angus was telling her where he was.

Then as she looked at the picture with its fat and joy-

215

ful angels, its worshipping women and lovely blending of light and colour, a conversation came back to her from the past.

Arthur had been showing Angus round the picture gallery at Avon House and they had paused in front of a portrait of Elizabeth painted by one of the leading Academicians of the year when she was first married.

It was a disappointing picture; it made her look frigid and aloof and much older than she was. Angus had studied it for some minutes and then unexpectedly had said:

"I would like to see you standing beside a picture by Rubens which hangs in the Church of St. Jacques at Antwerp."

Elizabeth had smiled politely at the remark, not knowing what he meant and not wishing to show her ignorance by asking. It was only later—much later—in their friendship that Angus, dining with them one evening, had remarked that of all painters he preferred Rubens.

"He is full of vitality and virility," he said. "It is fashionable at the moment to find him over-exuberant, but I believe that people and nations are happier, better and stronger, when they like exuberance both in their artists and in their politics."

Elizabeth had agreed with him without feeling deeply on the matter one way or another.

Arthur had answered in his clipped, indifferent manner:

"I'm afraid I know very little about painting. I only know that the Avon collection costs me a pretty penny every year in insurance."

There had been someone else there at the time. Looking back and searching her memory for what had occurred, Elizabeth could not remember who it was; but he or she—whoever it had been—asked:

"What do you think is the best example of Rubens' work, Mr. McLeod?"

And Angus had replied:

"My favourite picture of his is "The Virgin and Saints." I never go to Antwerp without going to look at it."

Elizabeth looked at the postcard for a long time, and then suddenly, with a mounting sense of excitement at her own discovery, she understood the remark he had made to her in the picture gallery.

There was undoubtedly a slight resemblance between herself and the central figure of the Madonna; her hair grew in the same way and there was an expression in the half-lowered eyes looking at the Holy Child which Elizabeth had seen echoed in her own photographs.

Yes, there was a resemblance, and Angus must have seen it. Was that the reason why he had first been attracted to her? Had the picture which held so deep an interest for him created in his mind an ideal woman?

How she wished then that she could talk about it to him. It was maddening to guess so much and to know so little! But he had sent her the postcard, that was enough in itself.

Yet even the happiness of that had the power to hurt, for she had but to glance at her newspaper to remember the bitter fighting that was taking place near Antwerp.

She could imagine him inspiring everyone around him, giving the fighting men courage and confidence by his very presence and assurance, performing miracles even on the battlefield. And in the midst of it all he had remembered her!

She looked at his writing again. What had he felt as he wrote her name? In writing at all he had very nearly infringed his own ruling that they must not correspond with each other.

He must have known just how much this voiceless message would mean to her and he had sent it for some reason she could not quite grasp. Had he a presentiment of danger, that it might be the last message he would send?

Somehow that seemed unlike Angus with his level-

217

headed Scottish outlook. No, perhaps it had been just an impulse of the moment, his desire and longing for her being stronger than his own resolution.

How often had she felt the same and yet had no way to assuage her longing because she did not know where he could be found! That much at least he had told her now—that he was in Belgium, that he was in the forward area and that he was alive.

She must be thankful for that, and thankful, too, for the message of the postcard which told her all too clearly that he loved her, that she was indeed enshrined in his heart.

Elizabeth turned from the rose tree, and as she did so a respectful voice behind her made her start.

"Mr. Askew is here, my lady."

Elizabeth turned so sharply that a large thorn from a crimson rose she held in her hand dug deep into her finger, drawing blood.

"How you startled me, Bates!" she exclaimed to the butler. "I didn't hear you approach."

"I am sorry, my lady. It must be the rubber soles I have on my shoes."

"Yes, of course. It wasn't your fault; I must have been day-dreaming."

Elizabeth put her bleeding finger into her mouth.

"Matron asked me to find you, my lady."

"I am coming, Bates. Would you take these flowers? I will do them later on."

"Very good, my lady."

Elizabeth handed the butler the basket and turned towards the house.

Mr. James Askew, who had taken the place of Angus in looking after the patients at Avon House, was also a famous surgeon. Elizabeth remembered that he had come down to perform a major operation on a man's arm.

The patient—a sapper—had been badly injured by a booby-trap. What was worse, immediately after his arm had been partially blown away; a counter-attack had driven the Allied Forces from the village they had captured and he had fallen into German hands.

His wounds had not been treated sufficiently carefully, and by the time he was recaptured by our own forces gangrene had already set in. He had been shipped back to England and operated on, but the man's general health was lowered and he had not rallied as was hoped.

They had aimed at saving at least the stump of the arm, but now another operation was necessary and Mr. Askew had come down to do it.

Elizabeth knew that as she had not been in her room on his arrival he would have already gone up to the wards. She found him in the small cloakroom adjoining the operating theatre.

They talked for a few moments, and then while he was still washing Elizabeth went into the operating room to see if everything was all right. Two of the nursing sisters had everything laid out.

"I wish we could have avoided this," Elizabeth said sadly. "I did hope we should be able to save poor Corporal Patrick another operation."

"So did I, ma'am," said Sister Evans. "He's been so brave about it too. If only it wasn't his right arm."

"Let's hope it won't be as bad as we anticipate," the other Sister remarked. "We've put out what we call 'the lucky scalpel,' ma'am."

"What is that?" Elizabeth asked.

The Sisters looked a little shamefaced.

"I suppose we ought not to be superstitious," Sister Evans remarked, "but it was the scalpel that Mr. McLeod always used—in fact he wouldn't work without it. It was the first thing he looked for when he came into the operating theatre, and after a while I suppose we all got superstitious about it. Anyway, let's hope it brings luck to young Patrick."

"Do show it me," Elizabeth said.

The Sister removed the top off a bowl of sterilised instruments and, taking a pair of curved scissors, took it out.

"That is it," she said. "I personally have never seen one exactly like it; have you, Sister Evans?"

Sister Evans shook her head.

"I think Mr. McLeod must have had it specially made for him," she remarked.

Elizabeth looked at it. She could imagine it held in Angus's sure and steady hand—a hand she could see so clearly with its square, well-kept nails and thin, surgeon's fingers.

"Are you quite ready?" It was Matron's voice from the door.

"Yes, Matron."

"Then I'll go and get the patient."

Elizabeth followed her down to the ward. Corporal Patrick was sleeping peacefully, having been given a drug earlier in the day. He looked very young and defenceless. Elizabeth felt a wave of pity pass over her.

It was hard to see these young men, so brave and so courageous, yet maimed and mutilated so that they must go through their life handicapped because of man's savagery and diabolical inventions.

"God bless you!" she wanted to say to Patrick as he passed her on the operating trolley.

But she felt that Matron, briskly efficient, would be surprised, so she said it in her heart and stood aside to watch him pass. They were all fond of the young corporal.

As she went into the wards the other men kept asking her:

"How do you think he'll get on? Will he stand it all right?"

"I'm sure he will," Elizabeth said.

At the same time she was not too certain. The boy—for he was not yet twenty-one—had already been through a gruelling experience and had been weakened considerably by the first operation.

220

They could only pray that the second would be successful and not too great a shock to the system. After all, he had youth on his side.

Elizabeth moved down the ward, once the Great Gallery where, when she was first married to Arthur, they had given balls and receptions.

She could see herself now wearing the heavy white satin gown which had been her wedding dress, receiving the County at Arthur's side. How nervous she had been, but at the same time a little elated to find how pleasant they were, how eager to receive her into their midst!

There had been a certain satisfaction then in being Arthur's wife. It was only gradually she began to realise how little she had in common with his particular friends.

They were all so old, so staid and set in their ways, and the young ones, while they were polite, made it quite clear that they did not expect her to mix with them or to become one of themselves.

"This is a happier place now," Elizabeth thought suddenly.

She knew it was true. The men, joking and laughing among themselves, greeted her with a smile and seemed to accept her gladly for herself. She was the Commandant of their hospital, but her rank mattered as little as her title.

Most of them called her "miss" and knew her by no other name.

"How's the garden looking, miss?" one greeted her now.

"Rather lovely, except that we haven't got any petrol to mow the lawns," Elizabeth answered. "You must hurry up and get well, Sergeant, and see for yourself."

"I'm hoping I'll be doing that soon," the sergeant answered. "But I'm wondering how my own little patch is getting on. The wife tells me that she's had to dig up a lot of the flowers to put in vegetables. I ask you, miss, onions where I used to have delphiniums! It's hard the things you have to put up with in war-time."

Remembering that the sergeant had had both feet amputated, Elizabeth agreed.

"I will bring you some roses in a little while," she promised. "I have just been cutting some."

"That'll be lovely, miss. There's something about flowers . . ." He paused. "Well, they helps."

"I'm sure they do," Elizabeth said softly and passed on down the ward.

She talked to the men and then went back to wait outsde the operating theatre. She was anxious about Corporal Patrick, and she kept wishing that Angus had been there.

Mr. Askew was clever and confident, but she knew that neither the nurses nor the men had the same faith in him as they had in Angus.

"If Patrick dies," she thought, "I shall always feel that it was my fault. If it hadn't been for me Angus would have operated on him."

It was silly and morbid to think of such things, she knew, and yet she could not help it. In the pocket of her grey uniform dress was the postcard she had received that morning. She put her hand on it, feeling that in some way it was a mascot.

"I'm getting as superstitious as the nurses," she told herself.

It did not seem long afterwards when the door of the operating theatre was opened and Corporal Patrick was brought out. There was the strong pungent smell of anesthetics, a glimpse of white-robed masked figures.

At last Elizabeth was able to ask the question,

"How did it go?"

James Askew pulled off his mask and smoothed back his hair with a slightly vain gesture.

"Extremely well, Lady Avon, extremely well! I must say I was surprised that it wasn't worse. I really think we have got to the root of the trouble this time. With careful nursing the lad should go right ahead."

"Oh, I am glad, terribly glad!" Elizabeth exclaimed.

She went into the operating theatre to find both Sisters smiling in relief.

"Mr. Askew really did it splendidly, Lady Avon," Sister Evans said in a low voice. "It was a beautiful operation, I'm sorry you didn't see it."

"And the lucky scalpel?" Elizabeth asked, feeling childish even while she felt she must ask the question.

"The very first thing he picked up," the Sister said with school-girlish glee. "Look!" She held out the bowl of blood-stained instruments.

Without thinking, Elizabeth picked up the scalpel.

"Oh, I shouldn't touch it, Lady Avon!"

But Elizabeth was looking at it with shining eyes.

"I feel as if Mr. McLeod has brought Corporal Patrick luck," she said.

Then because her heart was full and she felt she must tell someone, she added:

"I had a postcard from him this morning. He's in Antwerp."

There was a buzz of excitement from both Sisters.

"Well, that's interesting! What did he say? How's he getting on?"

"I think they are hard pressed there," Elizabeth replied. "He said little except where he was."

Yes, he had said little, but how much his postcard had told her!

"Tell him how much we are thinking about him when you write, won't you, ma'am?"

It was the little sister who spoke, now childishly eager. Elizabeth remembered she had always adored Angus.

"I certainly will," she replied, and put Angus's scalpel back in the bowl. "I must go and give Mr. Askew his tea," she said, "and congratulate him."

"He deserves it," Sister Evans approved.

Elizabeth went downstairs. Tea was laid in her own sitting-room and when the surgeon joined her there he

223

ate hungrily and quickly because he had to get back to London for an important consultation.

It was evening before Elizabeth had time to do her flowers and take them to the wards. The men were pleased to see her, and after she had talked to them she went to look at Corporal Patrick.

"He's just coming round," the Matron told her.

Sick and half conscious, Corporal Patrick was not a pleasant sight; but he was alive, that was what really mattered.

Elizabeth went to her own room feeling that in some indivisible way Corporal Patrick's operation and Angus were closely connected in her mind.

Two mornings later Lydia was woken at seven o'clock in the morning by Rose coming into her room. Sleepily she opened her eyes.

"Lord Avon wishes to speak to you on the telephone."

"Arthur!" Lydia ejaculated. "Surely he's very early!"

"Yes, ma'am, it's only seven o'clock. He said it was urgent and asked me to wake you."

Rose put the telephone receiver on the bed. Lydia took it up.

"It's Arthur speaking. Is that you, Lydia?"

Arthur's voice, rather too loud, boomed in her ear. He hated the telephone and could never use it properly.

'Yes, I'm speaking. Is anything the matter?"

"I thought you ought to know that Elizabeth is ill, very ill. She's got some infection in her hand and she's running a high temperature. The doctor is looking after her, of course, but as her nearest relation, I thought you ought to know."

"Thank you, Arthur. Is there anything we can do?'

"No, nothing. I'm hardly allowed to see her myself. Between ourselves, I don't think much of these damned doctors, but I suppose they know their job."

"How did she catch the infection?" Lydia asked.

"They think she must have picked it up in the operating room," Arthur boomed. "Of course she'd no right to be in there, not her job! But there, one never could stop Elizabeth doing what she wanted to do."

"I'm sorry, terribly sorry," Lydia said, distressed. "Would there be any point in my coming over?"

"None at all, I imagine. If there's any change I'll let you know."

"Thank you, Arthur, I'd like to know. Will you ring up this evening, anyway?"

"Oh, all right. Would about 9.30 suit you—after the news?"

"After the news" Lydia repeated gravely, thinking the remark was so like Arthur.

When he had rung off, it was quite impossible for her to go to sleep again. She lay awake worrying about Elizabeth until at 8.30 she put through a call to Matron.

"I'm sorry to bother you, Matron," she said, "but Lord Avon rang me up about my sister and I just thought I'd like to know a little more. You know how hungry one is for details."

"I quite understand, Mrs. Stanfield. In fact it was I who suggested that Lord Avon should telephone you."

"Is she really bad?"

"I'm afraid so. Apparently she was not alarmed at once and thought it was just a septic finger. The infection had already spread before she allowed me to see it, and then two of my sisters told me that Lady Avon had touched one of the instruments after an operation.

"Of course as soon as I knew that I sent for our chief operating surgeon and also for Lady Avon's own doctor.

"They are doing what they can and we're hoping that her temperature will come down; but it's a staphylococcal infection so we can't use sulphonamide."

"I must see her," Lydia said. "Will it be all right for me to come over? Lord Avon seemed to think it unnecessary."

"I think you would be quite right to come, Mrs. Stanfield," the Matron said,

From the tone of her voice Lydia realised how grave the situation was.

It was always rather difficult for her to go anywhere, as owing to petrol restrictions they could not use their own car, and hired ones were usually uncomfortable and made her terribly tired.

But with Rose as an escort Lydia managed to get into the local taxi and they started off across country for Avon House.

She felt glad that Ivan was not at home; she knew that he would have fussed and made objections about such an expedition; but his rehearsal the day before had gone badly and he had telephoned to say that he was tired and was staying at his Club.

Lydia had felt relieved at the time, for she was dreading to face him knowing the undercurrent of events between Philip and Thyra, hating to deceive the husband she loved and yet at the same time realising how impossible it would be to tell him the truth.

That he decided to remain in London gave them all a brief respite, and that he was not here this morning simplified her decision to go to Elizabeth.

It was a long journey and by the time the taxi drew up with a jerk at Avon House Lydia was tired and her back was aching.

The wheel chair was unstrapped from the roof of the taxi and Rose and the taxi-man helped her into it before the chair was lifted up the steps of Avon House. Matron was waiting to greet her.

"I'm so glad you were able to come, Mrs. Stanfield," she said. "I told Lord Avon and he left a message to say he would see you at lunch, that he had some work to do on the estate and he knew you'd understand if he wasn't here when you arrived."

"I'm glad," Lydia said. "I would rather see my sister alone."

"I am sure you would," Matron said understandingly, guiding Lydia's chair towards the luggage lift which would carry her to the first floor.

Elizabeth's room was in semi-darkness. A nurse rose from the bedside at their approach and made way for Lydia.

It took her a moment or two to accustom her eyes to the dimness and when she was at last able to see her sister's face clearly she had a shock. Elizabeth looked ghastly, there was no doubt about that.

Her cheek-bones were harshly prominent, and when she opened her eyes they were unnaturally bright.

"Elizabeth, dear," Lydia spoke softly.

Elizabeth did not answer for a moment and then in a very weak voice she replied:

"Why are you here? They must think I am very bad."

"Nonsense! I wanted to see you," Lydia said. "Besides, it's rather nice to have an excuse to come over."

"It's not nonsense." Elizabeth spoke very firmly now. Then suddenly she made an effort to clutch her sister's hand. "Lydia—tell Angus . . . tell Angus. He's in Antwerp."

"Yes, of course I'll tell him," Lydia said soothingly.

"You will? You promise?"

Elizabeth was getting agitated and Matron came out of the shadows. Lydia understood without words what Elizabeth was trying to say.

"I will tell him, I promise," she repeated to Elizabeth. "Now rest, darling, and get well. I mustn't talk to you any longer."

She propelled herself from the room, and as she went Elizabeth, tossing from side to side, was saying over and over again, "Tell him, tell him'; and it seemed to Lydia that she could hear her voice long after she had passed down the corridor. Matron joined her a few minutes later.

"I hope I haven't made Lady Avon worse by letting her see you, Mrs. Stanfield," she said, "but I expect Lord Avon told you she kept asking for you last night over and over again. I had the impression there was something she wanted to tell you and that was why I wanted you to come."

"I understand," Lydia said, "and I'm sure you did right. Do you think I could telephone?"

"Of course," Matron said. "Will you come to my room, Mrs. Stanfield?"

She took Lydia along to her own little sanctum near the wards.

"There's the telephone," she said, pointing to the desk, "and you'll get straight through to the Exchange."

"Thank you so much," Lydia replied, and waited until the door shut and she was alone.

She took off the receiver, gave a familiar number and waited. It seemed a long wait before she finally heard Lawrence Granger's voice.

"Hello, Lydia. I thought you'd forgotten all about me!"

Lydia spoke urgently. "Listen, Lawrence, I want you to help me."

"You know I'll do anything I can."

"I want you to find where Angus McLeod, the famous surgeon is. I believe he may be at Antwerp. He's with the Forces and I suppose his secretary would be able to give you the correct information. Anyway, will you trace him one way or another and send this telegram?"

Lawrence asked no question.

"All right," he said, "give it me, I'll take it down."

Lydia spoke slowly.

"Elizabeth desperately ill. Please come and see her if you possibly can. Lydia Stanfield."

17

Christine bent her head and prayed that Philip and Thyra might be happy together.

It was very quiet in the little church with its evidences of bomb damage in the boarded-up windows and grey stone monuments covered with scaffolding.

And yet Christine had no impression of emptiness or loneliness.

"This is how a wedding should be," she thought, as the clergyman's deep voice, clear and resonant, pronounced the words which made Philip and Thyra man and wife.

Christine thought of her mother and knew how bitterly she would regret not seeing Philip married. But things had planned out smoothly and easily, for Lydia had left the house early that morning and Ivan was away.

"Aunt Elizabeth's illness is a blessing in disguise," Christine had said to Thyra as they waited on the small empty station platform for a train to carry them to London. "You would never have deceived Mummy; you both look much too happy and excited."

"All the same, I wish she could have been with us," Thyra replied, and Christine liked her for the sincerity which she knew lay behind the conventional words.

The three of them had been very quiet as they travelled.

Yet Christine had been well aware of the undercurrent of tense excitement which made it almost impossible for Thyra and Philip to look at each other, which caused their breath to come quicker as their hands touched, and which created an aura of isolation round them, as if they moved in a world of their own.

It was obvious to the merest onlooker that they were overwhelmingly in love, and Christine was envious. They seemed so complete, so certain of the future and themselves.

Philip had chosen the church, a quiet, unpretentious one in a back street. Christine had never heard of it before, but when she entered through the heavy oak door she understood his reasons.

There was an atmosphere of deep faith and serenity in this small building. She was surprised at Philip's perception, for she had never thought him to be religious or particularly intuitive where such things were concerned.

But she knew that his choice of this church for his marriage to Thyra was not haphazard.

"How little one knows even about one's nearest and dearest!" Christine thought;

She wondered for the first time if she was responsible for such ignorance rather than those with whom she lived. How much there was that she didn't understand, how much which remained still a closed book even in her own home!

Quite suddenly Christine felt humble and insignificant. As she bowed her head and prayed for Philip and Thyra she prayed also for herself that she might have more understanding.

Philip and Thyra knelt at the altar steps and as they did so Thyra raised her head and looked at Philip. Christine saw the glance and the expression on Thyra's face. It was a look of ecstasy, almost of adoration.

And yet there was something else in it too—something vaguely familiar and to which for the moment Christine could put no name. Of what did it remind her? she asked herself.

Then suddenly quite clearly she remembered. It was the same expression she had seen on Ivan's face that night when he played to them in the studio.

As if it was another's voice speaking rather than her own thoughts, the explanation impressed itself upon her consciousness.

That is love, true love, an outpouring of what is within one, the giving of one's best and highest. Christine was startled at the idea. Thyra's love for Philip, Ivan's love for his music—each the giving out of what was within.

Strange that the two should be identical! And what of herself?

Was that same expression on her face when she helped those who were suffering? How did she appear in that moment of vision and intensity, when a power half physical and half mental poured through her? Was Love again the explanation?

Suddenly Christine felt herself uplifted, her whole being expanding in understanding and wonder. Love, that was the secret of it all. She was a channel through which it had poured, and she knew that these healing powers belonged not to herself but to something far greater and more virile.

Hers had only been the conductor's hand, harmonising and holding together the great forces so that, concentrated, they could restore strength to the weak.

Love! Christine felt it hard to breathe lest all that seemed to be unfolding within her mind should vanish and leave her once again in the absymal ignorance from which she had raised herself.

How stupid she had been, what a dunce not to have realised before that such an explanation was the only possible one!

How easy it was to remember only the narrow view and to think of love as essentially a physical emotion existing only between man and woman rather than as the expression of the universe itself.

Philip and Thyra, Ivan and his music, herself and her powers: one force lay behind them all, one power expressing itself through each of them in what amounted in reality to the same thing—Love!

And then just when it seemed to her that so much more could be hers—the secret of the universe, the wonder and glory of life and true living—the moment passed.

She was herself again, quivering with the experience and yet enriched, crowned and reborn with the wonder of that moment which had been hers.

Philip and Thyra were coming down from the altar now and turning towards the vestry.

Christine rose to her feet a little unsteadily, holding on to the pew in front of her with both hands, feeling as if she had passed through some great inspiring experience which had left her curiously weak.

Yet conscious still of that celestial lightness which comes when one has for a few moments escaped the heavy earthbound confines of the body.

She followed the others into the vestry. She kissed Philip and Thyra, shook hands with the clergyman, and watched them sign the register. There was a little catch in her voice as she said to them:

"I know you will be happy, I know you will."

Outside the church Philip hailed a taxi.

"We're going to lunch at the Savoy," he said. "You're coming with us, aren't you, Christine?"

"I'd rather not," Christine replied, and as they looked at her in surprise she added: "You want to be alone together, I know. You have a short enough time as it is, and I . . . I want to think."

"Are you all right?" Philip asked. "You look a bit pale."

"I'm perfectly all right," Christine answered, then added seriously: "Your wedding was a very beautiful one. It made me very happy. Don't worry about me; go and enjoy yourselves. You'll be coming home this evening?"

"We're coming home for tea," Philip answered, "to see Mummy and pick up our luggage."

Thyra gave a little cry of surprise.

"Did you think you were going to do without a

honeymoon?" Philip asked her tenderly. "I've made all the arrangements. We're going to stay at a little inn not far away from home but far enough for us to be alone."

"How lovely!" Thyra whispered, and her eyes were starry.

"In which case," Philip went on to Christine, "won't you change your mind and have lunch with us?"

Christine shook her head.

"You make me very envious," she said, "Bless you, darlings! I'll see you at tea-time."

She turned and walked down the street. She wanted to be alone; she wanted to try and analyse her experience in that quiet grey church. But now it was more difficult. What a few moments before had seemed so clear was now hedged about with questions; reason had returned to suspect ecstasy.

"I wish I was older," Christine thought suddenly. "I wish I had someone with whom I could discuss all this who would understand."

The thought came to her that she did know someone, and as a taxi crawled by with its flag up she hailed it and gave an address. It was only when she drew up at her destination that she wondered at her own impulsive action.

Harry Hampden was gazing idly out of the window, wondering if it was worth the effort to mix a cocktail for himself before luncheon, when Christine's taxi drew up outside.

He had been feeling bored and irritated with his own inactivity, longing fiercely for action, for the thrill and isolation of flying. In the air he knew himself master of his machine and of himself; now, crippled and grounded, he felt frustrated and impotent.

He wanted to live, but surely life was passing him by? Only being borne on wings could give him that elation and sense of supremacy which altered his whole prospect.

He told himself that the atmosphere in the house was

responsible for his mood of depression, but he knew that the cause was deeper than that of a superficial environment.

The long years in which Stella had lain unconscious—a living corpse—had taken their toll.

He loved Stella, and because he had lost his mother when he was young, all the tenderness of his boyhood and young manhood had been given to his sister.

She had clung to him and he had tried to make up in some little way for the parental love she had lost.

But without her companionship, her laughter and the demands she had made on him, Harry had grown older and graver in his outlook.

The shock of Stella's attempted suicide, and the reason for it, had made him take up a stern puritanical view of sex which was in reality alien to his temperament and personality.

He became afraid to love because he had seen a young love, sweet, fresh and exuberant, ravished and destroyed to become a thing of horror.

He shrank from love, and yet now, when he least expected it, love was stirring within him, fighting with all its strength and virility against the prejudices he had deliberately cultivated to safeguard himself.

At times he had hated women because they attracted him, hated them because often his body ached for the softness and sweetness of them while his mind held rigidly to his chosen path.

He was attractive, and it was inevitable that he should at times find temptation too strong for him. He was not without experience, but such experiences left him bitter and cynical.

Then unexpectedly he had begun to think of Christine.

He had found himself delighting in her reserve, in the natural dignity which gave to her a seriousness, and at times the impression that she was older than she really was, and in her beauty which, unobstrusive at first sight, drew and deepened an acquaintance like a brilliantly executed etching.

Christine's success with Stella left Harry breathless; then he realised that his gratitude and joy were but minor emotions compared with others she aroused in him.

He fought at first against the tide which threatened to sweep away the carefully erected structure which he had imagined was permanent. But it was useless.

Honest at last with himself, he acknowledged his love and then was afraid for new and very different reasons. Was he too old for Christine? Worse still, would she look at a man injured and inactive?

Wanting Christine with all the violence of a nature which has been repressed and disciplined too long, it seemed to Harry like an answer to prayer when he saw a taxi drive up to the door and glimpsed her face at the window.

The front door was opened as Christine reached the steps and she looked up to see Harry.

"I saw your taxi drive up," he said. "Have you come to luncheon?"

"If you will have me," Christine answered simply.

"But of course; I was just going to start."

"Are you alone?"

"Absolutely; do you mind?"

"Of course I don't," Christine answered. "But I wondered if I was interrupting a party."

Christine preceded him into the big sitting-room where they had first met.

"I ought not to be here," she said. "I ought to be lunching with my brother and sister-in-law. I have come here straight from their wedding."

"Their wedding!" Harry exclaimed. "How exciting! You didn't tell us anything about it. Why are you so secretive?"

"I didn't know anything about it myself," Christine replied. "They just decided to get married! I was the only member of the family present."

"It sounds intriguing," Harry said. "Tell me more."

Christine shook her head.

"It's a long and complicated story. Instead, tell me about yourselves. How is Stella?"

"Looking forward to seeing you as usual. She had a good night and informed me this morning that if I didn't get rid of the nurses soon she'd go mad. I must say I don't blame her."

"Nor do I," Christine agreed. "Why don't you get her away? A week or so at the sea or in Scotland would do you both good."

"It's an idea," Harry said slowly. And then he added: "You'll come with us, of course?"

"I?" Christine exclaimed. "Oh, I hadn't thought of that."

"But you'll come?"

Christine hesitated for a moment; then as she raised her eyes they met his.

"You'll come, won't you?" he repeated.

"Yes, I'd love to."

Christine said the words automatically, but something strange was happening to her as her eyes met Harry's. She felt a sudden breathless excitement sweep over her, and then as she waited, her lips parted, her eyes held by his, he moved across the intervening space between them.

"Christine," he said, and his voice was suddenly low and hoarse, "you know what I'm trying to say, don't you?"

She could not answer him and half turned away, feeling afraid of her own emotion, of the excitement which gripped her and the quick beating of her heart.

"Christine."

There was no mistaking the expression in his voice and in the tone in which he spoke.

She turned back towards him.

"Oh, Harry!"

The looked at each other and quite suddenly she was in his arms.

236

"I've wanted to say it for such a long time," he said, "but I thought it was too soon, too quick. I didn't see how you could care for a crock like me."

"You're not a crock!"

Christine spoke indignantly, her face hidden against his shoulder; and then as she raised it to his he bent and kissed her.

He felt the softness of her mouth beneath his and drew her closer and still closer until she felt herself tremble, weak beneath the strength of his possession.

"I love you," he said at length. "You're quite unlike any other girl I've ever met before. Can you really care for me a little?"

"Oh, Harry, it's all so exciting, so unexpected. I have never thought about it until now."

"And now?"

"I love you."

Harry held her closely to him.

"Darling, that's wonderful! Let's get married at once —today! What are we waiting for?"

Christine laughed.

"Please! Give me a chance to . . . to think. I've only just discovered that I love you."

"You are sure of that?"

Harry looked down at the flushed loveliness of the face against his shoulder.

"Luncheon is served, sir."

The voice from the door made them start apart guiltily, and then they both laughed.

"Another place for Miss Stanfield, Dobson," Harry said. "And by the way, you can congratulate us."

"Indeed, sir, that's splendid news, sir! My most hearty congratulations!"

Dobson left the room and Christine turned to Harry protestingly.

"But, Harry! You can't go about telling everybody! Not yet."

"Why not? I want the whole world to know. I want to shout it from the housetops."

He was elated like a boy—it was hard to recognise the serious man who had slightly awed her with his gravity.

"But, darling, think of our families," Christine pleaded. "We haven't even told Stella or my mother or anybody."

"We'll go and tell Stella now; and of course—your family! I'd forgotten about them. They won't mind, will they?"

"I hope not."

Harry stopped dead.

"Good Lord, are you suggesting they won't approve of me or something like that?"

Christine laughed.

"No, nothing so drastic. But I doubt whether they realise that I have grown up enough to marry anyone. It isn't so long since I came home from America."

"All the better, they won't miss you. I tell you quite frankly that I can't wait. I want you now, at once."

He put out his arms to catch hold of her, but playfully she eluded him.

"Let's go and tell Stella," she said. "Everything is happening too quickly—I'm afraid of losing my common sense."

But as Christine watched Harry go slowly up the stairs she felt her heart contract within her.

"I can do so much to help him," she thought. "There will be no point in waiting long. If Philip can get married, so can I."

Stella was delighted. She was sitting up in bed looking extremely pretty and a very different person from what she had appeared even a week before. Every day saw a new improvement in her as she took an interest in herself and in her surroundings.

Now at Harry's and Christine's news she held out her arms to them with a glad cry.

"Oh, it's wonderful! Absolutely wonderful! And now I shan't lose you, Christine. I was terrified that the day would come when you would go away and leave me."

"As if I should," Christine said scornfully.

"You might have other and more interesting patients."

"Now that she'll have two of us on her hands," Harry said, "she won't have time for any outsiders."

"I shall be a patient myself if I don't have something to eat," Christine said plaintively. "I'm ravenously hungry."

"So am I now I come to think of it," Harry agreed, "although I am not certain that it is not rather unromantic and does not show a lack of proper appreciation of this important moment in our lives."

He was teasing, but Stella took him seriously.

"I think important moments make one hungry," she said. And Christine, feeling that she was being championed, bent to kiss Stella's cheek. "We'll go and eat an enormous luncheon and then come back and talk to you."

"Be as quick as you can," Stella begged. "There's so much more I want to hear."

As they reached the top of the stairs Harry linked his arm with Christine's.

"Aren't you proud of what you've achieved?" he asked.

"The difference is wonderful, isn't it?" Christine answered.

"Do you imagine we could ever let you go after that?" he asked, his hand holding hers very tightly.

"I believe that's the only reason you're marrying me."

Harry stopped and put his arms round her.

"Take back that very unjust accusation."

His lips were very close to hers. Christine tried to laugh at him, but the sound stuck in her throat. There was something about his nearness and the tender masterfulness of his voice which made her feel shy and unsure of herself.

"Well?" he insisted as she did not speak.

"Oh, Harry, I'm so happy!"

239

He had barely heard her words before his lips found hers and they clung together oblivious of everything save themselves. A cough and the rustle of a starched apron brought them back to earth and they realised that Stella's nurse stood behind them on the little landing.

"Our lunch will be getting cold," Harry said.

Christine moved from his arms to catch sight of the nurse's astonished, tight-lipped expression.

"Good morning, Sister," she said brightly.

There was a moment's pause before the answer came, frigidly and with an underlying note of shocked disapproval behind the conventional words.

"Good morning, Miss Stanfield."

As they reached the dining-room Christine said:

"You might have told her. I know what she's thinking about us."

"As soon as I saw her face I made up my mind not to," Harry replied. "I have always disliked that nurse."

"All the same, I can't bear even to imagine what she's thinking."

"Then I'll tell her after lunch. But I enjoy giving her cause for complaint—she's that type of woman."

They finished their luncheon together, a meal during which they talked, laughed and ate and had no idea of what they ate. There was so much underlying the superficial gaiety of their conversation, so much that was being said by their hearts.

When they had finished, Harry lit a cigarette and then got up to open the door for Christine.

"Let's go and tell the dragon," he said. "I don't feel she'll be particularly elated by our news. At the same time it will dispel all her more vicious imaginings and set the seal of respectability on the house once more."

"I'm glad to hear you've always been respectable," Christine smiled.

She spoke lightly without thinking what she said, but Harry frowned and she had the idea that for a moment their closeness and intimacy was disrupted. It was as if

240

he withdrew from her and became a stranger. She waited.

Then putting out his hand to take hers he said seriously as if it were of paramount importance:

"You're the only girl I've ever wanted to marry—the only woman I've ever loved."

Christine felt a sense of relief flooding over her, warm and golden in its release, dispelling some secret minor fear which, she had not realised until this moment, had been at the back of her mind, taunting and tormenting her. Harry was not promiscuous—not like Ivan! Thank God for that!

When they reached the top of the stairs there was no sign of the Sister and they went straight in to Stella.

"I'm supposed to be lying down and having an afternoon nap," she told them, "but it's quite impossible for me to sleep; I'm far too excited. Pull up the blinds, Harry, and let's talk."

Harry did as he was asked and he and Christine sat down on the bed.

"I want to know everything," Stella said; "when you first fell in love with each other, what you said and what you felt."

"I've been in love with Christine for weeks," Harry said. "In fact, I think I fell in love with her the first day she came here."

"That's not true!" Christine exclaimed; "you disliked me intensely. You thought I was a charlatan; you didn't believe I could do Stella any good at all. Now, be honest."

"Well, I was extremely surprised when I first saw you," Harry admitted. "When Sir Fraser suggested bringing a healer, I imagined some fat old woman in home-woven clothes with an Arab 'control' or something like that. I have always connected faith healing with trances and such like."

"I wish I had known all this was going on," Stella said. "I would have loved to have seen Harry's face."

"And Dr. Dearman's!" Christine laughed. "There's

241

someone who is not one of my admirers. Poor old man, I'm afraid I've upset all his theories..

"Never mind about him," Stella said. "Tell me more about yourselves."

"There isn't very much more to tell," Christine replied. "I think the fact that I have been to a wedding this morning put the whole idea into Harry's head; otherwise he'd never have said anything."

"If you only knew how I have lain awake night after night thinking about you," Harry groaned.

"Why didn't you tell me?" Stella asked.

"I didn't want to worry you with my troubles," Harry replied affectionately.

"I'm afraid I've been awfully selfish," Stella sighed. "I've been thinking of myself all the time. Harry, it must have been dreadful for you all those years. I suppose you couldn't have people to the house or anything. Oh dear, what can I do to make up for it?"

"Forget all about it," Christine said quickly. " 'All's well that ends well,' and after all, if you'd been fit and the house had been packed with beautiful blondes, Harry would very likely have been married long ago and I should never have met him."

Stella put out her hand to take Christine's.

"That's true enough and I'm terribly glad you have met him, and frightfully, frightfully glad you are going to be my sister-in-law. '

"I'm glad too," Christine smiled.

"There's just one thing," Stella said. "If you are going to be one of the family, I think that we ought to tell you . . . about me." She glanced at her brother appealingly. "Don't you think so, Harry?"

"Do you want to talk about it?" he asked guardedly.

"I want Christine to know the truth."

"You are certain it won't upset you?"

"Not now," Stella said. "I'm better, so much better, and I'd like Christine to understand."

"Very well then," Harry agreed, "if you are sure it won't be too much for you."

242

"I'm quite sure," Stella said firmly.

She turned towards Christine, her hand in hers; "I want to tell you what a fool I've been."

Christine bent forward.

"Listen, Stella," she said. "Do you really want to talk about it? It all happened a long time ago. You're getting well; why can't you forget all that unhappiness and misery?"

"I want you to know," Stella said obstinately, and Christine was silent, only vaguely apprehensive of what she was about to hear.

Stella cleared her throat, a little dry sound, nervous and tense.

"I was twenty-one when . . . when it happened," she began. "It was in the middle of the London Season and I was having a perfectly marvellous time—at least I thought I was. I went to lots of dances and parties. And Harry and I filled this house practically every night with people, didn't we?"

Harry did not answer. He was lighting himself a cigarette. Christine, looking at him, realised how much he disliked this unfolding of the past.

Stella waited a moment and then went on:

"Well, there it was. I was a success and there seemed little more I could want. I was pretty—at least everybody told me so. We had plenty of money, Harry and I and no one to interfere with us.

"Several men wanted to marry me. I can hardly remember their names now; and while at the time I thought they were very sweet, I just wasn't in love. I didn't seem able to fall in love with anybody.

"I expect that sounds rather stupid and smug, but the men I met didn't affect me that way.

"I liked them to dance with, I thought they were awfully nice, but I was quite happy to come home alone with Harry and to feel that we were a family in ourselves, that we didn't need anyone else. And then . . ."

Stella paused and closed her eyes for a moment.

"Then?" Christine prompted, interested and curious despite a sense of embarrassment.

"Then I fell in love. It happened to me very quickly and quite overpoweringly. I went to a reception given by a friend of mine. I hadn't looked forward to it very much, it wasn't the sort of party I usually cared about; but Eileen begged me to come and so I went along—alone. And it was there I met . . . him."

Stella closed her eyes again and for a moment little lines of pain etched about her mouth.

"Must you talk about it?" Harry asked. "Let me tell Christine."

Stella opened her eyes.

"No, no, I want to do it myself. I shall feel better when I have. It doesn't hurt now—not much."

She took a deep breath.

"I can see him now as I walked into the drawing-room. He was standing by the mantelpiece and Eileen introduced us. As I put out my hand to touch his I felt a strange sensation. I can't describe it, it was rather as if he was magnetic and drew me to him.

"And then he spoke to me and I knew by the look in his eyes that he admired me—thought I was pretty.

"We talked for a little while and I felt my cheeks burning and a sort of wonderful tremendous excitement creeping over me. I can't explain it . . . but I was certain that he felt the same. Later in the evening he played the piano and I knew as I listened that he was playing to me . . . only to me . . . that the other people in the room didn't matter."

"What did he play?" Christine asked.

"I can't remember," Stella answered. "I only know that he spoke to me through his music, that he talked to me as intimately as if he were making love to me in words. Of course he was famous, I'd heard of him before, but never before this moment had I seen him or realised what he was like.

"All the time he was playing I felt as if he drew my heart from my body, that he took it and made it his. If he had asked me to go away with him at that moment, that very night, I would have gone . . . I was in love."

Stella suddenly put up her hands to her face.

"That's enough!" Harry spoke sternly. "I won't have you upsetting yourself."

Stella threw out her arms; the tears were streaming down her cheeks.

"I loved him . . . and God knows he loved me . . . at first. Yes, he loved me until I gave him myself body and soul . . . until I bored him with my love, my adoration and—why not say it?—my worship. I bored him . . . bored him, Christine; so he went away and forgot that I existed. I was too easy, too unsophisticated. I was desirable until I gave myself to him completely and utterly . . . After that he wanted more . . . more than I could give him—something perhaps that he will never find. When he left me, I died . . . yes, I died! The real me couldn't live without his love, his kisses, his music —I was dead, but my body, this body which had ceased to attract him, went on breathing, eating, walking and sleeping, so I . . . I . . . I . . ."

Stella's voice, which was little more than a whisper, broke.

"What was his name?"

Christine's question, sharp with terror, broke from her lips; but even as she spoke, even as the words seemed to echo round the room, she knew the answer.

18

Lydia was tired, so tired that every jolt and bump of the taxi on her way home from Avon House was like a physical wound. She was so tired that she felt irritated by Rose's solicitous ways.

"Better go to bed as soon as we get back, ma'am," Rose urged;

Lydia, because she craved for rest in every aching muscle of her body, must in her very tiredness argue.

"We will see about that. The Master may want me."

Rose said nothing, and Lydia sensed her disapproval. She knew only too well how much Rose disapproved of Ivan and his insatiable demands upon her strength.

Ordinarily it amused her, knowing that the reason lay in Rose's devotion to herself. But now, because she was as fractious as an over-tired child, she told herself that she would not be dictated to or tryannised over. Rose was only a servant; she must not try to impose her will over that of her mistress.

In silence they journeyed on—it seemed interminably—along the twisting lanes which were the quickest way across country from Avon House to Fairhurst. And then quite suddenly Lydia's irritation passed from her.

Dear Rose! It was comforting somehow to be looked after as though one were a child. Rose at heart was the eternal Nannie, always wanting to nurse and cherish someone, not only to do things for the person she tended, but to think for her as well.

"We're nearly home, Rose; I'm thankful that you came with me."

Lydia spoke to break the silence and to disperse the atmosphere of disapproval emanating from Rose. There was a warmth in her voice which never failed her where Rose was concerned, and now it worked like magic.

Rose pulled at the rug, shutting out imaginary draughts, and Lydia knew that all was well.

"I'll have to give you a massage tonight," Rose said grudgingly, "or you'll be fit for nothing tomorrow."

Lydia accepted the olive branch gracefully.

"Thank you, Rose. It makes all the difference, as you know."

The taxi drew up at the door and Rose got out to ring the bell sharply for the other maids. They helped Lydia into her chair and pushed her into the hall.

"Where is everybody?" Lydia enquired.

"On the verandah having tea, ma'am. Mr. Philip and Miss Jörgensen got back about twenty minutes ago, but the Master arrived soon after lunch, ma'am. He was very upset when he heard where you'd gone."

Lydia allowed herself to be taken to her bedroom; but as Rose left her by the dressing table and went to turn down the bed, she said firmly:

"I'll have tea on the verandah."

Rose's hands, which were moving over the lace-trimmed linen sheets, dropped.

"Let them come to you."

Lydia shook her head.

"I'll have my tea with them. And Rose, give me some of my drops."

For a moment she thought Rose was going to refuse. The drops were prescribed to be used only on very special occasions and in a case of emergency. Rose hesitated and then went without a word across the room.

Lydia felt a sudden spasm of impatience. If only people would do as she wanted and not fuss as to whether it was good for her or not! What did it matter?

What did anything matter besides the difficulties and problems which had got to be solved now at this very moment?

No one watching her fifteen minutes later as she made her appearance on the verandah would have sensed her anxiety or the uneasy sense of anticipation which possessed her. She took in the party with a swift appraising glance before she greeted them coolly, her voice undisturbed, her smile apparently unforced.

Ivan, who was stretched out on an easy chair, jumped to his feet.

"Lydia, my dearest, I had no idea you were back."

"I'm sorry you arrived home to find me gone," Lydia said, lifting her face to his kiss. "They told you the news?"

"About Elizabeth?"

"Yes."

"How is she?"

"Very ill. I'm worried about her."

"I'm sorry," Ivan said.

Lydia turned from him to the other two—Philip standing rather stiffly behind the tea-table, Thyra beside him. They were holding hands and one look at their faces told Lydia the truth.

Then Ivan with a sweeping gesture, his voice high and slightly brittle, cried:

"There's news for you here, darling, but good news. Philip and Thyra are married. Secretly, swiftly and without a word to any of us—they have been married."

"Thank God he's taking it like this," Lydia thought as she held out her arms to her son and daughter-in-law.

How she wished that they could have told her of their marriage without Ivan being present! But Ivan was behaving superbly! As they sat round the tea-table she was conscious of a slight sharpness in his tone and that occasionally his laughter and his somewhat elaborate chaffing of the young couple rang false.

But outwardly he was acting the part of a surprised but benevolent paterfamilias with an energy which at least showed his good-will.

"Where is Christine?" Lydia asked.

They had ceased for a moment to talk excitedly and

Ivan's extravagant compliments to the bride had brought a sudden silence with a sense of embarrassment.

"She left us at the church door," Philip replied. "I think she felt that we wanted to be alone."

"As of course you did," Ivan interposed.

"We should have liked to have Christine with us all the same," Philip answered gravely. "She hurried away; I thought perhaps she had come straight home. Anyway, I expect she will turn up before we leave. I've ordered the taxi for five o'clock."

"Taxi?" Lydia queried.

Philip explained his plans for a honeymoon. Lydia was not certain, but she thought she saw a faint expression of relief on Ivan's face. She had a moment alone with Philip when Thyra asked Ivan to choose her a few pieces of music to take with them.

"Whether he likes it or not, I'm going to play to Philip," she said mischievously; "he's got a lot to learn about music."

"Leave the choice to me," Ivan exclaimed. "I know the right ingredients for a love potion."

They disappeared together and Lydia knew Thyra had with exquisite tact engineered this moment in order to leave her alone with her son.

"Are you happy, darling?" she asked him.

"Terribly," Philip replied. "And, Mummy, thank you for everything."

"There wasn't much I could do."

Philip got up and put his arms round her shoulders.

"My only regret is that you weren't at my wedding— I thought of you."

Lydia felt the tears sting her eyes at the simple sincerity of his words.

"Bless you, my darling; I shall be praying for you. Thyra will have a good husband."

"If she has, it's entirely due to you; all the decent instincts I've ever had were given me by you."

"Oh, my darling!"—Lydia would have said more, only she was very near to tears, too near for speech.

She drew Philip's head down and kissed his cheek. With a little pang she thought of his birth. How thrilled she had been to have a son!

"Funny little beggar," Ivan had said a few days later, prodding him as he lay beside her; "I wonder what he will play when he grows up."

"He's my son, he won't be a musician," Lydia had replied.

She meant to tease Ivan but speaking more truthfully than she knew.

"I'm jealous of him!" Ivan had taken her into his arms, holding her closely, possessively, passionately.

Philip, as if he sensed that he was being neglected, had woken up and started to cry; but Ivan had refused to let her go, closing her mouth with kisses when she pleaded to be free.

"Ivan, the baby!" she gasped at length.

"Who comes first?" he replied. "Tell me quickly or I won't let you go."

"You—of course—you do," she answered, and only then had he released her to minister to the angry Philip.

Yes, Ivan had come first then and always, and yet she knew he had been jealous of his son.

When the parlourmaid announced that the taxi had arrived he sprang eagerly to his feet to see Philip and Thyra off, insisting at the last moment with a theatrical gesture on emptying a bowl of roses and placing the flowers at Thyra's feet.

"You will need them in your hotel," he said. "Besides, the bridal suite by tradition should be a bower of roses."

He took Thyra's hand and raised it to his lips, patted Philip on the shoulder and then waved to them as they drove off, his hand high above his head, the setting evening sun glinting on his fiery hair.

"He's doing it well," Lydia thought.

But she knew he was glad to see them go. With a little sigh she preceded him into the drawing-room. She sensed as she turned her chair round that now that his audience had gone his mood would change and the elation which he had so skilfully manufactured would die away from him.

She felt the dragging weariness which had been hers before she reached home encompass her again, and before Ivan could speak she said:

"I think I will go to bed if you don't mind. You and Christine can have trays in my room or dinner together, whichever you prefer. I am just a little tired; it's a long way to Avon House."

"If I had been here I shouldn't have let you go," Ivan said.

"I should have had to go," Lydia replied gently. "I didn't want to say too much in front of the children, but Elizabeth is really bad. Even Matron is worried. They will pull her through, of course, these modern cures are so marvellous. But all the same it's worrying for all of us."

"Yes, of course."

Ivan spoke gravely, but Lydia had the idea that he wasn't listening but was preoccupied with his own thoughts.

"I can't bear a scene at this moment," she thought. "I must lie down, I must go to bed."

Yet she hesitated to leave him. She sensed that he wanted her, and that was an instinct which she had never denied or refused.

He walked across the room and back again.

"Did you know anything about this?" he asked.

She knew only too well to what he referred.

"About Thyra and Philip?" she enquired. "I knew they were fond of each other; that was why Thyra wished to go away. She felt love might interfere with her career."

"Was that the only reason she gave?"

Lydia answered him steadily.

"As I expect you know, she wants to make a success

251

of her music so as to provide for her father and mother. Philip is very much against having a wife with a career, and at first it seemed as if their conflicting desires would prove a deadlock.

"But Thyra remembered that soon—very soon perhaps—Philip would have to return to his ship and to active service. She gave in, and as they both felt time was so short they arranged to get married at once and decided to tell no one till it was over, because it was obviously less trouble and quieter to have nobody there."

Ivan was disbelieving, Lydia could see that. He had his own ideas as to why the marriage had been so secret, and she guessed that he was trying to force her into accusing him.

"It is difficult to think of Philip as a married man," Lydia said. "But Thyra is a dear child. Like so many foreign girls she is far more sensible than one expects at that age. She will make Philip a good wife and they'll be happy."

Ivan said nothing. He turned his back on the room and drummed with his fingers on the window-pane. After a long pause he said:

"Go to bed and tell Rose to call me when you're ready."

He was suffering in some obscure way, but Lydia could not help him. She knew only too well the meaning of his restlessness and the nervous movements of his hands.

She propelled her chair from the room and outside the door found as she had expected, Rose hovering anxiously in the hall waiting for her.

Her face lighted at the sight of Lydia, but characteristically she grumbled at her, her voice gruff and uncompromising.

"I thought you were never coming. You'll be feeling so ill tomorrow that we shall have to send for the doctor."

"I may have to go over to her ladyship again tomorrow," Lydia replied. "Matron promised to telephone me after dinner tonight."

"If you want to kill yourself, you're going the right way about it," Rose said scathingly, but her hands were tender as she helped Lydia undress.

It was delicious to lie back against the soft pillows, to feel her tired body relax and the dull ache in her forehead lighten.

"I could sleep if I was left alone," Lydia thought; but she knew it would be a long time before she could hope for that.

"Will you tell Mr. Razoumovsky I am ready for him," she asked Rose. "And when Miss Christine comes in I want to see her at once."

Rose left the room and for a moment Lydia closed her eyes, thinking not of herself but of Elizabeth. Would Lawrence Granger be able to find Angus and how soon could he be with her?

Lydia had said nothing to Arthur of the telegram she had sent or Elizabeth's desire to see Angus McLeod. Arthur was worried about his wife but not unduly so. He thought all doctors and nurses were incompetent fools and said so innumerable times during luncheon.

At the same time Lydia had the impression that what really surprised him was that Elizabeth should be ill at all.

He was always careful of himself, knowing how much older he was than his wife, and the fact that Elizabeth was ill while he was well somehow struck him as incongruous and an idea to which he had in his slowness of thinking to adjust himself.

"I've never known her to have a day's illness," he said several times. "She must have been run down to let a little thing like this upset her so much. Can't understand these doctors letting it get to such a state. But there, I always said they were damn' fools. Now when I was a boy . . ."

He started off on a long and dull reminiscence of a country doctor who had attended his patients on horseback, and Lydia found herself wondering how Elizabeth could have stood this type of conversation so patiently and for so long.

Arthur Avon was a bore! There was no doubt about that. He was a bore in the way that so many elderly men of his particular generation and class were.

They were uneducated for one thing, having made no effort to improve their minds since they left their public school. The read *The Times* from cover to cover and occasionally scanned a biography or a book of sporting reminiscences.

Otherwise they were ignorant, and their ignorance was all the more abysmal because they despised what they did not know. They knew little history and less geography.

Their world consisted of their own estates, their own political party, their own class or the set of people with whom they had grown up.

Such men were the product of a generation who had produced as supreme examples of their muddled, unperceptive way of thinking the Prime Ministers who held sway in England between the wars—Stanley Baldwin, Ramsay MacDonald, Neville Chamberlain.

Listening to Arthur Avon droning on, Lydia knew that he was out of touch not only with the generations younger than himself, but with all the progress which had been made in the last hundred years by civilised mankind.

The world was crying for vitality, for strength, for leadership, for all those things which could revitalise and revivify the nations tired both by the catastrophe of war and by the nervous strain of speeded-up machinery.

What possible help could be found in Arthur Avon and his kind? Bloodless, without emotion and without imagination, they belonged neither to the virile buccaneers, the pioneers and aristocratic leaders of the past who had made a great Empire for Britain.

Nor to the strong forces of democracy striving to make themselves felt for the benefit of the generations to come.

"How I should have hated to be Arthur's wife," Lydia thought.

Ivan, with all his faults, with all the unhappiness he caused her at times, had at least justified his existence—would leave a legacy to the future. He was creative; he was also at all times—whether one judged him for his music or as a man—alive.

There was something about Arthur, droning on in the midst of his huge house, which reminded Lydia of a museum piece.

"I, too, am getting old," she told herself, "but I will never become like this, I'll never let myself get out of touch with life or be divorced from reality."

It was with a feeling of relief that she left the dining-room when luncheon was ended and went to seek Matron.

She felt more at home with the quiet, elderly woman who could not have been so many years younger than Arthur but whose personality seemed to exude efficiency and strength.

"Arthur is a very 'old' old man," Lydia thought, and wondered what the future could hold for Elizabeth.

She had at last learnt what love was, she had at last found what was worth having in the world, only to be force to relinquish it and live in this mausoleum, this tomb-like atmosphere with a man for whom she could have little emotion except respect and a childlike affection as for a kindly parent.

"Poor Elizabeth!"

Lydia sighed and opened her eyes to see Ivan coming into the room.

On an impulse, without considering her reasons for such an action, she held out her arms.

For a moment he hesitated and she knew that he did

255

not wish her to touch him because like a child who has been hurt he wanted to hide that hurt. Then he moved swiftly to her side.

She put her arms around his neck and drew his head down to hers. At first he did not kiss her, then gently he did so, but she did not release him and at last she felt his arms go round her.

There was no need for words. He held her tightly and the nearness of him gave her that familiar sense of wonder and happiness. He was hers—this splendid man, so different from the common clay of others.

She pressed her lips against his, giving herself utterly in a kiss. Lydia knew that in that moment Ivan understood that she expressed her sympathy and understanding and her yearning to help him.

Without words he had told her he was hurt, unhappy and unsure of himself; this was her reply.

At length they drew apart. Ivan held out his hand and drawing up a chair sat beside her, saying nothing, his face clouded, his eyes away from her.

"You will have to settle some money on Philip," Lydia said quietly, and she knew by the sudden tension of his fingers beneath hers he was surprised.

"I hadn't thought of that."

"He's a married man; he must support his own wife and it's a mistake to let him do it on an allowance."

"And suppose I don't give him any money?"

Ivan was being childish, playing with the idea of revenge.

"Then they would have to live on his pay. But you will?"

"Yes, I will."

Ivan got to his feet—how well Lydia knew those abrupt movements when he was perturbed! He walked across the room and back again.

"They are very much in love," Lydia said, speaking more to herself than to Ivan.

He stood still at the foot of her bed.

"Love!" He made an expressive gesture. "Love!

What is it? What does it mean? What is this thing called love? I've sought it, I've tried to understand it. What is it? Where is it?"

"You can't capture it or shoot it down."

Lydia's voice was faintly amused.

"Then what is it?"

"It is the only thing which matters, the rhyme and reason for our very existence."

Lydia spoke softly.

"And when men and women grow old," he asked, "what then? What happens to this love, of which you know so much?"

Lydia knew what he meant. That was the real question he wanted to ask her, the question which had been nagging at him. Torturing him:

"When *I* grow old—too old for love—what then?"

"If only I didn't feel so tired," Lydia thought. "If only I could express what I feel, could make him understand that he has had so much—that it is experience, not time, which counts."

She thought of Arthur, dried-up, withered and sapless. Ivan would never be like that, there would always be some fire and spark in him if he lived to be a hundred. But how to make him see it, how to tell him that the future would be no worse than the present?

Each stage brought its own problems, its own difficulties; it was only those who could not accept the passage of time who suffered. Ivan was like a professional beauty who concentrated only on her looks and thought that when they went all else must go too.

Lydia realised that Ivan was waiting. She answered him with the words that involuntarily came to her lips.

"In your case you will have your music."

"Without inspiration?'

"But you will have that too. What are you inspired by? Your own imagination. That is what never dies and that is what you can never capture, never reach, so you will always go on seeking it."

He understood, but some perversity prevented him acknowledging the truth of what she said.

"A charming outlook! Thank you, my dear, it's a comforting thought that I can use my imagination in common with every dirty old man who takes to pornographic literature when he is too old for anything else."

Lydia was not hurt; she only understood that Ivan's bitterness came from a desire to hide his own transparency. He turned to the door.

At that moment Christine came in. With a sense of relief Lydia turned towards her daughter.

"Hello, darling! We were wondering what had happened to you. Philip and Thyra wanted to see you, but they couldn't wait so they sent you their love."

Christine did not answer. She seemed not to have heard her mother. Instead she stood with her hand on the door-handle, looking at Ivan. The expression on her face was so intense and tragic that even he realised that something was the matter.

"Well?"

He met her eyes. It was as if a fierce and piercing tension vibrated between father and daughter; there was an atmosphere of violence, of an antagonism long repressed bursting to the surface and revealing itself.

Then Christine put up her hand and dragged off her hat with a sudden gesture which made Lydia think of a man drawing his sword.

"Christine!"

She spoke sharply to draw the girl's attention; she knew there was something sinister, something evil and dangerous in that silence.

Christine spoke at last.

"I have only one thing to say to you," she said to Ivan, addressing him as if they were alone in the room. "It's the last thing I hope I ever shall say, for I expect never to see you again and it will not be my fault if we meet. It is this:

"I hate you, I despise you, and I am utterly ashamed to be your daughter!'

258

19

Ivan did not answer. He stood looking at Christine, and Lydia, watching from the bed, saw suddenly a close resemblance between them that she had never noticed before.

At that moment when she felt almost suffocated by her own fear of what was occurring—of what was being enacted like a stage play before her—they appeared foreign, both of them alien to her own instincts of English self-control and good breeding.

She wanted to speak, she wanted to break the tension, but somehow the words stuck in her throat.

There was nothing she could say; she could only remain an unwilling onlooker, her heart beating quickly, feeling a dismay painful in its intensity and a desperate sense of impotence to prevent what she knew was about to be catastrophic.

Ivan spoke,

"Perhaps you would like to explain yourself," he said, his voice as hard as the expression in his eyes.

He seemed to have grown taller, but although Christine must look up to him, she did not appear to be dwarfed or overpowered by him.

"Is there any need for me to explain?" she asked; and the disdain and bitterness of her voice seemed to Lydia to cut through the air. "It is only that I've learnt a little more about you and your behaviour. I wonder if you've ever imagined what it must be like for a child to learn that the man she has to call 'father' is one of the basest creatures possible; a seducer, a man unfaithful both to his marriage vows and to the lowest code of decency?"

259

"How dare you speak to me like this?"

Ivan's temper was rising. He stepped forward and took Christine by the shoulders.

"Don't you dare touch me," Christine said defiantly and wrenched herself free. "I'm not afraid of you."

"Leave this room," Ivan commanded.

"I am leaving not only this room," Christine answered, "but also this house. You've destroyed my life as you've destroyed other women's lives. I'm going away to earn my own living. I shall change my name and I hope never under any circumstances to be forced to meet you or to have to admit that you are my father."

Ivan was consumed with rage. There was a fiery glint in his eyes which Lydia knew all too well. He stepped forward.

She knew what he was about to do and screamed even as he raised his hand and slapped Christine hard across the face.

Christine made no sound. She only stood looking at her father with a disdainful, cynical smile which hurt Lydia more than if she had burst into tears.

Ivan was breathing quickly. If he had heard Lydia scream he showed no sign of it; his eyes and his thoughts were on his daughter; and then suddenly, as if she had both defeated and routed him, he turned and went from the room.

The door slammed behind him and the noise of its closing echoed round the room, intensifying the silence which lay between the two women left behind.

Lydia cried out her daughter's name. Very slowly Christine raised her hand to her cheek which bore the red marks of Ivan's fingers and looked at her mother.

"What has happened?"

Lydia spoke tersely, but at the same time she felt a weakness and inertia creeping over her; unconsciousness threatened to envelop her and she lay back suddenly and closed her eyes. She opened them to feel

260

Christine's arms round her shoulders and the rim of a glass against her lips.

"It's all right, Mummy, drink this."

Christine spoke normally; the bitter note in her voice had gone. Lydia drank the water; she could feel the waves of darkness receding from her and her forehead was wet.

"I'm all right," she said at length. "There are some smelling salts on my table."

Christine fetched them and the strong aromatic smell restored her.

"I'm sorry, Mummy." Christine spoke tenderly. "It ought not to have happened in front of you."

"Did it have to happen at all?"

Lydia tried to sound severe, but instead the question pleaded.

Christine nodded her head.

"I'm afraid so. You see, I am going away now and at once; I can't stay here any more."

"But, darling,, I don't understand. What does it mean?"

Christine bent forward and took her mother's hand.

"I suppose really I ought not to tell you," she said, "but how can I help myself? I can't just leave home and not give you any explanation of why I am going. Can I?"

For the moment she was a child again, trying to justify her own actions.

"I want you to tell me the truth," Lydia said gently.

Christine's face hardened.

"It's going to hurt you, Mummy."

"We won't worry about that," Lydia replied. "Tell me what has happened."

Christine put her hand up to her cheek as if it still hurt her. The bitter, cynical twist of her mouth which had hurt Lydia so unbearably a few moments ago returned.

"I've just come from Stella Hampden's house," she said. "I told you about her. I told you how I'd brought

261

her back to life after four long years of lying unconscious and inanimate because she had tried to commit suicide.

"If it had not been for me, she would be in the same state at this moment, a state brought about because she was fool enought to fall in love with a man who took all she had to offer and then when she interested him no longer left her. That man was my father."

Lydia said nothing, but it seemed to her as if some wound opened within her body and drew from her all her strength, her pride and confidence.

There was a silence, there was nothing she could say. And then with an obvious effort Christine continued.

"That is not all. Today should have been the happiest day of my life. The man I love asked me to marry him. We were happy . . . terribly happy . . . for just an hour . . ."

Christine paused. For a moment Lydia thought she was going to break down, that the bitter hardness which seemed to make her a different person would vanish; but after a brief hesitation she continued:

"His name is Harry Hampden. He adores his sister and he is consumed by a violent, extremely understandable hatred for the man who ruined her life and who but for me would have been to all intents and purposes her murderer. Earlier today Harry asked to marry me; but when he asked me he didn't know the name of my father."

"Christine, my darling!"

Lydia would have held out her arms, but something in Christine's expression prevented her. This was not a moment for sympathy; it was not a moment when any tenderness she might feel for her daughter could touch this girl who was suffering so intensely.

Lydia understood the agony and humiliation which Christine must be feeling and yet she was powerless to comfort or console her.

She could only lie still, her face whiter than her pillows, conscious that she was cold all over with the shock of what had happened.

"If it had not been for you, Mummy," Christine went on, "I would never have come back here at all. But I wanted you to know what I had planned to do."

"Don't be in a hurry, darling," Lydia pleaded; "give yourself time to think—to try to understand and forgive."

"Forgive!" Christine spoke scornfully. "I will never forgive him, never! He is a beast, and I hope never to see him again!"

"But, Christine . . ."

"I'm sorry, Mummy. I love you, but even that can't reconcile me to staying here, to living on his money. I have been to see Sir Fraser Wilton. I told him what had occurred and he understood. He has arranged for me to go up to Scotland tonight.

"I'm going to be a probationer in St. Mary's Hospital, Edinburgh. Sir Fraser has spoken to the Matron on the telephone. Everything is arranged; it only remains for me to collect the few things I want and to say good-bye to you."

"But, Christine, I can't let you do this!"

Lydia spoke desperately.

"You can't stop me."

It was Christine who was calm and composed.

"I refuse to stay here. I know I'm not of age; but if I ran away the only thing you could do is refuse to support me, and I don't intend to take your money anyway. One day I hope to pay back to you and my father every penny you've spent on my upkeep since I was born."

Slowly the tears came into Lydia's eyes.

"Oh, Christine!"

"I'm sorry, Mummy," Christine said again,

But there was no tenderness in her voice and Lydia knew that any appeal she made would fall on deaf ears. There was nothing she could do but to accept Christine's arrangements. Nothing!

She felt stupid and tired, so desperately tired that she

could not find words to express her feelings. Weakly she asked:

"What time do you go?"

She had accepted the inevitable; but as if Christine had expected and had been prepared for a sharp fight, Lydia saw that she now relaxed a little.

"As soon as I have packed. And there's one thing more, I want you to promise to speak of me as little as possible to my father. I want him to forget my very existence as I pray that I shall one day forget his."

"And I pray that one day you will learn to understand," Lydia replied. "Yes, yes, I know," she added, as Christine made a hasty gesture. "There is little to be said in his defence. I am not attempting to justify his behaviour. I know that through him you have been hurt unbearably; but at the same time, darling, try always in life to understand others."

Christine turned away and Lydia knew that her words would go unheeded.

All that was strong and virile in her nature was concentrated at this moment in a bitter hatred. Christine was like Ivan in that there were for her few half-measures, few half-tones.

Her emotions were strong, far stronger than those of the average person, who in the majority of cases is indecisive and seldom positive.

In everything Ivan did he used his tremendous vitality, pouring forth energy with that mercury-like quickness which made him unforgettably alive. Christine was his daughter.

Lydia knew that her hatred was all-consuming; it semed to emanate from her so strongly and vibratingly that it amounted almost to a force. She herself was, Lydia felt, in danger from such a hatred.

It could not help reacting upon her whole nature. Yet what could she do, what could she say?

The flame which burned so clearly and vividly in such people as Ivan and Christine could not be easily dimmed or quenched. It was there, making its possessor outstanding, a personality, a power, too, either for good or for evil.

"However close we are to them," Lydia thought, "we are always outside."

Suddenly she held out both her hands to her daughter.

"Darling," she begged, "please don't shut me out. Once you were my baby."

Christine came forward to take her mother's hands. She held them for a moment and then bent her head and laid her soft cheek against them.

"Poor Mummy," she said. "I understand what you are feeling, but I can't do anything about it. I have got to go. Perhaps it was inevitable that Father and I could not live together in the same house."

She spoke softly with a perceptive note in her voice.

"What makes you think that?" Lydia asked quickly.

"I loathe him and I despise him," Christine said, "but I am more like him than I am like you. Philip is your child. He's English, very English. I am not."

"Can't you then try to understand?" Lydia asked.

But the moment of softness was past. Christine straightened herself.

"I love Harry Hampden," she said, and her voice was sharp. "I think it unlikely that I shall ever love any-one else or that I shall ever see him again."

Lydia would have spoken, but Christine turned away from the bed.

"I'm going to pack," she said. "I ordered a taxi as I came up from the station and I shall be leaving in about an hour's time. I will come in and say good-bye."

"But, Christine, wait!"

Lydia's words were lost. Already Christine had crossed the room, opened the door and was gone. She was alone.

She felt the full horror of her own thought descend upon her. "How could Ivan have done this? How could he?"

Yet she knew it was true. It was just one of the many episodes which seemed to him so unimportant, so trivial once they were past, carried away once they had gone from him on the swiftly moving stream of time. Ivan never looked back.

The past had no interest or fascination for him, he was concerned only with the present. He lived emotionally, and past emotions are hard to recapture.

What could she say to him, and what indeed could he say to her? There was only one thing she could do, and that was to cling to her understanding of him. If she lost that, she lost everything.

The door opened and Rose came in. She began to draw the curtains and Lydia knew by the sharpness of her movements that she was annoyed.

Always when there were scenes or upsets Rose would be angry, and the thought came to Lydia that Rose was the one true woman friend she possessed, the one woman who really cared for her selflessly and unceasingly, the one woman in front of whom there need be no pretence or hypocrisy.

"Where is the Master?" Lydia asked.

"In the studio, playing."

Rose came from the window towards the bed.

"Can I bring you something? You don't look well."

"Yes, I know," Lydia said quickly. "But I am all right. Don't worry about me."

"It's about time somebody did worry about you, if you ask me!" Rose exclaimed. "Upsetting you with all their selfish goings-on! If it isn't one thing, it's another! One day I shall give every one of them a piece of my mind!"

Lydia smiled. She was used to Rose grumbling on her behalf and somehow it was very comforting. Whatever else happened, Rose remained the same. Sharp, undemonstrative, yet with a heart of gold beneath it all, a heart which held her interests to be of paramount importance.

"I am all right," Lydia repeated.

Rose sniffed. She left the room without comment,

and Lydia felt that she was like a faithful watchdog whose hackles rose at the approach of danger.

All the same, she felt very tired. It had been a long day. So much had happened and all of it had hurt her in different ways. She sighed.

Only Philip was happy and she must try to be glad of his happiness, although it meant that the little boy whom she had loved and who had been so exclusively hers had become a man and belonged to another woman.

The door opened quietly and Ivan came in. For the first time in her life Lydia felt herself shrink at the sight of him.

This moment, she knew, had to be faced, and yet she would have given anything not to have to face it when she felt so tired, so weak, limp and unsure of herself.

Ivan was scowling. As he moved across the room Lydia knew that he had come to her against his own inclination.

He would want to forget what had occurred, he would want to lose himself in his music; and yet she knew some vulnerable part of him could not be repressed, that it had forced him back to her side to seek an explanation—perhaps even to make one.

He had not wanted to come; he was scowling because he was angry with himself and therefore in the most difficult of all his moods.

"Has she gone?"

He asked the question sharply.

"Christine is packing," Lydia replied. "She's going to Scotland tonight."

Ivan did not asked the expected question, so she continued:

"She's going into a hospital as probationer, she wishes to be a nurse."

"And she has told you why she has made this sudden decision?"

Lydia nodded.

"Yes, Ivan; I think you ought to know it too."

267

"Very well."

He sat down beside her bed.

Quietly Lydia told him of how Christine had healed the Negroes while she was in America.

She went on to tell him of Christine's visits to London when she first returned home and how she had been unable to establish contact with her daughter until finally Christine had told her of her success with the girl who had been lying unconscious for nearly four years.

"The girl's name was Stella Hampden," Lydia said.

She did not make the announcement dramatically; she told him quietly and waited.

Ivan repeated the name beneath his breath.

"Stella Hampden!"

"I expect you remember her," Lydia went on. "But that's not all. The girl has a brother, his name is Harry."

She saw by the look on Ivan's face that he knew this and she guessed that Harry Hampden would have told Ivan what he thought of him after Stella's accident.

"They have fallen in love with each other—Christine and he."

Ivan jumped to his feet.

"I forbid the marriage!" he said. "Do you understand? I absolutely forbid it!'

Lydia sighed.

"There is no question of marriage—now."

Ivan looked at her for a moment as if he had not really comprehended the whole implication of what had occurred. Then he looked away and Lydia knew that he understood.

"All the same . . ." he began;

Lydia felt with a sudden shrinking that he was going to try to deprecate Christine's behaviour.

Then quite suddenly, quite unaccountably, he capitulated. He turned towards the bed and kneeling down beside it put his face against his wife's.

"I'm sorry, darling," he said. "It's a mess, isn't it?"

"Oh, Ivan!"

Lydia was relieved at his capitulation and the childlike simplicity of his tones brought the warm tears flooding to her eyes. He raised his head and looked at her.

"I am no good,' he said. "I never have been, you know that. Why you've put up with me for so long I don't know."

"But, darling, I love you, I've always loved you."

"These women mean nothing. I think they've got something to give me, something that I need, something that I want. . . . I can't explain it; and then I find it isn't there, it's gone, it's vanished and there is only you—you who have never failed me, even when I behave to you like the swine I am."

Lydia put out her arms and drew his head down to her breast. She had no words to speak, her heart seemed too full.

This was the Ivan she understood, the man who had need of her; the little boy who came back ashamed of his naughtiness and making no attempt to pretend it hadn't happened.

She thought of the pain she had suffered because of him, the women whose hearts he had broken and the lives he had ruined. She thought of Stella Hampden and Christine. But somehow it was useless to pretend that any of them mattered beside Ivan—beside his love for her, hers for him.

"Why can't I behave normally?" Ivan went on. "Why can't I be like other men—stodgy and content, leading normal and uneventful lives? I can't, you know I can't.

"I've tried to tell myself it will never happen again, but it does. It's something in a woman's smile, the promise in her eyes, the touch of her hand; and I have to try to capture it, try to make it mine.

"It's the same thing as I hear sometimes in the wind—sometimes at night when I am half asleep. It's what we call 'music' for want of a better word; it's what I struggle to write down in crotchets and quavers, fool that I am—as if one can put something like that on paper!

"And yet I have to try; it draws me, it calls me, I need it with my whole being; I'm hungry for it and I would starve and if needs be die to find it.

"Then, if I am seeking it in a woman, quite suddenly it vanishes, it's gone, and I find that she is nothing but a body which no longer attracts me.

"I am ashamed—terribly ashamed, but what can I do—what?"

Lydia's arms twined around him. There was pain in his voice and she knew that he was opening to her his very heart.

"I have often wondered why you love me," Ivan said after a moment. "I've been unfaithful to you; I've been a bad husband and a bad father. Perhaps I ought never to have had children, they make me feel old."

He raised himself suddenly from her arms.

"That's what I am afraid of now—old age; of growing senile and infantile, of ceasing to hear my own music."

"Old age need not affect your powers."

He brushed the consoling words aside irritably.

"It will come. I've seen it with other men, other musicians. I've seen them try to hold their public; seen them afraid of their own instruments, of their own lack of inspiration.

"Sometimes now it's an effort for me to work; my brain feels tired, I become mechanical. Then I know that I am not as young as I was; soon it will be more difficult still."

"But, Ivan, you're frightening yourself," Lydia said.
"Yes, yes, I know."

He got to his feet and walked restlessly across the room.

"Can't you understand that's why I try to prove to myself that I'm still as virile, still as attractive? What I seek seems to be there in the very young. There is magic in their effortlessness, in their beauty—that is

270

why I wanted Stella Hampden. She was so fresh, so unspoilt. And it was the same with Thyra . . . ."

He paused a moment.

"You knew about Thyra?"

"Yes, darling, I knew she attracted you."

Lydia spoke steadily.

Ivan was still a moment and then he turned towards her again.

"I guessed that she thought I was too old," he said simply. "And yet I would not face it even to myself. When they came on to the verandah this afternoon and told me they were married, I felt as if they were both telling me what a damn' fool I had made of myself. I am getting old, Lydia.

"Very soon there is a likelihood of my being a grandfather. It would be funny if it were not tragic, and funny if I were not so afraid, so terribly afraid of myself."

Lydia did the only thing possible. She held out her arms once again and he dropped down on his knees beside her.

She held him close to her—the man who had never grown up, the genius who could not understand his own powers nor find out from where his own inspiration came.

"I love you."

She heard his lips whisper the words in the soft hollow between her breasts.

She was tired no longer, but possessed of an inexhaustible strength. Whatever the pain, whatever the heartbreak, her life was dedicated irrevocably to the man who loved her.

20

"The lines are still engaged; I'll call you as soon as they are free?"

Lydia put down the receiver with a sigh. She had been trying for over an hour to get through to Avon House.

It was a dull morning with a grey mist obscuring the horizon and she felt that the lowering sky echoed her own mood of depression.

She was desperately worried about Elizabeth and tired though she was she had lain awake all night, miserable and distraught by her anxiety about her sister and by thoughts of Christine hurrying northwards in the Scottish express.

Over and over again Lydia asked herself if she could have done any more, have made a more effective appeal to Christine, so that if she must adhere to her plan of leaving home, she might at least have done so in a more kindly and gentle frame of mind.

Her conscience reproached her, but Lydia knew if the truth was told, nothing and no one could have made Christine swerve from her purpose. She had done her best—but she had failed.

Rose had knocked at the door when Ivan was still there, and when Lydia asked her what she wanted she replied:

"Miss Christine wishes to say good-bye to you, ma'am—alone."

For a moment Lydia had been afraid that Ivan would refuse to go and would make some angry retort, but without a word—almost humbly, so that although Lydia knew he was in the wrong her heart cried out for him—he had gone from the room and a few minutes later Christine had come in.

She was dressed for the journey in plain, suitable travelling clothes and looked extremely pretty yet at the same time hard, composed and efficient.

"But she is so young in reality," Lydia told herself, and held out her hands pleadingly.

"Darling, I don't want to be a nuisance," she said. "I only want your happiness. But won't you reconsider your decision? Stay here just a few days so that you and I can talk things over."

Christine took her mother's hands in hers, but Lydia felt as if she touched a stranger.

"I have got to go, Mummy, you know that. Don't let's spend our last moments here together arguing."

"But I shall see you again soon, and you will write to me, won't you?"

"May I think about that before I make any promises?" Christine replied.

Lydia felt the tears gather in her eyes. This was her own child, her own baby going away from her, and going in anger and cruel bitterness of mind.

"Will you always remember one thing, Christine?" she said after a moment in which she grappled with her self-control; "that I love you. You meant a tremendous amount to me when you were a baby and before you went to America.

"Perhaps it was a mistake to send you away; we have grown apart. But I did it for your own good, and if you go out of my life now I shall miss you more than it is possible for me to tell you."

"I will try to remember that," Christine replied coldly. "At the same time, as long as you and my father live together it will be very difficult for us to be friends."

Lydia relinquished her daughter's hands, then with an effort she said:

"There is one thing in particular I want to say to you, one thing which I do want you to consider and consider very seriously. When you were telling me about your strange healing powers you said:

273

" 'I can't help thinking there must be a reason for them. Why should I be given this power? Why me of all people?'

"Have you thought now that the reason may be very obvious why you of all people should be chosen to heal Stella Hampden?"

Christine looked at her mother in a startled fashion. Lydia saw that the idea gripped her; and then, as if she did not wish to accept such an explanation and must thrust it from her, she replied:

"Surely to suggest that I have been sent into the world merely to make amends for my father's failings is carrying the idea of coincidence too far."

"Not too far for God?" Lydia suggested.

"I won't believe in a God who will let such things happen," Christine said hotly; and then suddenly her eyes dropped before her mother's. "I can't argue about it because I don't know what I think . . . Today when Philip was being married I felt . . . But no, it's impossible to put into words. . . ."

She frowned as if concentrating fiercely, then added as if to herself alone:

"Perhaps . . . perhaps religion is the answer to it all. . . . At any rate, one can but try it . . . as an explanation."

For the moment she had spoken simply and naturally; but the next, as if she regretted dropping her guard and revealing to Lydia even a brief glimpse of the bewilderment of her feelings and thoughts, she reassumed her armour of frozen bitterness.

"Good-bye, Mummy. Don't worry about me; I am going to be perfectly all right. I shall have a lot of hard work to do and one day it may be easier to forget the misery I have been forced to suffer."

"Good-bye, darling."

Lydia reached up her arms, but Christine dropped a light kiss on her cheek and turned away.

"You will take care of yourself?" Lydia pleaded; "very good care?"

"Does it matter one way or another?" Christine asked with a shrug of her shoulders.

"And money?" Lydia questioned frantically. "Have you got enough money, darling?"

"Plenty, thank you" Christine replied. "I have some left from what Aunt Johanna gave me for the journey home. But in case you are worried I have already made up my mind to sell my jewellery.

"I haven't got much, only the brooches and bracelets that you have given me since I was a child. Luckily I can consider them your gifts and not my father's because he certainly took no part in choosing them."

With Christine's hand on the door-handle Lydia tried to think of something to say, but she was choked by her tears. All she could murmur was:

"God bless you, darling."

"Good-bye, Mummy."

Christine raised her hand in farewell and then she was gone.

Lydia cried for what seemed to her a long time and then Rose came in, bringing her a cup of tea—Rose's invariable panacea for ills.

"Now don't you go upsetting yourself," Rose said, setting the cup down by Lydia's side and fetching her a clean handkerchief from a drawer of the dressing-table.

Lydia made no effort to hide her tears.

"She's so young," she said, "so terribly young, and desperately unhappy. And yet what can I do? There's nothing I *can* do."

"Miss Christine may be young in years, but she's older in her mind," Rose said wisely. "She's taken a hard knock, but she'll work out her own salvation. There's nothing you can do to help her except be ready to welcome her back when she chooses to return."

Lydia did not ask how Rose knew what happened. Rose always did know everything. If anything occurred in the house or to the household, it was known to Rose as soon as it happened.

As Rose tidied the bedspread she added:

"Miss Christine may be the last born, but Mr. Philip's younger than her in many ways; and what's more, those who travel the furthest suffers the most don't you forget that."

When Rose had gone from the room Lydia thought over her words. Would Christine travel far?

Yes, she supposed Rose was right. Christine had personality. The girl was—as she had put it herself—like Ivan in many ways. Lydia thought that Philip and she were the quiet ones, the home makers, the Marthas of this world, content with the small domestic circle, wanting only love and kindness and the peace of contentment.

They left it to Ivan and Christine to seek for ecstasies, to want more than it was possible to obtain, to aim at that which always lay just out of reach.

And yet, for all that, Christine was her child and it was for the baby she had nursed that Lydia yearned all night.

She was white-faced and weary-eyed when Ivan came to her room early next morning after breakfast. He was going to London and wanted to say good-bye.

He said it hurriedly and with a strange shyness as if he were ashamed both of himself and of the revelations he had made to her the night before.

It was so unlike him to trouble about anything that was past, however momentous, however soul-searing, that Lydia realised that on this occasion he had been shaken out of his egotism and that Christine's outburst had left a mark which for once had not been quickly forgotten.

And now she must wait for news of Elizabeth.

"Troubles never come singly," she thought.

And yet perhaps a multiplicity of problems kept them in their true perspective and pevented them from assuming mountainous proportions.

The telephone rang sharply. Lydia picked up the receiver quickly. But it was only a call for Ivan and she

276

told the enquirer briefly where he could be found in London.

She was worried about Elizabeth, but she told herself that perhaps no news was good news. If she had been really bad, Matron would have got through before this.

Lydia propelled her chair across the drawing-room to rearrange some flowers in a big silver bowl, and as she did so the parlourmaid opened the door.

"There's a gentleman to see you ma'am. He enquired for Miss Christine and when I told him she'd gone away he asked if he could see you."

"What is his name?"

"Wing Commander Hampden, ma'am."

"Will you ask him to come in?"

Lydia moved herself back to her favourite position a little to the left of the fireplace. She watched the door and saw Harry Hampden enter. She liked his grave, clear-cut face on sight. He moved slowly across the room to her, leaning heavily on his stick.

"It is very kind of you to see me, Mrs. Stanfield."

"Won't you sit down? I'm sorry that I can't rise to greet you."

She saw his surprise as he glanced at her wheel-chair.

"You've been ill?" he asked politely.

"Shall we say I'm permanently disabled?" Lydia replied with a smile.

He looked embarrassed.

"I'm sorry. I had no idea. Christine didn t tell me."

The word's slipped out and she thought that he changed colour as he mentioned Christine's name. He sat down in the chair she indicated.

"There is a box of cigarettes beside you," Lydia suggested.

"I won't smoke, thank you. I won't take up too much of your time. There's only one thing I want to know and I think you can guess what it is . . . Where can I find Christine?"

"Do you really want to see her?"

Harry looked at Lydia enquiringly.

277

"Has she told you what happened?"

Lydia nodded.

"Yes, she told me. It must have been a terrible shock for both of you."

She noticed that Harry's hands clenched suddenly as if he not only remembered the shock of what had occurred but reacted to his own anger and disgust. Then he relaxed.

"May I speak of it?" he asked. "I shall quite understand if you say no."

"I'd like you to talk quite openly," Lydia replied. "You see, Wing Commander, I am deeply distressed about my daughter. What happened to her yesterday at your house, what she learnt there, has caused her to go away—to leave home."

"For good?" Harry ejaculated.

"I'm afraid so," Lydia replied. "At any rate it is her present intention. Whether time will bring her a sense of forgiveness and a greater understanding is problematical. In the meantime I am powerless to do anything for her except to pray that she may be safe and well."

Harry smoothed back his hair from his forehead with an anxious gesture.

"Listen, Mrs. Stanfield. I'm afraid a lot of this is my fault. I said things yesterday which I didn't mean. . . . They burst from me because I was so surprised and astounded at the idea that Christine could be in any way connected with the man who ruined my sister. . . .

"You will understand, I think, when I tell you that when Christine told me her father's name I forgot everything but my own loathing of that particular man. . . .

"I forgot that I loved Christine . . . forgot she had just said that she loved me. I raged at her. I ought to have had more control of myself. . . . I see that now.

"It was only when Christine had gone out of the

278

house before I could stop her that I realised what I had done. . . .

"I've been through hell trying to find out where she was, where she lived. Finally Sir Fraser Wilton saw me this morning and after a great deal of persuasion he gave me Christine's address."

Harry spoke passionately and urgently with a compelling sincerity. Lydia's first impression that he was decent and trustworthy had deepened as he talked and now she knew that she liked him. He was straightforward; a man whom one could trust. She was as certain of that as she was certain of anything in life.

"I want to ask you something," she said. "You will forgive me if it sounds impertinent?"

"But of course."

"Do you still want to marry my daughter?"

There was not a moment's hesitation. Harry looked Lydia straight in the eyes and answered:

"She is the only woman I'll ever want to marry."

"And you think, knowing what you do, that there is a chance of happiness for you both?"

"I am certain of that," Harry answered. "I am not saying that I want to see Christine's father, that I should ever find it easy to speak to him or to be friendly. I loved Christine not knowing who her parents were. I can't see why, now that I know the truth, it should make any difference to my love."

"I agree with you," Lydia said. "At the same time it is going to be very hard for you to convince Christine."

"Why do you think that?"

Lydia paused for a moment in an effort to collect her words; then she said:

"Christine has had a tremendous shock. She is suffering very deeply. I can't help feeling that you will find it difficult to make her forgive you. She will not be easily convinced any more than at the moment she is in the frame of mind to forgive her father."

"Surely there is no parallel between us?" Harry asked quickly.

"Haven't you both failed her?"

Harry looked shamefaced.

"I realise now," Lydia went on, "that for a long time Christine has been feeling distressed and perhaps unnaturally curious about her father's behaviour.

"It is very usual for girls—and boys for that matter—when they are young to be extremely shocked at any irregularity that concerns sex.

"No one is more pure than the very young. I ought to have anticipated this and either explained things more comprehensively to Christine or kept her in ignorance of them.

"Now it is too late; her whole character, her whole life, will be affected by this.

"We have got to face the fact just as you must realise that when the shock came—when she was emotionally shattered by her father's behaviour—she could not turn for consolation to the man she loved, but must suffer from him further humiliation both to her pride and to her sense of decency."

"I understand," Harry said. "God knows how I could have been such a fool! But it was such a surprise to me too. Christine had never spoken of her father. If I had thought of him at all, I imagined him as some country squire living quietly in the seclusion of his estates."

"I understand your point of view only too well," Lydia said. "I am only trying to make you see that even when you find Christine things are not going to be easy."

"I will wait for her," Harry said. "I believe she loves me and that is all that matters."

Lydia's face lightened with one of her exquisite smiles.

"If you really believe that, then I promise you that everything will come right. It is the one thing that I am certain of in life, the one thing I have found to be irrevocably true—that love is the only thing that matters.

"Go on loving Christine, and if you love her enough,

if you care for her enough, one day you will find happiness together."

"Thank you," Harry said quietly. "And now, Mrs. Stanfield, will you tell me where I can find her?"

"She has gone to Edinburgh," Lydia replied. "I believe that Sir Fraser Wilton must have meant us to meet, and perhaps it was wise of him; he was the one person who knew that Christine would not be here this morning.

"He personally had arranged for her to go as a probationer to St. Mary's Hospital in Edinburgh."

"A hospital nurse!" Harry ejaculated. "Somehow I can't imagine Christine being a nurse."

"I do not think it will hurt her," Lydia said. "You have got to remember that she already has had an experience of sick people which is accorded to very, very few. There is a lot more for her to learn about people whether they are ill or well.

"Experience will do her good and she may find there among the sick and suffering her own peace of mind."

"I shall go to Edinburgh and see her at once," Harry announced.

Lydia nodded.

"Yes, I should do that. I should see her and tell her that you love her, but I should ask nothing in return. Give her time to find her feet, to recover a little from the shock of what she has experienced."

Harry looked at Lydia wistfully.

"Do you think if will be a long time before she will want to marry me?"

"Who can tell?" Lydia replied. "At the same time don't try to force her, let her come to you willingly. The young take things very hard. It's not until we get nearly to old age that we evoke a philosophy."

"And then?" Harry asked.

Lydia smiled.

"Things hurt just as much, but we try to convince ourselves they don't."

Slowly Harry got to his feet.

"You've been very kind to me, Mrs. Stanfield. Will you forgive me if I ask you a question?"

"Of course What is it?"

"Do you mind if I marry Christine?"

"I shall be glad if you do," Lydia answered. "I am going to be very frank with you, Harry—may I call you that? I know it is what Christine calls you. I have lost Christine; she can never feel the same about her father, and I have got to give up either him or my daughter.

"As he will always be my first and foremost consideration you needn't ask me which choice I shall make.

"Some day—perhaps when we are older, when we are wiser and realise how little in the sum total of existence all these tragedies and heartburnings matter—we may come together.

"But until then Christine will be terribly lonely—a girl without a background.

"I made the same choice myself once for a very different reason. It is not easy—and if you are there to look after Christine, to take care of her and to love her, I shall be very grateful."

"Thank you." Harry put out his hand and when Lydia put hers into it gripped it hard. "Thank you," he said again.

She knew that he was trying to express a gratitude for which he could find no words. He limped towards the door. It was only when he reached it that Lydia stopped him.

"Harry," she said urgently. "When you've seen Christine, when you've found her and heard what she has to say, would you feel it disloyal to write to me?"

"Of course I will," Harry replied.

He went out of the room, shutting the door quietly behind him.

Lydia looked up at the clock over the mantelpiece. Once again she gave the number of Avon House and this time after several minute's delay she was successful in getting connected. She was put through to the Matron.

"Oh, is that you, Mrs. Stanfield? I've been trying to get you all the morning."

"So have I. How is my sister?"

"I'm sorry to say that Lady Avon had a bad night. Abscesses are forming. I think if you can manage it, Mrs. Stanfield, you should come over as soon as possible."

"Do you mean that her condition is critical?"

"The doctor should be here at any minute," Matron replied, "and I'd rather you waited to hear his verdict, Mrs. Stanfield. At the same time I'd like you to be here . . . just in case."

Lydia knew only too well what Matron meant. She was not the type of woman who was prone to exaggeration or to making an unnecessary fuss. Lydia rang the bell for Rose and picking up the receiver again dialled the local garage.

She had been promised a car if she needed one, and now she was assured that it would be round in about twenty minutes.

Rose was prepared to argue as to the advisability of her making the journey once again, but Lydia silenced her.

"Her Ladyship's life is in danger. If anything happened and I was not there I'd never forgive myself."

After that Rose said nothing, but her silence was eloquent as she propelled Lydia from the drawing-room to her bedroom.

She got her ready and then went to fetch her own hat and coat while Lydia scribbled a note for Ivan in case he should be back before her.

"If Mr. Philip rings up, tell him where I have gone," she instructed the parlourmaid; and before eleven o'clock they had started off for Avon House.

They drove in silence for Lydia was preoccupied with her own thoughts. Somehow she felt a strange premonition about Elizabeth. She was afraid, a thing she had never been before.

She wondered if it was just her overwrought and

overtired nerves or whether she was in reality being clairvoyant.

She wondered if there would be any news of Angus. She had meant to ring Lawrence Granger but had kept the telephone free all the morning for her call to Avon House; and after it had come she had been too agitated at the thought of getting there as quickly as possible to remember to telephone Lawrence.

The dull mist of the morning changed towards mid-day to a fine rain. The countryside was obliterated and the window-panes of the taxi were spattered with rain-drops.

Memories of Elizabeth as a little girl kept coming to Lydia. Elizabeth climbing into her bed at night saying "I'se frightened. There's a bear peeping at me round the wardrobe."

Elizabeth coming to her for comfort when she had fallen down and hurt her knee. Elizabeth bringing her in from the garden the first snowdrops of spring and at another time a bird she had discovered with a broken wing.

She had been so busy leading her own life that it was painful now to remember what little time she had given to her younger sister.

Once, she remembered, Elizabeth, only a few years old at the time, had flung her arms round her neck and asked:

" 'Oo do love Lizabeth, don't 'oo, Lydia?"

"Of course I do, you little silly."

" 'Cause I love 'oo best in all the world. Better than Daddy, better than Nannie, better than Betsy Jane."

The last named was Elizabeth's most beloved doll and Lydia had laughed tenderly.

"That's a compliment. And what will Betsy Jane say about it?"

"Betsy Jane 'stands," Elizabeth replied solemnly, " 'cause she loves 'oo too."

Strange how such memories kept coming back over the years and how much they hurt.

"Have I failed Elizabeth also?" Lydia asked herself, and felt as if Elizabeth and Christine both accused her of deserting them. Ivan, always Ivan!

His name was the answer to everything she had done or not done. And yet was it enough excuse for having forgotten and deserted the little sister who had no one else to love her? for having lost—perhaps for ever—her own daughter?

"Now what are you worrying yourself about?"

Rose's voice broke in on her reflections.

"If it's about her Ladyship, she's young and she's strong. And anyway, if you worry yourself into the grave it will do no good to anyone."

Lydia tried to laugh.

"I know, Rose, but I can't help worrying. From what Matron said I gather she is very bad."

"She'll pull through, you mark my words," Rose said.

"But it would have to happen when you'd had a bad night—fussing over Miss Christine and her troubles. But there, young people are all the same, they think of no one but themselves."

"What did you think of the Wing Commander, Rose?"

Lydia was sure that Rose was longing to discuss him, for she guessed that he would not have come to the house and left it without Rose having had a good look at him.

"I showed him out, as it happens," Rose said composedly. "A nice young man, I should say, and one who'd be able to cope with Miss Christine. She'll not be easy to manage, so don't you imagine it."

"I don't," Lydia replied.

"He'll suit her when she comes round to marrying him," Rose said. "She says to me last night when she was packing:

" 'I'm never going to marry anyone, Rose. Men are beasts. I hate the lot of them!'

285

"And I answered her: 'Men may be beasts all right, Miss Christine, but don't imagine for one moment that women can get on without them, because they can't.' "

"What did she say?" Lydia asked.

"Oh, she replied sharp like.

" 'You've never married, Rose.' So I answers her honestly:

" 'That's not my fault, Miss Christine. You don't suppose I wouldn't have preferred to have a home of my own and children to being an old maid? I had the opportunity once and I let it slip. There's seldom been a day that I haven't told myself that I've deserved my punishment for being high and mighty.' "

"Oh, Rose, I'm sorry," Lydia exclaimed. "I had no idea."

"Who has?" Rose said. "I don't go talking about myself to everybody. But I don't want Miss Christine to get it into her head that she could be an old maid and like it.

"Of course, there's men and men," Rose added darkly, "and some of them I wouldn't touch with the end of a barge-pole, not if they went down on their knees to me.

"But that Wing Commander seemed a decent sort of chap, and I dare say that when she starts being sensible again Miss Christine will learn which side her bread's buttered."

"Oh, Rose, you're such a comfort to me," Lydia said, smiling, and then saw with relief that they were turning in at the Park gates of Avon House.

She could hardly wait while they got her wheelchair down from the roof of the taxi and carried her into the hall, where she saw Matron coming downstairs to greet her. Lydia held out her hand.

"Good morning, Matron. How is she now?"

She hardly dared to ask the question.

"Will you come upstairs, Mrs. Stanfield?" Matron asked, and both her face and her voice were grave. "I have a fire in the room opposite Lady Avon's."

286

"Shall I be able to see my sister?"

"In a few moments, I hope, but . . . someone is with her now."

There was a sudden gladness in Matron's voice which told Lydia all she wanted to know before the next sentence came.

"Mr. McLeod is here; he flew from Holland this morning."

"Thank goodness!" Lydia exclaimed; "now everything ought to be all right."

"I hope so, Mrs. Stanfield. I certainly hope so," Matron replied.

There was a fire burning brightly in a small dressing-room opposite Elizabeth's room. Matron pushed Lydia's chair near the fire and sent one of the nurses for a cup of tea.

"If you will forgive me," she said, "I will go back to the sick room. Mr. McLeod might want something."

"Where is Lord Avon?" Lydia asked.

"He was here a few minutes ago," Matron replied; and even as she turned towards the door Arthur came in.

"Hello, Lydia," he said. "I thought I heard a car drive up. I'm glad you've come. They seemed to think it was advisable to send for you."

"I'm sorry that Elizabeth had a bad night."

"Can't understand what's happening," Arthur Avon said testily. "These damned doctors don't seem to know their own business. Why, a little thing like that ought to have been cured days ago. I hear that fellow McLeod is here, and a good thing too. He's the best of the bunch, but I haven't got much faith in any of them. Now when I was a boy . . ."

He broke off suddenly. The door of Elizabeth's room had opened and Angus McLeod came out.

He walked slowly across the passage and through the open door. Lydia watched him come and saw the expression on his face.

She knew before he spoke that Elizabeth was dead.

21

Lydia sat on the verandah and looked over the garden
to where the pine trees were dark against the blue sky.

In the valley there was a gleam of silver from the
winding river and the sun touched the distant roofs,
making them sparkle and glint against the green countryside.

It was a day of sunshine, a day for happiness; and yet
Lydia's thoughts were with the sombre procession
which would at that moment be winding its way down
the long drive from Avon House towards the little grey
stone church where for hundreds of years the members
of the Avon family had been interred.

She would not have gone to the funeral even had she
felt well enough to stand the strain of the journey, and
Ivan had a big concert in London that afternoon from
which it was impossible for him to excuse himself.

Lawrence Granger, their ever faithful friend, had
gone to represent them both; and Lydia, alone with her
thoughts and prayers, regretted neither her own ab-
sence nor Ivan's.

She would have hated her last memory of Elizabeth
to be of the purple-palled coffin carried by the em-
ployees on Arthur's estate.

Lydia had chosen the usual conventional wreath of
white-lilies, and then at the last moment she had given
Lawrence a small bunch of red roses to place on Elizabeth's coffin.

He had taken the flowers without comment, but she
sensed his unspoken criticism and said meaningly:

"They *are* appropriate."

He had raised his eyes and looked at her and she
knew that he was wondering how she could say that,

considering the vast difference in Elizabeth and Arthur's age and the dull, pompous life Elizabeth had led.

Red roses were for love, for passion, for a rapture very far removed from Elizabeth's conventional, monotonous marriage.

"She learnt of love before she died," Lydia explained softly.

"I'm glad."

Lawrence Granger also spoke softly; it was obvious that simply and with an inbred trust he accepted her statement. Looking at him, tall, grey-haired and slightly austere in his well-cut mourning clothes.

Lydia felt a sudden warmth and affection for this staunch friend who had stood by her for so long and through so many difficulties.

"It's right that you should represent this family, Lawrence," she said impulsively. "You are one of us."

She saw the gladness that lit up his face before he replied:

"Nothing you could say, Lydia, could give me greater pleasure. Your friendship means so much to me."

"Sometimes I wonder if I ask too much of you."

He shook his head.

"You could never do that. I am content to be there when you need me—in the background, but when the occasion arises always and ever ready to help."

There were no words in which Lydia could answer him. Instead she put out her hand and he took it in his.

He had not gone alone to the funeral, for Angus McLeod had been with him.

After the first shattering shock of knowing that Elizabeth was dead Lydia had put aside her own grief to remember Angus and what this must mean to him.

She had known instinctively that he would not stay at Avon House under Arthur's roof and yet she felt that she could not let him go back alone to his house in London. She had drawn him aside a few hours after Elizabeth's death.

"Will you come home with me this evening?" she asked. "We should so like to have you."

"Won't you be staying here?"

Lydia shook her head.

"I don't think Arthur will need me," she said, "and I must go home to my husband; he would hate me to stay away without him even for one night. Please come."

"Thank you," Angus said simply.

Lydia had been correct in thinking that Arthur would not need her. Before they left the house, Arthur's own relations were arriving and there were telegrams and messages to say that more were coming.

It was quite obvious that Arthur intended to have a big family funeral for Elizabeth. It was in the tradition of the family that its members should gather when one of their members died.

Arthur would certainly not be alone and Lydia felt slightly nauseated at the eagerness with which his relations seemed to welcome the opportunity of meeting each other.

There was nothing she could do to be of further assistance to her sister. Through her action in telegraphing to Angus McLeod Elizabeth had died happy, and the thought of that was warmly comforting.

At first the shock of Elizabeth's death had left Angus silent and taciturn, and Lydia with her unvarying instinct and perception had known that he did not want to speak and found a relief in silence.

Wise as to the ways of men she had therefore left him alone.

When at last he was ready to talk he had sought her out and told her all she had longed to know of Elizabeth's last moments.

As Elizabeth had grown worse she had become at times delirious and had called for Angus, crying out for him with a yearning which revealed only too clearly to Matron and the nurses the secret of her love.

But they, well trained and as discreet as any priest in

290

the confessional, let no hint of this reach Arthur or any-one else in the house.

They had kept their patient as quiet as they could, only distressed and apprehensive at the turn her illness was taking.

Then at last Angus had arrived.

As soon as he got Lydia's telegram he applied to his Commanding Officer for compassionate leave and on receiving it had flown home from Holland, arriving at a South of England airport and motoring from there as swiftly as possible to Avon House.

The moment he entered the house, without waiting to give him more than the barest outline of Elizabeth's illness, Matron had led him straight to the sick-room.

One look at Elizabeth had told him the reason for Matron's haste.

She was half unconscious when he entered and he sat for a few minutes at her bedside taking in the details of her condition and wondering desperately, almost wildly—because it mattered so tremendously to him—what he could do to save her life.

Then she had opened her eyes. She had given a little cry of gladness and tried to hold out her arms, but she was too weak to raise them.

He knew what she wanted and he went down on his knees beside her, slipping an arm under her shoulders.

She looked at him for a long time and he saw the love in her eyes, a love spiritualised and intensified be-cause already physical things were slipping away from her.

There was no need for words; they spoke to each other with their hearts and she must have seen in his face the answer to all her questions, for at length she whispered:

"Now I don't mind dying."

"You are not going to die, my darling. I am here to make you well."

She had smiled at him tenderly, the kind of smile—

he told Lydia—that a mother would give a child who was talking delightful nonsense.

"I don't mind," she said again, her voice so low that he could hardly catch the words. And then as if she poured out her last remaining strength she said clearly: "Now I can be with you always."

A few seconds later she died.

When Lydia had gone in to see her sister she had been astounded at the radiant look of happiness on Elizabeth's face.

The lines of pain and suffering had vanished and she looked very young and, indeed, happier than ever Lydia remembered seeing her.

It was easy to understand how completely her love for Angus had transfigured her life, and Lydia seeking to comfort him said:

"You gave her the only real happiness she had ever known. I always felt that Elizabeth was like someone who was acting a part, but acting it because she did not know what else to do, how else to behave. When she met you she came alive for the first time."

Angus had waited a moment before he replied. Then in his calm, quiet way he said:

"I wonder if you will understand, Mrs. Stanfield, when I tell you that I believe she is alive now."

Lydia nodded.

"Elizabeth would not have said what she said to you at the end—that she would be with you always—unless she was very certain it was the truth. Elizabeth never exaggerated and seldom made a statement unless she was sure of her facts. I must acknowledge that at times her precision irritated me, but now. . . ."

Lydia paused.

"Now—it helps us both," Angus McLeod finished.

"I am so sorry for you," Lydia answered. "You knew her such a short time and when she told me how much she loved you, I felt that somehow, sometime, there must be a happy ending waiting for you both."

"Perhaps this is the only possible ending," Angus re-

292

plied. "I loved your sister, as you know; loved her with all my heart and soul; and yet I could not have asked her to spoil our love by committing what would have been to me a dishonourable act. As long as Arthur Avon remained alive Elizabeth could never have been mine."

Lydia sighed.

"Poor Arthur, I'm sorry for him; and yet he was content; Elizabeth gave him all he asked of her."

She thought even as she spoke how shocked Arthur Avon would have been at the idea of Elizabeth linked by death with the man she loved.

He would not understand it and therefore he would not be jealous, but only faintly disgusted at what would be to him false and sentimental emotionalism.

"What does death mean to you?" Lydia asked Angus suddenly.

He answered her without a pause as if he had already considered the question and was sure of his reply.

"An escape."

"To what?"

"To a state in which one can live more fully and—to speak a paradox—where one can be completely alive."

"Thank you. That clarifies something I have wanted to know for a long time," Lydia said. "I have thought about these things, but there are so few people with whom I could discuss them. May I tell you about my daughter?"

"Of course," Angus McLeod said.

Lydia, looking at him as he sat back comfortably in an arm-chair, saw that the lines of pain which had sharpened and altered his expression after Elizabeth's death were not so pronounced.

He looked like a man at peace within himself.

She told him Christine's story, leaving out all mention of the complications that had arisen over Ivan, but saying that for certain personal reasons she had chosen to go into a hospital.

"How do you account for such powers—if that's the right word?" Lydia ended.

"I don't account for them," Angus replied. "I accept them."

"But surely there must be some scientific or medical explanation of such phenomena?"

"You used the right word, Mrs. Stanfield," Angus answered. "Phenomena! Now the medical profession does its best to remain sane and sensible in a world in which it is being continually confronted with insanity, the supernormal and what is commonly known as the supernatural.

"Every day miracles happen; miracles which if they were recounted to the public would arouse a storm of excitement and speculation. We see, we hear, and we remain silent. Why? Because there is no language in which one can record such things.

"Words were invented as a vehicle and they prove themselves in most cases very adequate for our ordinary needs; but once get away from the ordinary and come up against the extraordinary and you will find a complete lack of words in which to explain it.

"We have an example of it here, between you and me. A few moments ago I told you that I thought Elizabeth was more alive than ever before.

"To the average person that is a complete contradiction in terms.

"You understood what I meant; you understood that I was trying to say that Elizabeth had at last through what we call death escaped from the confines of her body, from the environment in which she had always been repressed, into a state of spiritual activity.

"I know that Elizabeth is alive, I feel her near me. I believe with every fibre of my being that she will be with me always until I am allowed to join her.

"But can I explain that to the average person—the man and woman in the street, to the majority of my medical colleagues or to the people who have never experienced anything like it themselves?

"No, I could not explain it for the simple reason that I have no words—they don't exist. In trying to translate my faith into words I am attempting the impossible."

"Then you believe that what my daughter was able to do was just another instance of the encroachment of the supernormal upon the normal or commonplace?"

"That's the right word," Angus approved. "The supernormal is all round us, so near and so much a part of ourselves that to every one of us sooner or later in this life there comes some astounding experience, some sensation which we cannot explain or express and therefore keep to ourselves.

"I could no more begin to explain why your daughter—one particular individual—should be able to heal sick people than I could explain why amazing cures are performed day after day by some newly found drug and then in some particular case it will fail utterly.

"Conditions may be the same, the patients may seem to have the same degree of stamina, the same chance of survival, but as the Bible says:

" 'One shall be taken and the other left.' "

"Who can explain it by saying that these things are meant to be? They happen, and if we are wise we accept them."

"Do you think my daughter's powers will intensify as she gets older?" Lydia asked.

"On the contrary," Angus answered. "As her gift of healing is entirely instinctive and without skill, there is every likelihood of the power leaving her or of its being transmitted into other channels.

"I have heard of cases where a healing force is at its strongest during adolescence, then as the transmitter grows older it becomes spasmodic and in old age vanishes altogether. But of course there are no rules or regulations and every case is different.

"My advice to you is to let your daughter's life develop without interference or argument; sooner or later she will discover the meaning of it all for herself; no one can do that for her.

"It is, I believe, a more spiritual than physical condition and therefore almost entirely personal."

"I must remember to tell Christine that," Lydia thought.

She decided that, whether she had an answer to her letters or not she would write to her daughter.

"Perhaps they will help her," she thought humbly, "but at any rate *I* shall have kept in touch."

She was startled by the next question that Angus McLeod asked her.

"Has your daughter ever tried to heal you?"

"No, of course not," Lydia said quickly; then added: "I don't know why I say it so vehemently, but I never thought of such a thing. Anyway, I am past all healing. The doctors made that very clear to me."

"Who were they?"

Lydia mentioned the names of two eminent and extremely well-known surgeons.

"Um. I know them both," Angus said. "Clever men, but already old-fashioned and high enough on the pinnacle of their fame for them not to take a chance unless it is absolutely necessary."

"What do you mean by that?" Lydia asked.

Angus leant forward in the chair in which he was sitting and reached for a cigarette.

"Will you let me examine you?" he asked casually.

Lydia hesitated a moment. She guessed that his air of indifference and his concentration on the lighting of his cigarette were merely a ruse to give her time.

"Why?" she asked after a moment.

"I am curious," Angus McLeod replied. "I have seen various cases which appeared as bad as yours and yet yielded effectively to an operation and treatment. Am I raising your hopes?"

Lydia shook her head.

"I wouldn't let them be raised," she replied. "You can see the X-ray photographs if you like. They are in the top drawer of that big chest over there. They mean very little to me, but when the surgeons showed them to me they assured me it was very obvious why nothing more could be done. Have a look at them and then you will understand."

Angus fetched the X-ray photographs and looked at them for a long time. When he had finished he said:

"I would still like to examine you."

"Not this evening," Lydia said quickly. "Ivan might be home any time. Please don't say anything in front of him. He was so bitterly distressed by my accident; he hoped against hope that I might get well.

"He told the surgeons that he would take me any-where—anywhere in the world, if there was a chance of my being able to use my legs again; but they told him it was hopeless.

"At first he railed against Fate even more than I did, but now he has accepted it as inevitable and I should hate him to get excited again merely to be disappointed."

"I understand," Angus said sympathetically.

Instead he had come to Lydia's room early that morning before he left for the funeral. Ivan had gone to London immediately after breakfast and Lydia, with her breakfast tray beside her, had not been expecting a visitor.

"What are we waiting for?" Angus had asked when Lydia looked surprised. "My leave won't last indefinitely. Besides, I want to give you something to think about today when you are here all alone."

She had let him do as he wished without much hope in her heart, quite certain that after his examination he would agree with the previous verdict.

He took a long time, and when he had finished he went into her bathroom to wash his hands.

"Well," he asked as he returned, "are you curious?"

"I suppose so," Lydia smiled. "Tell me the worst."

"On the contrary. I can tell you the best," he replied. "I am absolutely convinced that if you will allow me to operate on you there is every chance of your being able to walk again."

Lydia caught her breath.

"Do you mean that?"

"I do," he replied. "I will mean extensive treatment and manipulation and it will be of course a very slow business. I am not going to tell you that you will ever be particularly active—stairs, for instance, may prove an impossibility for many years; but with hard work and much perserverance on your part you will be able to walk and move about."

"Oh, Angus!"

It was the first time she had used his Christian name and it slipped out unexpectedly.

"Yes, Lydia," he replied with a smile. "It is a bit of a shock, isn't it? But knocking down other people's pre-conceived ideas is one of my specialities. Are you going to let me do it?"

"How soon would I be able to walk?"

"It's difficult to say. Three months . . . six. . . .It depends a great deal on how much swelling there is and how quickly the unused muscles react to treatment. If only I could have operated on you when the accident occurred . . . but, still, it's no use having any regrets; we can only look forward."

"And when would you want to operate?"

"Just as soon as I can. I have got to get back to the front, so there is every reason for speed. If you will give me your permission to go ahead I will arrange for you to go into a nursing home tomorrow or the next day."

"And if the operation fails?"

"There is, of course, always the chance of that happening," Angus said seriously, "in which case you wouldn't be any worse off than you are now. You will suffer a certain amount of inconvenience, a little pain; but at least you will have taken a fighting chance. Surely it is worth it?"

"Tomorrow or the next day," Lydia repeated reflectively. "You must give me time to think. I shall have to tell Ivan."

"Now listen, Lydia." Angus put his hand on hers as if to quell her agitation. "You can take as long to think about it as you like. I am not going to rush you into anything. But I believe I can help you, and you know as well as I do that I would do anything that is within my power for—Elizabeth's sister."

Sitting alone, Lydia wondered now if she had dreamed this, if it was really true that there was a chance of her being herself again, being able to move about, being beside Ivan, doing things with him as she had done before her accident.

It seemed too good to be true, too marvellous to realise; and yet she knew that Angus would never have spoken with such assurance unless he had been certain. She rather shrank from the idea of the long time it would take.

She had a vision of herself, slightly ludicrous, trying to hobble about on sticks, moving slowly and ponderously from room to room.

She had lost her figure; that was inevitable; and she wondered if she would have the courage to show Angus the depths of her vanity and ask how that too could be restored to her.

She thought of herself, slim, pliant, quick-moving, as she had been before her accident; she thought of Ivan holding her close to him, her head level with his shoulders.

How often had she raised herself on tiptoe to meet his lips—hungry, passionate, possessive. At such times they had been like gods, glorious in their beauty and in their strength.

She had been a fitting mate for him, bringing him a body as perfect as his own, his equal in gifts, yet always utterly content to know him master—he the possessor, she the possessed.

Could they be hers again? Could she rouse again in Ivan that flame of desire, that rapture and ecstasy which had been theirs until her accident?

He loved her still, but now it was a love mellow and

299

sweet, a very different emotion to that wild, fiery, pagan love which ravished her body, her senses and seemed to demand her very soul.

Her whole being cried out for what she had thought had gone for ever. Her pulses throbbed in anticipation of what might be hers once more.

"To walk again!"

She almost said the words out loud; and hearing a step on the verandah looked round to see Ivan approaching her.

"Ivan! I am so glad you are back!" she exclaimed and heard the excitement in her voice.

"So am I."

"Did the concert go off well?"

"Yes, it was a great success," he answered; but she knew from his tone that he was thinking of something else.

She wondered what it was that perturbed him and raised her face eagerly as he came towards her. She offered him her mouth, but he kissed her cheek.

"There's a bit of a wind out here," he said. "Shall we go indoors?"

"If you like," Lydia replied, knowing that even on the warmest days Ivan often felt cold after a concert.

Without waiting for her to propel herself he turned her chair and pushed it into the drawing-room.

The light was dim and translucent from the half-lowered sunblinds. The fragrant heady scent from great bowls of flowers greeted them.

Looking up at Ivan, Lydia thought how handsome he was with his red hair vivid against the soft colourings of the room. He dominated everything; it was impossible not to feel that ordinary clothes and an ordinary environment confined him.

He was frowning, his fingers moved restlessly.

"What is worrying you, darling?" she asked.

Ivan sat down beside her in a low chintz-covered chair.

"I've got something to tell you."

"What is it? Good news or bad?"

"I am not quite certain how to answer that; it's a little bit of both."

"Tell me," Lydia pleaded.

Ivan drew a letter from his pocket.

"No," he said, as Lydia stretched out her hand for it, "I don't want you to read it. I want to tell you. I have been asked—and I know we should consider it an honour—by the Soviet Union at the personal direction of Marshal Stalin to take my orchestra to Russia."

Lydia gave an exclamation.

"Yes, I know," Ivan said. "I was surprised myself. They have invited me to give a short season in each of their three great cities opening in Moscow just as soon as we can get there. It means, of course, that I shall be away for at least three months."

"But, Ivan! Russia!" Lydia exclaimed.

"Yes, I know," Ivan said. "I felt like that myself, and then I saw it from this point of view. I am now a British subject; and although I have always thought of myself as a White Russian my parents were killed not for any sins of their own but because, however much we may deprecate the action taken, the Russian Revolution was the result of much that was wrong and evil in the old regime.

"Today we are looking for a new democracy, a new standard of civilisation, not only in Russia but everywhere in the whole world.

"In returning to the land which murdered my father and mother I go not as an individual, but to demonstrate the highest art to which mankind has yet attained.

"I go to speak to a young nation—not in the language of the old, but in the language of all free men, all civilised men and all progress.

"There is only one universal language, only one Esperanto which touches not men's tongues, but their hearts, and that is—music! Do you understand?"

"Of course I understand," Lydia cried.

Then she reached out her arms.

"Darling, I am glad, glad for your sake. It is a great honour and I know what you will feel in returning if only for a little while to your own land."

"I may be disappointed," Ivan said. "It's difficult not to idealise any place when you are in exile. And yet, how often have I dreamt of my own people! How often have I dreamt of the thick snow in the streets, of the sun gleaming on the golden turrets of the Kremlin!

"How often have I longed for the magic that is only to be found in the air of Russia! But how can any English person understand?"

"You must go, of course you must go," Lydia said half to herself, as if she over-rode her own arguments.

"And you?" Ivan asked. "I hate to leave you alone for three months—it may even be longer."

He rose from his chair and knelt down beside her.

"You're everything to me," he said, "everything that matters in my life. Today when I was thinking I must leave you I realised, perhaps for the first time, how much I love you, how much you mean to me.

"And as I was thinking of you the thought came to me that your accident was a blessing in disguise; because through it I have found my home—for my home is with you.

"In your tranquillity and in the knowledge that you are always here waiting for me, I have found the only security I have ever known in my life.

"Always I have been a man without roots, without a country, a wanderer—an adventurer if you like—looking and seeking for what has always remained out of reach.

"Thus have I thought of myself, sometimes in bitterness, and only now today have I realised that is no longer true. When I came home last week and found you had gone to Avon House—to your sister—I could hardly bear it.

"At first I thought it was jealousy; then I believed it was my own anxiety at the journey you were undertaking; but now I know it was because I have grown so used to coming home—to you.

"Do you understand, my beloved, that it means the whole world to me—to come home, to find you sitting waiting for me, to know that you will always look the same, that you will hold out your arms and there within them I shall find the intangible wonders of real love?

"It may seem selfish to you, it may almost seem cruel; but I love you now more than I could ever have loved you had our lives not been shattered by your injury. Now you are mine, completely and inescapably mine, and I am yours—I belong to you.

"I shall always return to you. Darling, if I must go away to Russia, the thought of you will be there always at the back of my mind, always close in my heart, the thought of the woman whom I love, waiting for me patiently, tranquilly—the one really beautiful, unchanging thing in a world of turmoil and unrest. I love you, Lydia, my wife, I love you!"

Ivan stopped speaking, and pressed his face against the softness of her neck in a tender, familiar gesture. She held him close, looking with unseeing eyes over his head and across the room.

She understood all that he had tried to say in the fullness of his heart, and she knew in that moment what her answer would be to Angus when he returned.

She knew, too, that, whatever the pain of renunciation, the sacrifice of self was worth the love and deep emotion in Ivan's voice.

Then Ivan's lips became more insistent.

"I love you," he said again kissing her eyes, her hair, her ears, the hollow between her breasts and again her neck.

"You love me!" he cried triumphantly as he felt her quiver beneath his mouth. "You love me—now tell me so—tell me you love me as you could never love another man—with your body, your heart, your soul. Tell me!"

It was a command. The demand of a conqueror, invincible, competent and utterly sure of the answer.

But because of the ecstasy and interminable happiness he aroused within her, Lydia could hardly bring the answer to her lips. How could words ever express her love?

"Say it," Ivan insisted fiercely, "say it."

Then slowly after a faint almost imperceptible hesitation Lydia whispered:

". . . I . . . love . . . you . . . darling . . ."

His mouth on hers blotted out the words and she did not realise that the tiny panic, that second's hesitation, was to tantalize him, irritate and worry him. He had not yet completely captured her. She was not entirely his!

She was still irresistibly, enticingly, maddeningly—out of reach!